Clair Dolan was the most beautiful girl Harry had ever seen. Blue-black hair falling down over her shoulders, pretty face, the longest legs in the world. She lived in a beautiful flat in a classy area; she wore elegant clothes and had a glamorous job as a model. When she took Harry back to her place, she fixed him a meal fit for a king, food and wine like he hadn't seen in years. Clair was certainly a classy lady . . . such a pity she was a pickpocket . . .

Also by James Hadley Chase

AN ACE UP MY SLEEVE
JUST ANOTHER SUCKER
I WOULD RATHER STAY POOR
LAY HER AMONG THE LILIES
DOUBLE SHUFFLE
YOU FIND HIM — I'LL FIX HIM
THE GUILTY ARE AFRAID
HAVE A CHANGE OF SCENE
NOT SAFE TO BE FREE
YOU'RE LONELY WHEN YOU'RE DEAD
A LOTUS FOR MISS QUON
THERE'S ALWAYS A PRICE TAG
EVE
KNOCK, KNOCK! WHO'S THERE?
SAFER DEAD
THE WORLD IN MY POCKET
SO WHAT HAPPENS TO ME?
THE WARY TRANSGRESSOR
MAKE THE CORPSE WALK
THE THINGS MEN DO
YOU'VE GOT IT COMING
GOLDFISH HAVE NO HIDING PLACE
THE FLESH OF THE ORCHID
BELIEVE THIS YOU'LL BELIEVE ANYTHING
SHOCK TREATMENT
YOU NEVER KNOW WITH WOMEN
LADY HERE'S YOUR WREATH
MISS SHUMWAY WAVES A WAND
THE JOKER IN THE PACK

and published by Corgi Books

James Hadley Chase

But A Short Time To Live

CORGI BOOKS
A DIVISION OF TRANSWORLD PUBLISHERS LTD

BUT A SHORT TIME TO LIVE
A CORGI BOOK o 552 10477 9

Originally published in Great Britain by
Jarrolds Publishers Ltd.

PRINTING HISTORY
Jarrolds edition published 1951
Corgi edition published 1977

This book is set in 10pt Plantin

Corgi Books are published by Transworld Publishers Ltd.,
Century House, 61–63 Uxbridge Road,
Ealing, London, W.5.
Made and printed in Great Britain by
Hunt Barnard Printing Ltd., Aylesbury, Bucks.

PART ONE

CHAPTER ONE

I

The fat woman smiled self-consciously at Harry as he gave her the card. It was a pity, he thought, that she had let herself go. Her uncared for hair straggled from under a hat that didn't suit her, her eyes were heavy and tired, and there was a shine on her face that made you think she had just this moment finished cooking a stodgy, uninteresting meal. But she seemed pleased that Harry had photographed her, and she read the card carefully before putting it in her bag.

'And to think I didn't see you,' she said as she closed the bag. 'I bet I'll look a proper fright.'

'No, you won't,' Harry returned. 'People always look their best when they don't know they're being photographed. It will be ready by tomorrow afternoon. There's no obligation to buy, only I hope you'll go along and see it.'

'Oh, I'll go,' the woman said. 'Link Street's somewhere near the Palace Theatre, isn't it?'

'That's right. First turning on the left as you go up Old Compton Street.'

She thanked Harry and gave him a smile. Some of the lost prettiness came back like a transparency you hold up to the light, and as she walked away, she tucked up the strands of hair that escaped from under her hat.

That was the last photograph for the day. Thank goodness for that, Harry thought as he wound off the film, slipped the spool into its metal case and put the case in his pocket. He felt chilly and tired. To be on your feet for four hours at a stretch wasn't so bad if the sun shone and people were pleased to be photographed, but today heavy clouds had hung over the West End and there had been a cold East wind. The crowds moving in a steady stream up and down Regent Street weren't in the mood to be photographed, and some of them had scowled at Harry and his camera, refusing to take his cards, or if they did, threw them away after an indifferent glance. He had taken over a hundred photographs and considered he would be lucky if twenty-five of them found buyers.

He put the camera in its case, slung the case over his shoulder and as always at this time found he had nothing particular to do. He could return to his bed sitting-room in Lannock Street, off Sloane Square or return to the studio and listen to Mooney's moans and groans about how bad business was or he could go to a pub and read the evening paper. He decided to go to a pub. He liked pubs. He liked to get in a corner with a pint of beer and watch and listen. It was surprising what he heard and saw in the West End pubs. He overheard the most extraordinary scraps of conversation, and it amused him to try and place the speakers, to guess what they did for a living, whether they were married, whether they lived as he did in a boarding-house or whether they owned their own homes. He found that if he sat long enough, listened hard enough and kept his eyes open wide enough he could learn a lot about the people around him, and he liked to know about people. Besides, there wasn't much else for him to do: not on six pounds a week with forty shillings of that going out on bed and breakfast.

He paused on the edge of the kerb for the traffic lights to turn red. There was nothing about him to attract attention. He wore a shabby tweed sports coat, a pair of old flannel trousers and a dark blue shirt. He was twenty-four, and had a thickset, strong, broad shouldered figure. His eyes were big and grey and friendly, and his mouth wide and generous. His hair, cut short and inclined to curl, was fair, and his complexion, exposed to all kinds of weather, was the colour of old mahogany. He could have been mistaken for a medical student, and the people whom he photographed often looked at him curiously as if wondering why a young fellow of his stamp hadn't found himself something better to do than to stand at street corners and take photographs for a living.

When the traffic stopped, he crossed Regent Street and walked slowly up Glasshouse Street where he bought an evening paper. He went on, moving more slowly as he scanned the front page, indifferent to the threats of another war, disinterested in the worsening of the dock strike, held for a moment by a smash and grab raid in Shaftesbury Avenue, and then giving his undivided attention to the latest sensational murder trial which covered two pages of the paper. He was still reading as he pushed open the swing doors of the Duke of Wellington's public house in Brewer Street. He liked the Duke of Wellington: it had a pleasant homely atmosphere and its beer was good: quite the best beer in London.

He ordered a pint of bitter, pulled up a stool and sat down, still reading. This chap hadn't a hope, he thought. What jury would believe a yarn like that? Why even a kid wouldn't believe it!

He read to the end, turned to the stop-press to see if there was any more of it, and then reached for his tankard. The beer went down well and he gave a sigh of satisfaction as he savoured its taste and stretched his tired legs.

The bar was crowded; voices blended in one continual sound, punctuated by the shrill bell of the cash register, the banging of tankards on the counter and the continual shuffling of feet.

Harry folded his paper and leaned his shoulders against the wall, tilting back his stool at a precarious angle. He surveyed the crowd hopefully. The usual faces were there. The three men in black homburg hats and overcoats huddled together in a corner, drinking whiskies and whispering. They were there every evening about this time: mystery men. Harry had never been able to pick up one word of their conversation, and had no idea what they did or who they were. The grey-faced man and his perky, shabby wife were sitting at a table close by, drinking port. Harry knew something about them. They were caretakers of a block of offices in Regent Street, and the woman was always trying to cheer the man up. He had an ulcer, and seemed in need of a great deal of cheering up. There was an elderly couple who wrangled good naturedly about dog racing. There was a heavily built man who bored his two companions with his political theories. There was a young couple who drank shandy and sat in a corner and who never paid any attention to anyone except themselves. The girl was flat-chested and plain and held the man's hand with fierce possessiveness and scarcely said a word while the man talked in low continuous murmur, and kept waving his free hand at her as if he were trying to persuade her to do something against her will.

Harry regarded all these faces without enthusiasm. He thought it was high time he found someone new to interest him. Hopefully he stood on the rungs of his stool and looked over the heads of the crowd before the bar and surveyed the little group of tables against the far wall. And then he saw her: the most attractive-looking girl he had ever seen in his life.

She had a mass of blue black hair which fell in a heavy wave to her shoulders. She seemed to him to be prettier than any film star, and as bright and glittering as a diamond. She wore no hat. Her sky blue blouse with its high collar looked as immaculate as if she had only this second put it on, while her black full-pleated skirt was neither too short nor too long as if it had made up its mind to strike a compromise between the Old and the New Looks and succeeded uncommonly well.

He stood on the rungs of the stool, gaping at her, thinking how marvellous she was: just the kind of girl he would like to take out if he had plenty of money. He knew a girl with her looks and her way of dressing was certain to cost a packet of money if he did take her out. It would be unthinkable as well as unreasonable to expect her to go to any old restaurant or to travel by bus or go in the three and sixpenny seats at a movie. Obviously only the best of everything would do for her. It would be unreasonable too to expect her to take any interest in a fellow who stood at street corners and took photographs for a living, and Harry sighed.

But what was she doing in a pub like the Duke of Wellington? he wondered. Not that there was anything wrong with the Duke, but after all it wasn't quite the kind of place – pleasant as it was – in which you'd expect to find a girl who dressed so smartly and was so bright and glittering. Then he saw she was drinking whisky, and that rather shocked him. He looked to see who she was with and received a second shock. Her companion wasn't the polished Stewart Granger type Harry expected to see, but a short, fat elderly man whose face was the colour of port wine and who was as near being intoxicated as made no difference.

Here, Harry thought, sitting down on his stool again, was a problem worthy of his undivided attention. Who was the man? Who was the girl? Were they related? What were they doing here? And as he began to puzzle how best he could get within earshot of these two and overhear a word or two of their conversation that might supply a clue to these questions someone suddenly lurched violently up against him and upset his tankard of beer.

Startled, Harry turned and found himself face to face with

8

the fat, elderly man he had been thinking about.

'My dear sir,' the fat man said, clutching Harry's arm. 'I offer you my profound apologies. I really am very sorry indeed.'

'That's all right,' Harry said cheerfully. 'Accidents will happen. There was only a drop left, so there's no harm done.'

'It's very nice of you to take it like this,' the fat man said, breathing heavily. 'But you must allow me to buy you another drink. It's the least I can do. What will you have?'

'No, it's all right, thank you,' Harry said hastily. 'As a matter of fact I wasn't going to finish what I was drinking anyway. It's really all right.'

The fat man looked hurt. He screwed up his bloodshot eyes and peered closely at Harry.

'You mustn't fob me off you know,' he said. 'Can't go knocking people's drinks over. I wouldn't like it if it happened to me. Have a whisky. Nothing like a whisky to cement friendship,' and he thumped on the counter to attract the barman's attention. 'A large Scotch and soda for this gentleman,' he went on as the barman raised his eyebrows at him.

'Well, thanks,' Harry said, and tried to wriggle his arm out of the hot, clutching hand. 'You needn't have bothered. It was an accident. Anyone could have seen that.'

'It wasn't,' the fat man said, and lowering his voice, went on, 'Just between you and me, would you say I'm a little tight?'

Harry hesitated. He didn't want to hurt the fat man's feelings, nor did he want him to fly into a rage. You never knew with drunks just what they were going to do.

'Oh, I don't know,' he said cautiously. 'Perhaps you've had enough. Let's put it that way.'

The fat man seemed quite pleased as if he had formed this opinion for himself and was glad to learn he hadn't been exaggerating his condition.

'You're right,' he said and patted Harry's arm. 'I like a chap who tells the truth when he's asked. But the trouble is she hasn't had enough,' and he jerked his head in the direction of the table against the wall. 'These modern girls can put it away,' he went on, lowering his voice. 'Mind you I had a good few before I met her. Now look here, why don't you join us? That'll give me a chance to drop out for a round or so. You wouldn't mind doing that, would you?'

Harry said he wouldn't mind at all.

9

'But she might,' he pointed out. 'She mightn't like me to barge in on your party.'

'Don't you believe it,' the fat man said. 'She's a nice girl. She'll like you. You bring your whisky and come over. S'matter of fact I'll be glad of your arm. I'm not as steady as I ought to be.'

Harry picked up his drink and grasped the fat man's arm.

'How's that?' he asked, excited at the thought of meeting this girl.

'Very good,' the fat man said and blinked up at him. 'My name's Wingate. Sam Wingate. What's yours?'

Harry told him.

'Now we know what's what,' Wingate announced gravely. 'Wicks, eh? All right, Wicks, let's go.'

'Ricks,' Harry said. 'Harry Ricks.'

'That's it – Wicks. Now, come on. Best leg forward. Steady does it. Off we go.'

And they set off on the short but precarious journey from the bar to the table against the wall where the girl was sitting.

II

The girl – her name was Clair Dolan – watched them come with a cold, set expression. She sat still, her legs crossed and one elbow resting on the table, and looked pointedly at the distant bar, dissociating herself from the approaching two.

'This is Mr Wicks,' Wingate said, sitting down heavily beside her. 'The truth is, little girl, I brought him over because he was lonely. If you don't want him we can always send him away, but I thought you wouldn't mind. He's a nice young man, and I was clumsy enough to upset his drink.'

Clair gave Harry one brief glance and looked away again. She didn't say anything.

Harry stood uneasily before her. Her manner and bored expression made him feel uncomfortable. He wanted to go away, but was afraid Wingate might make a scene.

'I'm afraid I'm intruding . . .' he began, nervously fingering his tie.

'Bosh!' Wingate said loudly. 'Sit down, old chap. I said she'd be pleased to meet you, and so she is; aren't you, my dear?'

Clair looked fixedly at Harry.

'Of course, I'm delighted,' she said sarcastically. 'But I'm sure Mr Wicks has other things to do than bother with us.'

Harry turned a fiery red.

'The name's Ricks,' he said, determined at least she should know who he was. 'Harry Ricks. I'll be getting along if you don't mind. Thank you for the drink,' he went on to Wingate. 'I'll say good-night.'

'You'll do nothing of the kind!' Wingate said, turning a deeper shade of purple and struggling to his feet. 'You haven't even tasted your drink. What's up? Don't you like her? Damn it! You sit down or I'll lose my temper, damned if I won't!'

Heads turned and eyes stared at them.

'Oh, sit down and make him shut up!' Clair said furiously, in an undertone. 'I don't want a scene even if you do!'

Harry sat down, feeling hot and embarrassed and immediately Wingate beamed on him, slapping him on the shoulder.

'That's the way, old boy,' he said, sitting down himself. 'You talk to the little girl. I've a bit of a headache. Don't mind me. You keep her amused while I have a little nap.' He rubbed his face with his handkerchief. 'S'matter of fact, old boy, I'm a bit under the weather. You look after her while I close my eyes.'

And he did close his eyes, swaying on his chair and looking as if he was going to pass out at any moment.

Clair gave him a disdainful look and turned her back on him, and in doing so faced Harry.

'I'm sorry about this,' Harry said in a low voice. 'I didn't want to come over. I'm sorry to have barged in. I really didn't mean to.'

She lifted her shoulders in an impatient shrug.

'Oh, it's all right. If the old fool doesn't pull himself together in a moment, I'm going,' and she stared at the bar as if it was the only thing in the place that interested her.

In spite of her bored, sulky expression, Harry still thought she was marvellous, and even though she was snubbing him so pointedly, he was pleased to be sitting next to her.

'Can I get you something to drink?' he asked, seeing her glass was empty.

'No, thank you,' she returned, not looking at him. 'You don't have to make conversation, so please don't try.'

'I wasn't going to,' Harry said, a little nettled.

They sat in silence for several minutes, while Wingate snored gently and swayed to and fro in his chair.

Harry studied Clair's face, trying to think how he could break down her bored indifference. It was absurd to sit like this without saying anything to a girl as beautiful as she was. His scrutiny irritated her and she jerked round and frowned at him.

'Must you stare like that?' she demanded. 'Haven't you any manners?'

Harry grinned at her.

'Well, yes,' he said. 'I suppose I have. But you're worth staring at, you know, and there's not much else to do.'

'Oh, be quiet!' she said angrily, and turned away.

Inspired suddenly by an idea, Harry said softly as if speaking his thoughts aloud, 'She walks in beauty like the night, of cloudless chimes and starry skies, and all that's best of dark and bright, meet in her aspect and her eyes.'

She didn't move or turn, but after a moment or so, he heard her try to suppress a giggle.

Encouraged, Harry said, 'I don't suppose I'll ever see you again so perhaps you won't mind if I say you're the most beautiful girl I have ever seen.'

She swung round to stare at him.

'I think you're crazy, and what's worse, you're sloppy too.'

But he could see she was looking at him with a little more interest, and the cold, bored expression had gone from her eyes.

'Is it sloppy to say you're beautiful?' Harry asked. 'Anyway, I don't care if I am; it's the truth.'

She studied him. He was a species of male which had entirely gone out of her life: a young man without money, with a pleasant, engaging smile, and without that hot intent leer she was used to seeing in a man's eyes when she met him for the first time. And unlike the other male pests he was shabbily dressed, and this she found quite a novelty after the padded shoulders and flashy ties of the numerous men she knew. She particularly noticed how clear his eyes and skin were and how white his teeth were, and rather surprised at herself, she felt less hostile towards him, and even began to think he was rather nice looking.

'What did you say your name was?' she asked.

'Harry Ricks. What's yours?'

She frowned at that, not sure if she wanted him to know her name, then said distantly, 'I don't really know if it's your business, but if you must know it's Clair Dolan.'

'I knew it would be something like that,' Harry said, determined not to lose an opportunity to soften her towards him. 'I once made a study of names. Did you know Clair means bright and illustrious?'

She looked sharply at him.

'Who do you think you're kidding?'

'But I'm not. I have the book at home. I'll lend it to you if you like.'

'Well, I don't like,' she said shortly.

There was a pause, then he asked, 'Do you come here often?'

She said, no, she didn't. In fact she had only once been here and that was during the last big blitz on London. So they began to talk about the blitz, and Harry told her he had been an Air Raid Warden before he went into the Army and had been in charge of a shelter not three hundred yards from where they were sitting. That was one of the reasons why he came to the Duke of Wellington. Every night during the blitz he and a fellow warden used to have a beer here before beginning their night's duty.

'Gets you into the habit,' Harry said, pleased to see she was showing interest in what he was saying. 'It's a friendly place, and it has memories.' He looked at her admiringly. 'What did you do in the war?'

'Oh, nothing,' she said, shrugging her shoulders, and remembered how she used to gad about the West End with American officers and drink their whisky and dance with them and struggle with them in taxis, and she giggled. 'A girl can't do anything very important, can she? Besides, I was too young.'

Harry had known some girls who had done a great deal more than he had, and they had been young too. He had known a girl who dropped into France, and had been caught by the Gestapo and shot. But it was unthinkable, of course, that a girl like Clair should be mixed up in looking after people in shelters or to be bossed around in the WRAF or the WRAC or spoil her hands working in a factory. Some girls could do that sort of thing, but not Clair. Harry saw that all right.

Then suddenly a discordant note sounded. Wingate had shaken off his fuzziness and had decided it was time to have another drink. He put his hand in his pocket and discovered his wallet had disappeared. Still feeling dazed, he groped carefully through his other pockets. His movements were so deliberate

13

that both Clair and Harry broke off their conversation to stare at him.

'Have you lost anything?' Harry asked, wishing Wingate would go to sleep again.

Wingate didn't reply. Instead, he stood up and emptied everything he had in his pockets on to the table. He continued to go through his clothes with growing alarm.

'I've been robbed!' he exclaimed violently. 'My wallet's gone!'

The two barmaids and the barman, the grey-faced man and his perky wife and the three mysterious gentlemen in homburg hats all turned to stare at Wingate.

Harry felt the colour rise in his face. He was young enough to be acutely embarrassed by a scene like this, and was also aware the three mysterious men in homburg hats were looking suspiciously at him.

'Robbed!' Wingate repeated in a hard, angry voice, and turning to Harry, pointed an accusing finger at him. 'All right, young fellow, a joke's a joke, but this has gone far enough. Hand it over or I'll send for the police!'

'Hand what over?' Harry asked, turning crimson.

'My wallet!' Wingate snapped. 'Hand it over and I'll say no more about it. There's fifty pounds in that wallet and I'm not going to lose it!'

'I don't know what you're talking about,' Harry said, getting to his feet, confused and embarrassed. 'I haven't taken your wallet!'

The barman appeared from behind the counter. He came over and planted himself before Wingate, a heavy scowl on his blunt-featured face.

'Now then,' he said, 'what's all this in aid of? What are you complaining about?'

Wingate welcomed his appearance. He felt ill and dizzy and the loss of the wallet was a disaster. He pointed a trembling finger at Harry.

'That young man has stolen my wallet. Make him hand it over.'

The barman eyed Harry's confused face suspiciously.

'All right, son, don't let's 'ave any trouble. 'And it over and be sharp about it.'

14

'But I haven't got it!' Harry declared. 'He's drunk. You can see that, can't you?'

'And that's all the thanks I get,' Wingate wailed. 'I befriend this young man and he robs me and says I'm drunk. Call a policeman.'

'All right, all right,' the barman said hastily. 'We don't want any trouble. The three of you – just step this way. We'll soon see who's who and what's what. Come on. Just step this way.'

And he seized Harry's arm in one hand and Wingate's arm in the other, and jerking his head at Clair, conducted them to a room at the back of the bar where the manager received them with a set smile which threatened to disappear at the first sign of unpleasantness.

'Gent 'ere says this 'un's pinched 'is wallet,' the barman said, jerking his head at Wingate and his thumb at Harry.

The manager rose from behind his desk. His smile fairly jumped off his face.

'And who's this?' he asked, looking at Clair.

'The gent's friend,' the barman explained, and gave Clair an admiring glance.

The manager also seemed taken with her. He pushed a chair forward and invited her to sit down.

'Right-ho, Bob,' he said to the barman when Clair was seated, 'just stand by the door while I sort this out.'

When Bob had taken up his position before the door, the manager asked Wingate what he had to say for himself.

'My wallet's gone,' Wingate said. He was pale and shaken. 'I spoke to this chap who is a complete stranger to me, and a moment or so later I found my wallet gone. It contained fifty pounds.'

The manager stared hard at Harry who had now recovered from his embarrassment and was getting angry. The manager liked the look of Harry. It seemed unlikely that he was a pick-pocket. He just didn't look the type, and the manager decided to treat him cautiously. He had seen him often enough in the bar and wasn't going to lose a regular customer if he could help it. He had never seen Wingate before and noticed he was scarcely sober, and that sort of thing was bad for business. So he asked Harry in a mild voice what he had to say.

'I don't know anything about his wallet,' Harry declared, growing red in the face again. 'And I can prove it!'

Before anyone could stop him he emptied the contents of his

15

pockets on the desk in exactly the same way as Wingate had but a minute or so ago piled his possessions on the table in the bar. The manager, the barman, Wingate and Clair looked at the articles which lay on the desk with interest: they were a miscellaneous lot. There was a packet of 'You've Just Been Photographed' cards, three metal cases containing films, a handkerchief, a penknife, a half eaten bun, some crumbs from the other half that had been eaten, three half-crowns and a piece of string.

The manager peered at the collection, shook his head doubtfully, looked at Wingate and asked him if he was satisfied.

Wingate turned even paler, licked his dry lips and then suddenly turned and pointed an accusing finger at Clair.

'Then she's got it!' he exclaimed. 'It's either one or the other. I – I picked her up in Regent Street. I've never seen her before. It was her idea we should come here and he was waiting for her. That's it! They're working together. He took my wallet and passed it to her.'

Clair rose to her feet. She looked surprised and inclined to laugh. She walked up to Harry and stood by his side, facing Wingate.

'So we're working together, are we?' she said. 'Well, that's funny, considering you knocked his drink over and introduced him to me. Can't you think of a better yarn than that?'

'Now, steady on,' the manager broke in, frowning at Wingate. 'You can't go accusing everyone like this. You just said this young man had it. Well, he hasn't. You'd better be careful.'

Wingate thumped the desk.

'I want my wallet. If he hasn't got it, then she has!'

'If you don't watch out,' Clair said, smiling at the manager, 'he'll be saying you took it next. Oh well, I may as well set his mind at rest,' and in spite of the manager's growl of protest, she opened her handbag and dumped its contents on the table side by side with the articles that had come out of Harry's pockets.

Now it was Harry's turn to peer with interest. There was a gold powder compact and cigarette case combined, a gold cigarette lighter, a fountain pen and cheque book, several pound notes and a lot of silver, some letters, a comb, handkerchief, a lipstick in a gold holder and a number of keys on a ring.

There was a long and heavy silence, then Clair said brightly,

16

'I'll take my clothes off if it'll satisfy him. I only want him to be happy.'

The manager went red and the barman lost his scowl and looked hopeful.

'That won't be necessary at all,' the manager said hastily. 'It's quite all right, miss. There's obviously been some misunderstanding.' He turned on Wingate and went on in a cold, unfriendly tone, 'When did you last use your wallet?'

Wingate sat down heavily. He looked old and feeble and very stupid.

'I don't know. I can't remember.'

'Did you take it from your pocket while you were in the bar?' the manager asked. 'Now come, sir. Think carefully. Did you pay for your drinks with the change in your pocket or did you pay with a note?'

Wingate admitted he hadn't taken a note from his wallet while he was in the bar.

'Then you could quite easily have dropped the wallet or had it stolen before you came in here,' the manager said, pleased with his reasoning.

While this was going on Harry began to put his possessions back into his pocket and Clair joined him and began to put hers back into her bag.

'That's a nice case,' Harry said as she picked up the gold cigarette case.

'Oh, it's all right,' she said and smiled at him. 'Have one?' and she offered him a cigarette.

Harry took the cigarette and she lit it for him, and as she did so she looked right into his eyes.

'Excuse me,' the manager said sharply, 'when you two have quite done I'd like to get on with my work.'

Harry started and looked blankly at the manager. He had been so carried away that he had forgotten where he was.

'I'm so sorry,' Clair said, smiling. 'Well, I suppose we can go now or does he still want to send for the police?'

'Of course you can go,' the manager said. 'And I hope you'll both accept my apologies. I don't like this sort of thing to happen in my house, and I hope you will both continue to come here. You'll be very welcome.'

'Thank you,' Clair said.

Wingate, who was listening with a dazed expression on his face, made an effort to pull himself together.

'Now listen, little girl . . . ' he began feebly, but Clair ignored him.

She turned to Harry. 'Well, let's go. He thinks we're working together so let's keep up the illusion,' and to Harry's surprise, she linked her arm through his and made for the door.

The barman opened it for them with a flourish and winked at Harry as they went past.

Wingate called feebly, 'Hey! Don't go away. I want to apologise . . . '

But they didn't look back and went on through the bar and into the street. Then they paused and looked at each other. Harry hated to think in a few seconds they would part, and he would probably never see her again.

'I'm awfully sorry that happened,' he said, putting his hands in his pockets and kicking the edge of the kerb. 'It was really my fault. I shouldn't have barged in.'

'That's all right,' she said, and he was suddenly aware of a change in her. She wasn't smiling, and she even seemed a little bored with him. 'The old fool was drunk. We'd better be going before he comes out. I don't want to see him again.'

'No,' Harry said awkwardly. 'Well, then I suppose I'd better say good-bye.'

Still unsmiling, her eyes expressionless, she stepped closer and offered her hand.

'Good-bye,' she said abruptly.

Harry took her hand, and as he did so she appeared to stumble, and she caught hold of his coat to steady herself, and he felt a little tug at his hip pocket. He stepped back and something fell on the pavement at his feet. Clair bent swiftly, snatched it up and put it with one lightning movement into her bag. But Harry had seen it: a worn, bulky leather wallet.

They stood looking at each other.

'That – that came out of my pocket,' Harry said.

'Did it?' she said, and continued to look steadily at him.

'So you did take it,' Harry said. 'You put it in my pocket before you showed them your bag.'

She bit her lips, looked uneasily at the swing doors of the Duke of Wellington, and then at him.

'Yes, I did,' she said suddenly. 'I took it to teach him a lesson. I'm going to give it back to him. You don't think I'm a thief, do you?'

Harry was so shocked he didn't know what to think, but he

said, 'Why, no, I don't think that. But – well, hang it, you shouldn't have taken it. There's fifty pounds in it –'

'I know I shouldn't have,' she said, and again looked uneasily at the swing doors. 'Look, let's walk on, shall we? I'll tell you why I took it as we go along.'

'But you've got to give it back to him,' Harry said, not moving. 'You can't go off with his fifty pounds.'

'I can't give it back to him when he's drunk,' she said impatiently. 'You can see that, can't you? He'll give me in charge.' She suddenly linked her arm through his. 'I know his address. I'll send it back to him. Come on back to my place. We can talk about it there.'

'Your place?' he said, surprised.

She smiled up at him.

'Why not? It's not far. Don't you want to come?'

'Well, yes,' Harry said, falling into step beside her. 'But are you sure we should leave him without his money?'

'I'll send it back tomorrow,' she said, and again looked uneasily at the swing doors of the Duke of Wellington. 'Let's go to my place, and I'll tell you how it happened.'

He went with her down Glasshouse Street towards Piccadilly.

III

As they made their way through the crowds along Piccadilly, she kept up a flow of conversation that took Harry's mind away from Wingate and his wallet. She walked quickly, holding on to his arm and hurrying him along. If Harry had had a chance to think he would have realised she was trying to get away from the Duke of Wellington as fast as she could without actually running, but she didn't give him the chance. Nor did she give him the chance to ask about the wallet.

'Where do you live?' she asked, tossing back her thick wavy hair from her face and looking up at him as if she was really interested in what he was going to say.

'I have a bed-sitter in Lannock Street. It's a turning off Sloane Square,' Harry told her.

'I have a flat off Long Acre. You'll like it.' She gave him a swift smile. 'Have you got a girl friend?'

'A – what?' Harry gaped at her.

'A girl friend. Someone to go around with.'

'Well, no, I haven't. Of course I know a few girls, but I haven't a regular one.'

'I should have thought you would. What was that you said about me: something about she walks in beauty . . . '

'Yes. She walks in beauty like the night, of cloudless chimes and starry skies, and all that's best of dark and bright, meet in her aspect and her eyes. It's fine, isn't it?'

'I bet you've said that to dozens of girls.'

'I haven't. It's a thing I learned at school, and I only remembered it again when I saw you. It fits you, somehow.'

'Does it? You're a funny boy, aren't you?' She touched the small camera hanging from the strap on his shoulder. 'Do you take photographs?'

'Yes.' Harry felt himself grow hot, wondering what she would think of him if she knew what he did for a living.

'It's a very small camera, isn't it? Is it a Leica?'

He said it was.

'A friend of mine had a Leica. He was always pestering me to pose for him in the nude. Have you ever taken nudes?'

Harry shook his head.

'I can't get anyone to pose for me,' he said, and grinned.

'Well, girls aren't mugs these days,' she said. 'One thing leads to another, doesn't it?'

'Not necessarily.'

'Perhaps not, but a girl can't be too careful.' She paused to open her bag. 'This is it. I have a flat above the shop.'

They had stopped outside a tailor's shop, and Harry glanced at the window display. Looking at the various suits displayed on the immaculate dummies made him suddenly aware of his own shabbiness.

'I'm afraid I'm in my working clothes,' he said. 'I hope you don't mind.'

She found a key and opened a door by the entrance to the tailor's shop.

'Don't be a dope,' she said shortly. 'I couldn't care less what you wear. Come in. It's just at the top of the stairs.'

He followed her up the stairs, and couldn't help noticing what slim, neat legs she had as she moved from stair to stair. And as if she could read his thoughts, she glanced over her shoulder and made a face at him.

'Like them?' she asked. 'Most men do.'

Harry was so surprised that he blushed.

'They're wonderful. What are you – a thought reader?'

'I just happen to know men. Whenever I walk up stairs with a man behind me I know he's trying to see further than he should. It's not my mind, you know. It's really what he's doing.'

She paused outside a door and, using the same key, opened it and entered a large airy room which was Harry's idea of the acme of luxury. It was furnished with taste and comfort: the big armchairs, the settee and the divan were all built to give the greatest possible ease. They were covered with fawn corduroy material, off-set with scarlet piping. There was a big table in the bay window, a radiogram, an elaborate cocktail cabinet, several prints of Van Gogh's country scenes on the walls and a large fireplace where a bright fire was burning.

'This is nice!' Harry exclaimed, looking round. 'Have you been here long?'

She dropped her handbag on the table and crossed the room to inspect herself in the mirror above the fireplace.

'Oh, about two years,' she said carelessly. 'It isn't bad. Well, sit down. I'll get you a drink. What would you like? Gin, whisky, or beer? I'm going to have whisky. Have one with me?'

'Thank you,' Harry said, 'but can't I get it?'

'If you want to. You'll find the things over there. Are you hungry? I am. I haven't had a thing since breakfast.'

'Haven't you?' Harry said. 'But, why?'

'Oh, I couldn't be bothered. When you live alone as I do, meals are such a bore. You get the drinks. I won't be a moment.'

Harry was surprised to see the number of gin and whisky bottles in the cabinet. There were twenty full bottles of whisky and twelve full bottles of gin, and he whistled under his breath.

'Wherever did you get all this whisky?' he asked, raising his voice as she had gone into another room, leaving the door open.

'Oh, I got it. There's not much I can't get. You can have a couple of bottles if you like.'

'No, thank you,' Harry said hurriedly. 'I seldom drink it.' He poured a small whisky into a glass. 'How do you like yours?'

'About two fingers,' she called back. 'Don't be mean with it. There's some soda at the bottom of the cupboard and I'm bringing the ice.'

In a very short time she came back with a tray containing plates of cold chicken, brown bread and butter, lettuce, a Camembert cheese and biscuits.

'Will this be all right?' she asked as she dumped the tray on the settee. 'I have some tongue if you'd prefer that.'

Harry gaped at the food.

'Why, it's a feast!' he exclaimed. 'I can't rob you of this. I can't really.'

She stared at him, raising her eyebrows, and when she did that it was extraordinary how hard she looked.

'My dear idiot, what are you yammering about? You're not robbing me. It's here to eat, so eat it.'

'But will you be all right tomorrow?'

'All right? Of course I will. What do you mean?'

'Well, I'm eating you out of house and home, aren't I?'

'You talk as if there's no food in the country.'

'Well, is there?' Harry asked, and grinned. 'I don't find much.'

'That's because you don't know where to look for it,' she said, and patted the settee. 'Sit down and stop acting like a fugitive from a ration book. And for goodness' sake give yourself a better drink than that. That wouldn't drown a fly.'

'Oh, it's all right. I'm not used to whisky,' Harry said, sitting down. He took a plate of chicken she gave him and rested it on his knee. 'You know this is a bit like a dream. Do you usually take compassion on people and feed them like this?'

'No, I don't, but you're rather a special case, aren't you?' and she gave him a quick searching look.

Her remark and look reminded him of the wallet which had gone completely out of his mind.

'Did you really take his wallet?' he asked anxiously.

'Of course I did,' she said, and pointed her chin at him, her eyes defiant. 'He needed a lesson and he's got it. I know where he lives and I'll send it back tomorrow.'

'But it's – it's not my business, of course,' Harry said, worried. 'If he had fifty pounds in it, wasn't it rather reckless to take it? I mean anyone might think –'

'Might think I meant to keep it?' she asked and laughed. 'I suppose they might. Why else do you think I palmed it off on you? I was scared out of my pants when the old fool found it had gone. I didn't think he'd find out until we had parted.'

'But why did you do it?' Harry asked, staring at her.

'He was a filthy old man. He thought I was a tart, so I pretended I was, and when he put his wallet on the table I hid it in my bag. He was so tight he forgot all about it. I meant to

22

give it back to him after he had had a shock, then I forgot I had it. Then when he made a scene about it I decided to keep quiet. That's all there's to it. I'll post it back to him tomorrow. I bet he's in a proper old stew now, and serve him right.'

Harry didn't like that kind of thing, but he didn't say so. In fact he felt sorry for Wingate.

'Would you like me to take it back tonight and explain?' he asked. 'I will if you like.'

'Certainly not!' she snapped, and for a moment a cold, angry look came into her eyes, then she forced a laugh. 'Don't be such a fuss-pot. He'll get it back, but he's going to sweat first.' She held out her empty glass. 'Give me another drink and have one yourself. Chicken all right?'

Harry said the chicken was fine, although he had scarcely tasted it, and as he got up he looked at her questioningly.

'Fuss-pot!' she said. 'Do you always worry about such little things?'

'Well, no but —'

'Tell me about yourself,' she said, interrupting him. 'What do you do?'

Harry hesitated. It was no use being ashamed of your job, he thought. If he was going to see her again she would have to know. Now he was beginning to get used to her he had a feeling that perhaps she wouldn't care what he did as she obviously didn't care about his shabby clothes.

'I work for Mooney's Camera Studio in Link Street,' he told her, pouring out a drink. 'I stand at the street corners in the West End and take people's photographs.' He purposely made it sound as bad as he could and watched her as he said it but her expression didn't change.

'Is it fun?' she asked.

'Well, it's all right. Of course it's not much, but one of these days I hope to set up on my own.'

'I shouldn't have thought there was much in it. Is it worth doing?' she asked just as if you could pick and choose a job, and choose one that made a lot of money.

'Well, yes.' Again Harry hesitated, then plunged on, 'I make six quid a week to be exact.'

'No wonder you don't drink whisky.'

They sat in silence for a minute or so. She was staring into the fire, and there was a little frown on her face.

'Isn't there anything better you can do?' she asked suddenly.

23

'I mean something where you can earn more money?'

Harry was surprised at the interest she seemed to be showing in his affairs.

'Well, I don't know,' he said. 'The trouble is I don't know much about anything except photography. I'm not ready yet to set up on my own. I took a couple of pictures while I was in the Army in Italy and sent them in for a competition run by a Sunday newspaper and I won the first prize. That encouraged me and I went in for other competitions. During the past three years I've collected three hundred pounds in prize money.'

Clair gave him a look of surprised interest.

'That's good. You must be clever at it.'

Harry smiled.

'Oh, I don't know. More luck than anything else. I seem to strike on the right picture. Anyway, my boss, Mooney, wants me to put the money into his business. He says he'll make me a partner and put me in charge of the portrait side of the business. We haven't gone in for taking studio portraits, and Mooney wants to, but he knows nothing about it, and wants me to equip the studio and run it.'

'That's a good idea, isn't it? Why don't you do it?'

'It's not as easy as it sounds,' Harry said, stretching out his long legs towards the fire. He had never felt so comfortable or so happy in his life. He had forgotten about Wingate's wallet and couldn't believe he wasn't going to wake up suddenly and find himself in his cheerless bed-sitter in Lannock Street. 'You see, I'm not convinced it would be a good idea to open a studio in Link Street. It's not much of a district, and I don't think we'd get the right kind of trade. Mooney swears we would, but I'm not sure about it. Then you see I've been awfully hard up. I lost my parents when I was fifteen and have had to look after myself ever since. It's a pretty nice feeling to have three hundred pounds in the Post Office. I feel if anything went wrong, if I got ill, if I lost my job, I'd have something to fall back on. And besides, I have to think of my old age.'

Clair gaped at him.

'Old age? That's ridiculous! Why, you're only a kid. You have years and years before you need worry about your old age. And you might win other prizes. I've never heard such rot.'

Harry looked doubtful.

'Oh, I know. Mooney keeps telling me that. But I can't help being cautious. That's the way I'm made. One of these days I might do something about it, but I'm not going to do anything in a hurry. I believe in saving as much as I can. Don't you?'

'Me?' Clair laughed scornfully. 'Good Lord, no! I've never saved a farthing. The past is gone – forget it! The future hasn't arrived – to hell with it! The present's here – use it. It's a short life and a merry one. That's my philosophy. I have a good time while I can.'

'Well, I suppose that's all right,' Harry said, thinking it was far from being all right. 'Girls are a bit different. They get married; so it doesn't matter so much.'

'You're really the most old-fashioned boy I've ever met,' Clair said as she put the plates on a tray. 'I shan't get married. That's the last thing I want to do. The idea of having to run a home and darn a man's socks and cook and be at his beck and call doesn't appeal to me. And children! No, thank you!'

Harry's face fell. She was right, of course, he thought. It was impossible to imagine her washing dishes and standing in queues and pushing a pram. And yet, Harry felt, it was a pity in a way. He supposed she might be right. He was old-fashioned. He liked to think a woman's place was in the home doing just those things she didn't want to do. But then why was he feeling like this? If she was the marrying kind he wouldn't be sitting in this marvellous room, enjoying her company and having the best evening he could remember.

'Finish your drink and have another,' she said. 'And pass the cigarettes. They're on the table.'

'I won't have another drink, thank you,' Harry said, getting the cigarettes. He handed her the box and lit her cigarette.

'Can I help you wash up?' he went on, nodding at the plates on the tray.

'My goodness!' she exclaimed. 'You're the first man who's ever offered to do that. It's all right. I have a woman who comes in every morning. She'll take care of it.' She handed him her glass. 'Well, if you won't, I will.'

While he was mixing another drink, she asked, 'Tell me about your place. Did you say it was in Lannock Street?'

'Yes. It's not bad. Not like this, of course.' Harry gave her the drink and sat down again. 'I share the room with another chap. By splitting the cost we get a big room.'

'Who's the other chap?' Clair asked, surprised she was asking these questions: surprised at her own interest.

'His name's Ron Fisher,' Harry told her. 'He writes articles and things. At the moment he's working on a series of articles on London night life for a Sunday paper. He'd make quite a bit of money only he sends most of it to his wife. They're separated.'

'There you are, and you talk about married life,' Clair said, and grimaced. 'That's what generally happens. Not for me! I prefer to be free to do what I like.'

'What do you do if it's not being rude?' Harry asked; then added hastily as he saw her frown, 'But perhaps I shouldn't ask.'

'I don't mind,' she said, not looking at him. 'I'm a model. It's a pretty good job and it pays well.'

'What do you have to do then?' Harry asked, interested.

'Oh, you know, I'm on all the big agencies' lists. Whenever they want a girl to advertise anything, they send for me. The money's good, and the things I pick up are even better. I did a whisky advertisement last month, and they gave me a couple of dozen bottles as well as a fee. Last year I did a series of pictures advertising the M.G. sports car, and instead of a fee I asked for a car and got it. That radiogram over there was given to me as part fees. It's a good racket to be in, and the work isn't hard.'

Harry thought this was marvellous, and said so. When he had come into the room he had wondered how she managed to live at such a standard, and had been a little uneasy about it.

'I bet you thought I was a tart,' Clair said, smiling at him. 'I saw the look on your face when you saw all this. You did, didn't you?'

'I wish you wouldn't talk like that,' Harry said. 'I didn't. I spend a lot of time in the West End, and I know a tart when I see one. They're unmistakable. I don't like to hear you say that even if you are joking.'

'Don't you want to know how I ran into Wingate?' she asked. 'Now, admit you're curious.'

'Well, I suppose I am,' Harry said. 'But that doesn't mean I expect you to tell me.'

'I was feeling lonely,' she said, and leaned forward to poke the fire. 'I hadn't anything to do and this place got on my nerves and I wanted to do something reckless. Do you ever want a violent and complete change? I don't suppose you do, but sometimes I feel I want to do something crazy – to take my clothes off and swim in the fountain in Trafalgar Square or smash a shop window or knock a policeman's helmet off. You don't ever feel like that, do you?'

'Well, no,' Harry said, startled. 'I can't say I do.'

'I can't imagine you would,' she said and laughed. 'I was walking along Piccadilly looking for trouble and Wingate turned up. He followed me all over the place and finally propositioned me. I thought it would be fun to lead him on, but he was so damned crude and horrible I lost my temper and decided to teach him a lesson. There, now you know all about it.'

'I shouldn't have thought a girl like you would ever be lonely,' Harry said seriously. 'You must have hundreds of friends.'

'I suppose I have,' she said. 'But sometimes friends are a damned bore.' She looked at the clock on the mantelpiece. 'My goodness! Look at the time! I have a date in half an hour and I haven't changed.' She jumped to her feet and smiled at him. 'You don't mind if I turn you out now? I'm sorry. It's been fun, hasn't it?'

Harry stood up.

'I think it's extraordinary nice of you to have given me such a grand evening,' he said. 'I've enjoyed it. And thank you for the meal and – and your company.'

She made him a little bow.

'I liked it too,' she said, and moved to the door.

'I wonder if I'll see you again,' Harry said hopefully as he followed her. 'I don't suppose you have much time to spare, but if you ever feel like going to the movies and would like me to take you . . . '

She laughed as she opened the door.

'I'll remember. You can always find me here. Give me a ring sometime. I'm in the book.'

This was too vague to satisfy Harry.

'I suppose we couldn't fix up something for next week?' he asked, standing in the doorway and looking hopefully at her.

She shook her head.

'Not next week. I'm booked up. You ring me sometime. I won't forget you.'

'All right,' Harry said, and took a slow, reluctant step into the passage. 'It's been a wonderful evening, and thanks a lot.'

She held out her hand, smiling.

'Good-bye. I must fly now. And don't fuss, will you?'

He took her hand.

'No,' he said. 'Well, good-bye.'

As he still didn't move, she gave him a bright smile and closed the door in his face.

'What an extraordinary boy,' Clair thought, leaning against the door, her hand still on the door-knob as she listened to the sound of Harry's footfalls as he ran down the stairs. 'But he's nice. A bit soft, of course, but nice.'

She walks in beauty like the night...

No one had ever said anything like that to her before, and no man she had ever invited to her flat had left without at least trying to kiss her.

She frowned, and moved over to the table where she had left her bag. She picked it up, still thinking about him. She wondered if he would telephone, and if he did whether she should go out with him or not. A boy like that could make life complicated. But what a change from the other men she knew! She couldn't ever remember spending an hour alone with a man without being pawed. And he was good looking too. She wondered what he would look like in a good suit, and immediately felt a surprising urge to buy him one: to give him a complete outfit.

'I'm getting as bad as Babs,' she thought, resting her hips on the edge of the table and staring at her reflection in the mirror over the fireplace. 'She buys Teddy his clothes, gives him pocket money, and takes him out. Of course Teddy's a stinking little rat. There's no comparison between him and Harry. The trouble would be to persuade Harry to accept anything. But it might be fun to try.'

Her thoughts were abruptly interrupted by her bedroom door opening. She stiffened and pushed away from the table. A tall, fat man, smoking a cigarette, appeared in the open doorway. His face was pink and smooth shaven. His hair was ash blond and grew in two heavy wings, brushed carefully above his ears. His eyes were pale blue, almost colourless, shrewd, hard and steady. He wore a light grey suit that had cost him fifty guineas, a white silk shirt, a yellow tie ornament with horses' heads in dark brown, and reversed calf shoes.

His name was Robert Brady.

'Hallo, darling,' he said, and smiled, showing a mouthful of gold-capped teeth. 'How very pensive you look.'

'Have you been in there all the time?' she demanded, her face hardening.

He nodded.

'All the time, precious, with my ear glued to the keyhole.' He dug his finger into his right ear and grinned. 'Keyholes are beastly draughty things,' he complained, sitting down before the fire. 'Did you have to bring him here?'

'I was nearly caught,' she said shortly. 'If you were listening you must have heard all about it. I had to be nice to him or he might have been difficult.'

'It didn't seem such an unpleasant task,' he said. 'Did you have to give him chicken? I was going to eat that myself.'

'Oh, shut up!' Clair said crossly. 'How did you get in here?'

'With a key,' Brady said. 'You know, one of those metal gadgets that lock and unlock doors. Didn't you know I had a key?'

'No, I didn't!' Clair said. 'Give it to me at once! I'm not going to have you in and out just whenever you like.'

'After all it's my flat,' Brady said mildly. 'I'm entitled to come in and out, precious.'

'If you don't give me that key I'll have the lock changed,' Clair said furiously. 'And as long as I'm here, this is not your flat.'

Brady studied her; his fat, pink face expressionless. Then, because he had two duplicates of the key, he dipped a fat finger and thumb into his waistcoat pocket and produced the key.

'Have it your own way,' he said. 'We won't quarrel about it. Where's the wallet?'

'That's all you think about!' She opened her bag and threw the wallet at him.

'Darling, couldn't you try to cultivate a few manners?' he asked as he bent to pick it up. 'Do you always have to behave like the gutter-bred whore that you are?'

'Oh, shut up!' she said, and walked over to the cellaret and poured herself out a drink.

'I'm afraid your new friend has had a disturbing influence on you,' Brady said as he counted the five-pound notes he found in the wallet. 'Was he very romantic?'

'Oh, shut up!' she repeated, sitting down.

'Fifty quid!' He glanced up and showed his gold teeth in a meaningless smile. 'That's not bad.' He took six of the notes and folding them into a compact packet, stowed them away in his waistcoat pocket. The remaining four notes he took over to Clair. 'There's a reward for a clever girl.'

She snatched them from him, and pushed them indifferently into her purse.

'You really are in a sour temper tonight, precious, aren't you?' he said, and patted her face with his finger-tips.

She jerked away.

'Take your paws off me!' she said. 'I'm not in the mood for mauling tonight.'

'Considering your trade, you should always be in the mood,' he said, chuckling. 'What was the young man's name?'

'I don't know,' she said, not looking at him. 'Harry. He didn't say what his other name was.'

'Never mind,' Brady said, moving about the room, his hands in his trouser pockets. 'We can always find out. I think he said he worked for Mooney's Camera Studio in Link Street, didn't he? I know the place.'

She jumped to her feet and went up to him.

'What do you mean? What are you planning?' she demanded, catching hold of his arm.

'Why, surely,' he said, smiling down at her. 'He has three hundred pounds. It should be fairly simple for you to get that from him, shouldn't it? You're not going to miss a chance like that, are you?'

'Don't be ridiculous,' she said. 'I'm not likely to see him again. It's not as if he carried it around with him. He keeps it in the Post Office.'

'It doesn't matter where he keeps it. He'll spend it on you if you give him the chance, and you'll see him again. He'll phone. It's funny how these nice boys always fall for a bitch. They just don't seem able to help themselves.'

Clair clenched her fists, and looked for a moment as if she was going to hit Brady, then she turned away with an angry shrug.

He pulled her round.

'Let's forget about him for the moment, precious. I thought it would be nice if we spent an hour together. You mustn't get temperamental with me, Clair. You couldn't get along without me, you know. You mustn't ever forget that.'

She tried to jerk away, but he held her easily.

'Come along. Let's go into the other room.'

'No!' she said furiously. 'I'm not going to! Let me go, you fat swine.'

He gave her a little shake, jerking her head back.

'Don't be silly, darling,' he said, and the colourless eyes hardened. 'Let's go into the other room.'

They stared at each other for a long moment, then he released her and took her face in his moist, soft hands.

'Lovely Clair,' he said, and drew her face to him. Shuddering she closed her eyes, letting his lips rest on hers.

'Imagine I am him,' he whispered into her mouth. 'All cats are grey in the dark, darling, and it'll be good practice for you.'

He led her unprotesting into the other room.

V

A strong smell of cod fish on the boil greeted Harry as he opened the front door of No. 24 Lannock Street and groped his way down the dark passage which led to the stairs.

Somewhere in the basement Mrs Westerham, his landlady, was mournfully singing an unrecognisable song. It could have been a hymn or a ballad, and pausing to listen, Harry decided it was a hymn. Mrs Westerham was always singing something.

'When you live alone,' she had once told Harry, 'you've either got to talk to yourself or sing. Well, I don't hold with talking to myself. People who talk to themselves are a bit cranky. So I sing.'

Listening, Harry felt sorry for her, and as he mounted the stairs it occurred to him that he never felt lonely, and because he hadn't ever thought of this before it surprised him. He spent a lot of time on his own, but he was never conscious of being alone or wanting company. There was so much going on that interested him. That, he supposed, was the answer to loneliness. If you could interest yourself in other people, if you could be entertained by hanging out of a window, watching people go by and wondering what they did and who they were, if you could sit in a pub and listen, if you could lie in bed and wonder about things like what the young couple in the pub who drank shandy found to talk about, and who the three mysterious men in black homburgs were, you hadn't much time to feel lonely. It was a good thing, he decided, to be interested in people. He wouldn't

31

care to get like Mrs Westerham. It couldn't be much fun to sing hymns all day, and he wondered if he ought to go down and have a word with her. She liked him to visit her. Only the trouble was once he was there it was so difficult to get away.

The sound of Ron's typewriter decided him. He felt in need of male company tonight. Only another male would understand how he was feeling. He felt somehow Mrs Westerham wouldn't approve of Clair.

He found the air in the big room he shared with Ron heavy with tobacco smoke. Ron always forgot to open a window, and there he was now, seated at the rickety bamboo table, his coat off, his pipe smoking furiously as he hammered away at his typewriter; the floor around him was littered with sheets of paper in a fug that proclaimed he had been at it for hours.

He waved his hand at Harry and said, 'Shan't be a tic; just finishing,' and continued to hammer away with a speed and dexterity that Harry never ceased to admire.

Harry opened the window a few inches at the top and bottom, put his camera away, pulled up an easy chair to the spluttering gas stove and sat down.

He was suddenly conscious of the drab shabbiness of the room. Its only redeeming feature was its size, but comparing it to Clair's flat, Harry thought sadly that it was little short of a slum.

The walls needed repapering, the carpet was worn, the two armchairs were long past their prime. The vast marble topped washstand with its two floral bowls and jugs gave the room a Victorian atmosphere that made Harry think of hansom cabs and mutton-chop whiskers. How unlike Clair's sophisticated luxury flat, he thought, and wondered how much she paid to live in a place like that.

He had no idea a model made so much money. Thinking of her gold cigarette case and lighter he wondered if those were also gifts from satisfied advertisers. And a car! It just showed you, he thought, how little you know about what goes on in other businesses.

Ron suddenly pushed the table away and got to his feet.

'Done!' he exclaimed, running his fingers through his untidy hair. 'Phew! I've been working like a dog all the afternoon. Well, that's that. I've had enough for tonight. I'll correct the blessed thing tomorrow.'

Ron Fisher was a tall, lanky, shock-headed fellow of about

thirty-four or five. His face was long and thin, his eyes dark, his chin square and determined. People who met him for the first time jumped to the conclusion that he was irritable and unfriendly for he had a bitter, cynical tongue, and no patience with people who bored him.

Harry and he had met at a demobilisation centre, and while waiting their turn, had struck up a conversation that had led them to joining forces as they came out of the centre, civilians again. Ron had a large room he was willing to share. He had taken a fancy to Harry as Harry had taken a fancy to him. Ron was anxious to economise, and suggested Harry might like to split the rent of the room and take over the spare bed. They had been together now for nearly four years.

'Have you had supper?' Ron asked as he gathered up his papers.

'You bet,' Harry said, stretching out his legs and grinning up at the ceiling. 'Haven't you?'

Ron looked up sharply and regarded Harry with a puzzled frown.

'And why are you looking so damned smug? Fallen in love or something?'

'What's that?' Harry demanded, sitting bolt upright and turning a fiery red. 'Fallen in – what!'

'Oh, my stars!' Ron exploded, staring at him. 'Don't tell me that's what's happened? Come on; get it off your chest. It's a girl, isn't it?'

'Well, in a way,' Harry said, piqued that Ron should have arrived at the truth so quickly.

Ron put the pile of papers on the table, picked the table up and carried it to a far corner. Then he went to a cupboard, opened it and surveyed the contents with a scowl of disgust.

'The cupboard's practically bare,' he said. 'Well, I'm not going out so I'll have to make do with what's here.' He carried a loaf, butter, cheese and a bottle of beer to the armchair opposite Harry's and sat down.

'Sure you have eaten?' he asked, taking out his penknife and sawing off a hunk of bread.

'Yes, thank you,' Harry said a little stiffly. He thought Ron at least might have asked more particulars about the girl. 'As a matter of fact I had a pretty good dinner.' He stared up at the ceiling and waited hopefully, but as Ron didn't say anything, he

3   33

went on, 'chicken, lettuce, Camembert cheese with whisky to wash it down.'

'That's fine,' Ron said with his mouth full. 'Observe me, I'm eating oysters with a grilled dover sole to follow.' He poured the beer into a tooth glass and drank half of it with a grimace. 'Can't think what they put in this stuff. It gets worse every week.'

'I'm not joking,' Harry said, thumping the arm of his chair. 'I went to this girl's flat, and that's what she gave me.'

Ron frowned and put down the tumbler.

'What are you babbling about? What girl?'

'The girl I met,' Harry said. 'Her name's Clair Dolan. She has a flat near Long Acre.'

'Has she? Well, that's very nice and central for her. How did you meet her?'

'I know it sounds a bit odd,' Harry said, fumbling for his cigarettes, 'but she really is a nice girl. She's lovely too. Honest: talk about glamour! She's just like a film star. I wish you could have seen her.'

Ron gave a low groan.

'For goodness' sake!' he exclaimed. 'Spare me the details. I asked you how you met her. That's all I want to know.'

Harry grinned and told him how he had gone to the Duke of Wellington, how Wingate had upset his drink, how he had been introduced to Clair. But he didn't tell him about the wallet. Even now the wallet worried him. He was quite sure that Clair was all right, but he did think she had been foolish to have taken it. He didn't want Ron to know about it. Ron was so cynical. He would probably have said the girl was a thief. So he left out the wallet and said after they had had a few drinks, Wingate had had to go off somewhere and Clair had invited him to her place for supper. Once he had got over the dangerous ground, he went into the fullest details, describing the flat and what Clair did for a living, how she looked, what she said and what he had said. It was nearly ten-thirty by the time he had finished.

Ron had long ago finished his supper, and was smoking a pipe now, his legs stretched out before him, a thoughtful expression on his long, thin, face. He didn't interrupt Harry all the time he was talking, and Harry was so enthusiastic about Clair that he didn't notice how quiet Ron had become.

'Well, that's that,' he concluded, lighting yet another cigar-

34

ette. 'She said I could ring her up. Of course I'm going to. I'm going to see if I can take her out next week. She did say she was booked up, but there's no harm in trying.'

Ron sank lower in his chair and stared at Harry from over his knees.

'I don't want to be a wet blanket, Harry,' he said quietly, 'but watch your step with this young woman. One can so easily come a cropper, especially when you're young and inexperienced. I know that sounds damned pompous, but it happens to be true. So be careful.'

Harry stared at him.

'Be careful of what?'

'Of her,' Ron said, yawned, stretched and got to his feet. 'Well, I'm going to turn in. I've got a long day before me tomorrow, and I can do with some sleep. How about it, Harry?'

'I'm ready,' Harry said, frowning. 'Look, Ron, if you could see her, you'd know at once she was all right.'

'Really?' Ron said, as he began to undress. 'I judge a girl by her actions, not by her looks. It seems a little odd that a girl who lives entirely on her own should invite a strange young man to supper with her after knowing him for only half an hour.'

'Now you're talking rot,' Harry said heatedly. 'She took me back to . . . ' He broke off hastily, realising he couldn't tell Ron just why she had taken him back to her flat. 'She was lonely,' he went on a little lamely. 'There was nothing wrong about it.'

Ron sat on the bed, kicked off his shoes and pulled off his socks.

'I like you, Harry,' he said, without looking up. 'You're a nice, clean kid, and I like to think that's the way you'll always be. I don't want you to get mixed up with glamour girls: they always spell trouble sooner or later. I know. I thought I was being smart when I married Sheila. She was a glamour girl. Her idea of a good time was getting tight, dancing, going to the movies four times a week, and doing as little work as she could. She was cute and pretty, and I thought she would settle down, but she didn't. They never do.' He pulled on his pyjamas and rolled into bed. 'There are some girls, Harry, who are no good. They're no good to themselves, and they're no good to anyone else. Their values and outlook are all wrong. They want the fun without the responsibility, and that kind of outlook doesn't work. At least, it works for them, but not for the poor mug who marries them or goes around with them. Be careful of this girl.

35

Make sure she isn't another Sheila. Maybe she isn't, but watch out.'

Harry pulled the bedclothes up to his chin and scowled up at the ceiling.

'You're talking through your hat, Ron,' he said. 'Clair isn't like Sheila at all. I spent the whole evening with her, and it didn't cost me a penny. You never spent an evening with Sheila without it costing you a packet, now did you?'

'That's true,' Ron said sadly. 'Well, all right, let's see what happens; but watch your step.'

'The trouble with you is you're a damned cynic,' Harry said. 'You're always crabbing about women. Just because you had a thin time with Sheila you think every girl is the same. Well, they're not, thank goodness.'

'Ask her her views about marriage,' Ron said. 'That'll give you an indication of her character. From the start I mended my own socks, got the meals, washed up, did the housework while Sheila sat around and let me do it. Find out if your girl's keen on keeping a home or if she wants children when she's married. I'll bet a bob she doesn't want any of that. That type of girl never does, and the sad thing about it is the mug who goes around with her thinks it wouldn't be right for her to spoil her pretty hands or the shape of her pretty figure by having children. Anyway, ask her and see.'

'You talk as if I was going to marry her,' Harry said, snapping off the light. He was thankful he hadn't told Ron about Clair's views on married life. 'How could I marry a girl like her? She must earn ten times as much as I do.'

'I wonder,' Ron said, out of the darkness. 'I suppose I am over suspicious, but this yarn about being a model sounds a little far-fetched to me. I can't see any firm giving a model such expensive gifts – not these days. An M.G. sports car runs into a good many hundreds. Doesn't that sound a bit steep to you?'

It did sound odd to Harry, but he wouldn't have admitted it to save his life.

'Oh, rot!' he said shortly. 'How else do you think she got it?'

'Even in these days of austerity there are still a few rich men left who set girls up in flats and give them expensive presents. There are also still a number of girls in the West End who sell themselves and make big money. That seems a far more likely explanation than the one she's given you.'

'Oh, I knew you were bound to say that sooner or later,'

Harry said heatedly. 'But you're absolutely wrong. There's nothing like that about her at all.'

Ron sighed.

'All right, Harry, I'm wrong. I hope I am. But watch out. Don't get in a mess, and if you do, don't be a mug and keep it to yourself. Maybe I could help.'

'I don't know what's the matter with you tonight,' Harry said crossly, thumping his pillow. 'You're making a cockeyed fuss about nothing. I'm going to sleep. Good-night.'

But he remained awake long after Ron had fallen asleep. His mind was in a whirl. He wished now he hadn't told Ron about Clair. He might have known Ron would have been sour about her. Ron was talking a lot of bosh. Clair wasn't like Sheila at all. She wasn't like anyone. She was marvellous; the most wonderful, the most attractive girl in the world. Of course, it was awkward she had so much money. If he was going to see her often – and he was determined he was – then he'd have to do something about getting more money himself. He had been working for Mooney now for three years. It was time he had a rise. He decided to ask Mooney for another ten shillings a week. But that, of course, wouldn't help him much if he was to take Clair out regularly. Ten shillings went nowhere these days. He would have to think of some other means of making money, unless he drew on capital. After all, if he couldn't manage, he could always draw a pound or two from the Post Office. With this thought to comfort him, he went to sleep.

CHAPTER TWO

I

Alf Mooney had once overheard a girl say he reminded her of Adolph Menjou, and he had never forgotten it. Perhaps he was a little like Adolph Menjou. He had the same sad expression, the same heavy bags under his eyes, the same drooping moustache and the same pointed chin.

Because of this resemblance, Mooney habitually wore a soft slouch hat at the back of his head, and a hand-painted American tie which he knotted loosely below the open V of his collar. He seldom wore a coat in the studio, and went around in his shirt sleeves; his waistcoat hanging open and held together by his watch chain. A dead cigar which he kept in the corner of his mouth, and which often made him feel sick, completed the American pose: a pose that fooled no one except Mooney himself.

For the past forty years, Mooney had struggled unsuccessfully to make his fortune. He had tried most things. He had been a bookmaker, a sailor, a door-to-door salesman, a taxi-driver, a space salesman and a manager of one of Woolworth's stores. He had made money and lost it, made it again and lost it again. One year he was up, and the next he was down. One week he was driving about in a second-hand American car, the next week he was travelling on buses. Things never went right for him for long. He was either in the money or out of it. There seemed no happy medium for Mooney.

At the moment he was going down hill again. Three years ago he had won five hundred pounds from a football pool promotion, and had opened the Camera Studio in the hope that if someone else did the work, his luck might change. He employed three young fellows – of whom Harry was one – to take people's photographs in the streets, and a young girl, Doris

Rogers, to develop and print the films and handle the customers. Mooney limited his own activities to lounging in the shop doorway, imagining he was giving the shop what he called 'character'.

Somehow the business had held together for three years. This was a record for Mooney, but he could see the red light now, and he was already wondering what the next move was to be.

So when Harry asked him for a ten shilling rise, he just lounged back in his desk chair and laughed bitterly.

'Have a heart, kid,' he said, waving his dead cigar at Harry. 'It just can't be done. Business is so lousy it won't be long before I put the shutters up. Look at that lot you brought in yesterday. How many suckers do you think'll come in and buy prints? Not a dozen! I'll tell you something, Harry. This racket's washed up. There are too many at it. Besides, money's tight. People haven't got half a dollar to throw away on a photo.'

Harry liked Mooney. In all his dealings with him he had never known him to go back on his word or tell a lie. If he said business was bad and the shop likely to be shut down Harry knew he wasn't just saying it to avoid giving him a rise. The news dismayed him. If Mooney went out of business, Harry would lose his job and six pounds a week, and the thought alarmed him.

'Then what will you do, Mr Mooney?' he asked, sitting on the edge of the desk. 'How much longer do you think you can carry on?'

'The thing I like about you, Harry,' Mooney said, 'is you're unselfish. I can talk to you where I couldn't talk to those other jerks. All they think about is what's in it for them. Now look, kid, how about putting some money into this business? I've talked about it before; but if you want to save your job, now's the time to do something about it. You have a natural eye for a good photograph. You understand the finer points of the racket. If we could set up a portrait studio I'm pretty darned sure we'd hit the jack-pot. This street corner stuff's no use. It's a novelty people can do without. But a good portrait – that's another thing. We could clean up in a big way if only you'd get wise and come in with me. Now look, suppose I give you fifty per cent of the take and five per cent on your capital? How's that, kid? That's fair, isn't it? We could get rid of the other jerks. Doris could stay, but she'd have to take a cut in salary. We could get our overheads down to fifteen quid a week. You should clear that for yourself after a month or so. What do you say?'

Harry shook his head.

'I'm sorry, Mr Mooney, but I can't risk my money. It's all I have, and I'm sticking to it. This isn't the district to set up a portrait studio. It's a West End trade; not Soho.'

'That's where you're wrong,' Mooney said. 'Okay, I know I'm stuck with this lease, but even at that, these spicks around here have got money. They're as human as the rest of us, and they'll want a nice picture of themselves. We could break new ground if only you'd use your head.'

'I'm sorry,' Harry repeated firmly, 'but I'm not convinced.'

Mooney lifted his shoulders helplessly.

'Well, all right, kid, it's your dough. But I'm warning you unless something crops up within the next month I'll have to make a change.' He hoisted his feet on to the desk and tilted back his chair. 'As a matter of fact I might do worse than go into the dyeing and cleaning racket. I know a guy who's looking for extra business in that line. I could use these premises as a clearing house and send the stuff to him to handle. But there wouldn't be anything in it for you. I'd have to run the place on my own.'

'That's the way it will have to be then, Mr Mooney,' Harry said, gloomily, 'but perhaps it won't come to that.'

Leaving Mooney staring up at the ceiling in what he called his suicidal mood, Harry went into the darkroom to discuss the crisis with Doris Rogers.

Doris was short and plump with a mass of frizzy black hair, a turned-up nose and a smile that made you her friend the moment you saw her. Harry knew little about her, for she never talked about herself. She was a tremendous worker, and Mooney imposed on her, paying her badly and shifting as much of his own work on to her plump young shoulders as he could. She never grumbled, never seemed to mind if she had to work late, and didn't appear to have any private life of her own.

Harry liked her. She was the kind of girl you could be friendly with and confide in without any of the usual complications. He admired her quickness and skill, and her natural talent for spotting a good picture, and he always listened to her opinions with respect.

As soon as she saw his gloomy expression she knew what the trouble was.

40

'Has he been moaning again?' she asked, as she stirred a batch of prints in the hypo bath.

'Worse than that. He says he's going to shut down next month if things don't get better.'

Doris sniffed scornfully.

'Well, it's his own fault. He never does anything; never gets any new ideas.' She transferred the prints to the washer. 'What will you do, Harry?'

'I don't know. I suppose I could try Quick-Fotos, but they may not want me. I don't know. I wish I did. What will you do?'

Doris shrugged.

'Oh, I'll find something,' she said cheerfully, and paused in her work to smile at Harry. 'Something always turns up. Why don't you tell him about that idea of yours – taking photos at night? We've talked about it for months and never done anything about it. Now's the time. I'm sure it would work. You might even screw some more money out of him if you try hard enough. After all, you'd have to work much longer hours.'

'I'd forgotten all about it,' Harry said. 'I'll have a word with him right away, Doris. If he falls for it I'll make him put me on a percentage basis.'

'That's right,' Doris said. 'Don't stand any nonsense from him.'

Mooney was still lolling in his chair, feeling sorry for himself, when Harry came in. He gave Harry a bleak look, and asked, 'Now what's the trouble? Never have a minute's peace in this place. It's a wonder I'm not worn out.'

'I have an idea, Mr Mooney, that might be worth trying,' Harry said. 'I've been thinking about it for some time. Why not switch from day to night photography? Let's give them something new. They might be more interested to have a picture of themselves at night; at least, it's a novelty.'

Mooney saw the possibilities at once, but as he hadn't thought of the idea himself he curbed his enthusiasm. Instead, he closed his eyes and looked gloomier than ever.

'It's not a bad idea, of course,' he said grudgingly, 'but there are snags. For one thing you'll need a flash-gun, and that costs money. Then there are flash-bulbs, and they cost money too. The trouble is I haven't the money to spare.'

'I have a flash-gun,' Harry said. 'I bought it years ago, and seldom use it, and I'll pay for the bulbs.'

41

Mooney opened his eyes and sat up.

'What was that again?'

Harry repeated what he had said.

'That's fine,' Mooney said, then suddenly looked suspicious. 'Where's the catch?'

Harry grinned at him.

'I want a third of the profits, Mr Mooney, as well as my salary. You see, it'd mean I'd be working much longer hours, and I'd be supplying the flash-gun and bulbs, and it's my idea too. I wouldn't do it unless you gave me a third.'

'Have a heart, kid,' Mooney protested. 'A third! Look, don't let's quarrel about this. We'll make it a quarter, and you pay for the bulbs. How's that?'

'A third or nothing. I need the money. It's got to be a third or nothing.'

'Suppose I said nothing?' Mooney said craftily. 'Where would you be then?'

'I'd take the idea to Quick-Fotos. They'd jump at it.'

Mooney nearly fell out of his chair.

'Quick-Fotos?' he bellowed. 'They're just a bunch of crooks. What's got into you, Harry? You wouldn't leave me for a cheap-jack firm like that, would you?'

'There's nothing cheap-jack about them, Mr Mooney,' Harry said firmly. 'They're doing first-class work. If you can't see your way to pay me a third, then I'll have to go to them. That's all there's to it.'

Mooney began to bluster, but seeing the determined look in Harry's eyes realised he wouldn't be persuaded, so reluctantly he gave way.

'All right, kid, if that's how you feel about it. You can have a third. But who's turned you into a business man? What do you want money for?'

'Who doesn't want money?' Harry said, turning red.

Mooney studied him for a moment, and then exclaimed: 'Suffering cats! You're not thinking of getting married, are you? Is that why you want the money. Some dame, eh?'

Harry edged towards the door.

'We don't have to go into that, Mr Mooney. I'll go home now and get the flash-gun. May as well make a start tonight.'

'All right, kid. When you're through come along and tell me how you've got on. I'll stay here until ten-thirty. Don't be later than that.'

'All right,' Harry said and made for the door.

'Oh, Harry . . . ' Mooney said.

Harry paused in the doorway.

'Yes, Mr Mooney?'

'What's she like, kid? Pretty, huh? Have you made her yet?' And Mooney closed one eye and leered.

'I don't know what you're talking about,' Harry said indignantly, and almost ran out of the office.

Mooney tilted back his chair and began to sing in a loud, unmusical voice: 'Love is the sweetest thing.'

II

The night turned out to be moonlight and dry. There was a chilly wind blowing, but Harry didn't mind about that. The important thing was that it was dry. He had chosen Leicester Square for his work, and now, at ten o'clock with only three flash-bulbs left, he knew the idea was a success.

He had taken over fifty pictures, and was confident he wouldn't have more than five per cent failures. He had been careful to pick his subjects, and in every case he had had no trouble when he handed out his card. The novelty of the flashlight seemed to appeal to the crowd. Perhaps it was because so many film stars had been photographed in Leicester Square that the boys and girls Harry took imagined they had suddenly become celebrities overnight. Harry was sure that had something to do with it.

'This'll please Mooney,' Harry thought as he turned the film winder on and screwed in another flash-bulb. 'Two more, and then I'll pack up.'

In a few more minutes the crowds would be coming out of the cinemas, and there'd be no point in trying to get any more photographs with so many people about. And besides, Harry felt chilly. He had been standing against a lamp post opposite the Warner Cinema for the past two and a half hours. It was cold work, and he wouldn't be sorry to get home.

He looked towards the London Hippodrome. There weren't many people about now. In the distance, coming from Long Acre, he caught sight of a man and woman. He watched them, holding the camera in readiness, and then as they passed under the bright lights of the Hippodrome, he recognised the girl: it was Clair!

It was extraordinary how, at the sight of her, his blood seemed to rush through his veins, and his heart began to pound.

For a second or so he hesitated, not sure whether he wanted her to see him or not. But what did it matter? he thought. She knows what I do, and what have I to be ashamed of? Besides, it would be a wonderful opportunity to have a photograph of her.

They were only a few yards away now. She was walking by the man's side, her light coat slung over her shoulders, the empty sleeves flapping in the wind.

Harry had scarcely time to notice the man, except he seemed tall and bulky. He swung up his camera. Clair appeared in the camera sight. She was looking right at him. He couldn't see her expression, but he had the impression from the sudden tilting of her chin and a slight falter in her stride that she was aware she was about to be photographed, then he pressed the combined shutter release and flash-gun.

He had a lightning glimpse of her face in the brilliant white flash. She was looking right at him; then, smiling, he offered her his card.

She walked by him, looking sharply away, brushing past his hand and knocking the card out of his fingers. She went on, not looking back, as if she had never met him before; as if he was a complete stranger.

He looked blankly after her.

A hand touched his arm. He turned quickly to find the tall, bulky man at his side.

Harry took an immediate dislike to the pink, fat face and the hard little eyes.

'I don't think I like this,' Brady said softly. 'What exactly do you think you're doing?'

Harry bent quickly, picked up the card and offered it to Brady.

'Sorry if I startled you,' he said, wondering who this fat spiv was. 'You've just been photographed – you and the young lady. If you care to call tomorrow at that address, the prints will be ready. There's no obligation to buy.'

'How very interesting,' Brady said, and showed his gold-capped teeth. 'I have a mind to call a policeman. You hawkers are a damned pest. You shouldn't be allowed on the streets.'

44

Harry felt the blood rise in his face.

'You needn't have the photograph if you don't want it,' he said, trying to control the anger in his voice. 'Most people like to be photographed.'

'But I'm not most people, my funny little man,' Brady said, ignoring the fact that Harry was an inch or so taller than he. He tore up the card. 'If you ever bother me again I'll give you in charge.'

Before Harry could think of a suitable retort, Brady had walked away, his black square-shouldered overcoat open and flapping in the wind, his hands in his trouser pockets, his homburg hat tilted rakishly over one eye. He disappeared up a side street, leading to Lisle Street, leaving Harry, hot and furious, staring after him.

The incident spoilt Harry's evening. Why had Clair cut him like that? Perhaps she hadn't recognised him. Surely she wouldn't have walked past him without a word if she had recognised him? Who was this fat spiv who looked as if he was made of money and someone in the black market? Could he be one of Clair's advertising clients? Somehow Harry couldn't believe that.

Angrily he wound off the film and put it in his pocket. Well, anyway he had a picture of Clair now. That was something.

The crowds were beginning to pour out of the five cinemas around Leicester Square, and Harry decided to go to the studio and then get off home.

He, too, turned up the side street, leading to Lisle Street, wondering if he would be lucky enough to catch sight of Clair again; but apart from a couple of middle-aged women standing at the corner who called out to him, Lisle Street was deserted. He continued up Wardour Street, turned down a narrow side street that would bring him to Old Compton Street.

He had only walked a few yards down this dark little street when someone whistled softly behind him. He looked around, peering into the darkness.

A squat, thickset man came quickly out of the darkness. As he passed under a dim street lamp, Harry saw he was hatless and had a mass of tow-coloured hair. He appeared to be wearing a black suit and a dark shirt. Except for the dim blur of white that was his face, the rest of him was almost as dark as the night.

'Did you want me?' Harry asked, thinking probably he had lost his way and wanted to ask Harry where he was.

The man came to a standstill a few feet from Harry. The light from the street lamp reflected on his extraordinary mop of hair, but the rest of his face was in shadows.

'Were you the fella who was taking photographs just now?' he asked. He had a faint lisp, and his voice was low-pitched and nasal.

'Why, yes,' Harry said, surprised. 'Was there something . . . ?'

He broke off as the man stepped closer, instinctively feeling that he was up to no good. A fist shot out of the darkness towards him and he ducked, twisting to one side, knowing with a sudden pang of fear that the blow was merely a feint to get him out of position. He tried desperately hard to jump clear, but he was already off balance, and he only succeeded in stumbling back and in his endeavour to regain his balance he slipped off the kerb and fell on one knee.

Something hit him on the side of his head. A vivid streak of light blinded him, and then he seemed to be falling into thick, suffocating darkness.

III

Clair had recognised Harry. She had spotted him too late to steer Brady away from him, and her heart sank when Harry let off his flash-gun. She knew Brady would be furious. She had walked past Harry, pretending she didn't recognise him because she was anxious Brady shouldn't know who he was. She had made up her mind that Brady was not going to get his hands on Harry's three hundred pounds, and somehow or other she was determined to keep them apart.

She didn't look back when Brady stopped to speak to Harry. She knew if she showed any interest or annoyance Brady would immediately guess who Harry was, so she kept on, hating to walk away, uneasy and alarmed as to what Brady was saying.

She walked up Lisle Street to the Tamiami Club, paused for a moment to look over her shoulder, and then climbed the stairs to the club. She wanted to go back to see what Brady was doing, but restrained herself. She hoped he wasn't being too beastly to Harry, and wondered how she should explain him away to Harry when next they met.

The bar was deserted. The white-coated barman moved along the horse-shoe shaped bar towards her and raised plucked eyebrows at her. His thin, white face was disinterested, and his eyes, under mascara-coated eye-lashes, were jaded.

'Hallo,' he said, leaning an elbow on the counter and simpering at her. 'Isn't it quiet? None of the boys have come in yet. A new one came yesterday. He was terribly intense. Wait 'til you see him.'

'Give me a whisky and shut up!' Clair said, and turned her back on him.

A girl came out of the Powder Room: a plump blonde with eyes like granite and a mouth like a trap. She waved to Clair and joined her at the bar.

'Hallo, Babs,' Clair said indifferently. She offered her cigarette case.

'Hallo, darling,' Babs gushed, examining Clair's dress enviously. 'What a lovely thing. Suits you too. Every time I see you you have something different. I don't know how you do it.' She took a cigarette. 'Where's Bobby?'

'He'll be along,' Clair said, pushing a ten shilling note over the counter. 'Have a drink?'

'Well, I don't mind. A large whisky, Hippy,' she said to the barman. 'How nice your hair looks.'

'Do you really think so?' Hippy said, stretching up to look in the mirror. 'I'm so glad. I had it trimmed yesterday. It's not bad, is it? The beast nipped off a bit too much I think, but they always do unless you watch them.'

'Will you shut up and go away?' Clair said.

Hippy served the drink, scowled at Clair and moved down the bar.

'You shouldn't talk like that to him,' Babs said. 'You'll hurt his feelings.'

'I want to,' Clair said viciously. 'I hate his kind.' She handed the whisky to Babs, thinking how awful she looked. 'How are you? You look a bit tired.'

'Oh, I am, darling. I'm an absolute wreck. I don't know what's the matter with me. I get a most awful pain sometimes. It scares me to death.'

Clair studied the round, unhealthy little face and grimaced. Babs drank too much, took drugs, was seldom off the streets, and had been leading a rackety life for years. It wasn't to be wondered at that she didn't feel well.

'You should see a doctor.'

Babs shook her head.

'I'm scared to,' she said, lowering her voice. 'I keep thinking it's cancer. I do really. I'd rather have the pain and not know.'

'Don't be a fool,' Clair said sharply. 'It's probably indigestion.'

'That's what Teddy says,' Babs sighed and looked sentimental. 'You know, Clair, darling. I've often wondered why you haven't a regular boy. It makes such a difference. Teddy's an absolute pet. The things he does for me! He always waits up for me, and he has a drink ready and my slippers warming before the fire. I used to be so lonely and get so fed up with myself, but he's changed all that. You ought to get some boy – some nice boy to have around. You ought, really.'

'But Teddy's pretty expensive, isn't he?' Clair said, doubtfully.

'Well, darling, the poor lamb must enjoy himself sometimes. Of course he does like the most expensive things, but that's a good fault, isn't it? I mean it shows he has taste?' Babs's dark-ringed eyes grew dreamy. 'He's made all the difference to me. You should find a boy, Clair.'

'Bobby's enough for me,' Clair said curtly.

'Oh, but he doesn't count. A woman should have someone she can look after. No one could look after Bobby. He's got too much money, and he's so independent, and he's a little bit overbearing, isn't he, darling? You don't mind my saying so, do you?'

'I don't mind,' Clair said indifferently.

'You want someone like Teddy. Someone who'd be grateful for all you did for him. It makes you feel – well, as if you're doing something worth while.'

Clair finished her drink. Not so long ago she had told Babs she was a fool to keep Teddy, but now she wasn't so sure. Life was lonely. She hadn't been able to get Harry out of her mind. The more she thought about him, the more she liked him, and wanted to do something for him. What Babs had said was true. To look after a boy like Harry would be worth while.

Brady came in and joined Clair at the bar. He gave Babs a quick scowl.

48

'All right, girlie,' he said. 'Run along. No use hanging about here. You have a living to earn.'

'Oh, leave her alone,' Clair said.

'It's all right; I'm going,' Babs said, and smiled hopefully at Brady. 'You're looking ever so well, Mr Brady; and so smart.'

'Yes,' Brady said, and showing his gold-capped teeth. 'Just run along.'

When Babs had gone, Clair said, 'Where did you get to?'

'That chap took my photograph,' Brady said, and his fat face darkened. 'I had to fix him.'

Clair stiffened.

'What do you mean? Why?'

'There are times, precious, when you don't always use your brains,' Brady said patiently. 'How would it look to have a photograph of us together in some shop window for every copper in London to see? Would you like that?'

'What did you do to him?' Clair asked, turning cold.

'I tipped Ben to take care of him. Ben has the film by now. It's all right. Ben just tapped him.'

Clair's empty glass slipped out of her fingers and smashed on the floor.

Brady looked searchingly at her, and then laughed.

'Why, of course, your new boy friend! Well, well, I should have thought of that. It's all right, darling, there's no need to get excited. Ben only tapped him.' He reached out and patted her cheek with moist, soft fingers. 'You are excited, aren't you?'

'No!' Clair said violently, 'and don't do that, damn you!'

IV

Mooney dozed in his chair. His feet rested on his desk, and there was a strained, worried expression on his face. He was dreaming, and whenever Mooney had dreams they were always concerned with his own personal problems.

The sharp sound of knocking on the outer door woke him, and he sat up, blinked round the tiny office, still only half awake, and not sure if he had heard anything.

The knocking was repeated, and he lowered his feet to the floor.

'That'll be Harry,' he thought, yawning. He moved to the

door. 'Well, now we'll see if his idea's any good. Shouldn't be surprised if it was. That boy's no fool.'

When he opened the shop door he was startled to find a policeman standing on the step.

'Mr Mooney?' the policeman asked.

'That's me,' Mooney said respectfully. He was always respectful to policemen. 'What's up?'

'Young fella named Harry Ricks work for you?'

Mooney groaned.

'Don't tell me he's been pinched. I haven't got the dough to bail him out if that's what you want.'

'He's been hurt,' the policeman said. 'You're wanted at the station.'

Mooney changed colour: in sentimental moments he regarded Harry as a son.

'Hurt?' he repeated. 'Is he bad?'

'No, he's not bad; a bit shaken up, you know,' the policeman returned. He was big and mooned faced with a fresh complexion and sandy hair, and had a quiet, mournful manner; the kind of manner, Mooney thought, feeling a little sick, that would do credit to an undertaker. 'He wants to go home, and said you'd look after him.'

'Of course I'll look after him,' Mooney said. He was surprised how upset he felt. 'Here, wait a second while I get my coat and lock up.'

He ran back to the office. His knees felt wobbly and his hands shook.

'The trouble with me is I'm getting old,' he thought as he struggled into his coat. 'Getting worked up like a blasted old woman. But it's a shock. I like that boy. I wish I'd got a bottle of something here. I could do with a nip.'

He pulled open his desk drawer, but the whisky bottle he found under a pile of papers was empty, and had been empty for the past year. He sighed, turned off the light, returned to the shop, closed and locked the door.

'I'm ready,' he said. 'What happened to him?'

'Got knocked on the head,' the policeman said. 'I found him lying in the street just up the way. He wouldn't go to the hospital so we fixed him up at the station.'

'Knocked on the head?' Mooney repeated blankly. 'You mean someone hit him?'

'That's right.'

'Who was it?' Mooney demanded. 'I hope you caught him.'

'I didn't catch anyone,' the policeman returned. 'The inspector's talking to Ricks now.'

Mooney suddenly stopped and clutched at the policeman's arm.

'Don't tell me his camera's pinched? Cost me forty quid before the war, and I couldn't get another for three times that amount.'

'I don't know anything about a camera,' the policeman said, freeing his arm. 'If you'll step out, we'll get there all the sooner.'

Although Mooney didn't feel like stepping out, he did his best to move along briskly. He felt suddenly depressed and deflated.

'When a chap reaches my age and can't have a drink when he wants one,' he thought gloomily, 'the writing's on the wall. It's no use, Mooney, old kid, you've had it. Fifty-six and can't spring to a bottle of Scotch. You've had it all right. If there's ever a man heading for the workhouse, it's you.'

He was feeling very low by the time they reached the police station. He had now come to the conclusion that he was not only a failure, but that Harry wouldn't be able to work again, and the camera had been stolen.

'No more bright ideas,' he thought as he mounted the steps and followed the policeman's broad back down a passage. 'This settles it. I shouldn't have let Harry work at night. I might have known some drunk would have got annoyed and hit him. Not everyone wants to have a flashlight let off in their faces. I ought to have thought of that.'

He was shown into a large office. Two plain-clothes officers were standing by an empty fireplace, smoking, and Harry was sitting in a chair.

'Jeepers, kid,' Mooney said, going to him. 'How are you? What did they do to you?'

Harry gave him a wan grin. There was a broad strip of sticking plaster across his forehead, and he looked shaky and white.

'It's all right, Mr Mooney. It's not half as bad as these chaps are trying to make out.'

One of the plain-clothes officers, a fat, good-natured looking man in a shapeless tweed suit came over.

'He said he wanted you so we sent a constable round for

you,' he said to Mooney. 'He's had a nasty crack on the head. By rights he should be in hospital.' He looked at Harry and frowned at him. 'You can thank your stars you have a head like a flint stone, my lad,' he went on. 'Otherwise there'd have been a lot more damage.'

Harry touched his forehead and winced.

'There's been quite enough damage already, thank you,' he said. 'If it's all the same to you I'd like to go home now.'

'We'll run you home in a few minutes,' the plain-clothes officer said. 'There's a cup of tea coming. You don't want to be in too much of a hurry.' He turned to Mooney. 'I'm Inspector Parkins. Sergeant Dawson, over there,' he waved to the other officer. 'Sit down, Mr Mooney. You don't look over grand yourself.'

Mooney sat down, and because he suddenly found himself momentarily the centre of interest, he passed a hand wearily across his face and endeavoured to look on the point of collapse.

'As a matter of fact, I feel pretty bad,' he said. 'It's been a great shock. I don't suppose you have a little brandy?'

Parkins smiled.

'I might find you some whisky, unless you'd rather have a cup of tea,' and seeing Mooney's expression, he laughed and produced a bottle of Scotch from a cupboard. 'Always handy in case of illness,' he said and winked. He gave Mooney a good stiff drink. 'There you are, Mr Mooney. That'll set you up.'

Mooney took the drink gratefully. And to think he had always sneered at the police! He'd never do that again. 'Damned good chaps,' he thought, and drank half the whisky at a gulp.

'That's a lot better,' he said. 'I wanted that badly.'

Just then a constable brought in three huge mugs of tea, and put them on the table.

'Now you get outside this, my lad, and you'll be right as ninepence,' Parkins said, putting a mug within Harry's reach. 'Have a cigarette if you fancy it.'

Harry accepted the cigarette, and although his head ached, he enjoyed the novelty of being entertained by a police inspector.

'Harry,' Mooney said, 'did you lose the camera?'

'No, I've still got it, but I lost the roll of film.'

Mooney heaved a sigh of relief.

'That doesn't matter. It was the camera I was worrying about.'

'All right, Mr Mooney,' Parkins said. 'I just want a word with our young friend, then he can get off home. Mr Ricks,' he went on to Harry, 'if you feel like it, perhaps you'll try to help us. This fella who hit you. You say he was short, thick-set and had a mop of tow-coloured hair. You didn't see his face. Is that right?'

'That's right,' Harry said, sipping his tea.

'Can you give us any more details. How was he dressed?'

'Well, I couldn't see much. It was too dark. He seemed to be in a dark suit, and he wore a dark blue or black shirt. Oh, yes, I remember now, he had a sort of lisp when he spoke, and he talked through his nose.'

Parkins looked at Dawson who shook his head.

'Well, he's a new one to us, but we're anxious to catch him,' Parkins said, turning back to Harry. 'He's been doing quite a lot of bashing lately. He uses a bicycle chain. When you get that plaster off you'll see the marks. We've had three or four people in here recently with the same marks on their faces. In their case it's been robbery, but somehow I don't think it was robbery in your case. I think you took his photograph, probably without knowing it, and he knocked you out to get the film.'

'Oh, no,' Harry said. 'I'm positive I didn't take his photograph. That mop of hair is unmistakable. I never saw him all the evening until he attacked me.'

Parkins stirred his tea with a pen holder and stared down at the blotter on his desk.

'You're sure of that?'

'Absolutely.'

'Well, he wanted that roll of film for some reason or other. Perhaps you took someone he's working with. Do you remember anyone objecting to being photographed?'

Well, of course, Harry did. The bulky figure of Clair's companion loomed up in his mind. But he wasn't going to get Clair mixed up with the police. That's the last thing he intended to do.

'No,' he said, and unable to meet Parkins's steady stare, looked away. 'No one objected.'

'Don't rush at it,' Parkins said quietly. 'There's plenty of time. Just think about it for a few minutes.'

'There's nothing to think about,' Harry said curtly. 'No one objected.'

There was a pause, then Parkins lifted his massive shoulders.

'Well, that's that then,' he said. 'A pity. This fella's dangerous, Mr Ricks. We want to catch him.'

'Well, I'm not stopping you,' Harry said, and because he had told a lie and his head ached, he was angry with the inspector and himself.

Parkins looked at him for a long, uncomfortable moment.

'Think it over,' he said. 'You may remember later on, and if you do I hope you'll let me know. This chap's dangerous. One of these nights if he goes on as he's been going on, he'll hit someone who has a thin skull, and then there'll be trouble. Any little clue might lead us to him. You're still quite sure no one objected?'

Harry felt his face redden.

'Yes, I'm sure,' he said. 'But if I think of anyone I'll let you know.'

Parkins rose to his feet.

'All right. Well, I don't suppose a good night's rest will do you any harm. There's a car outside to take you home. Mr Mooney will go with you. Do you think you would recognise this tow-headed chap again?'

'Oh, yes,' Harry said grimly. 'I'd know him anywhere.'

'Well, that's something. If you do see him again, call a policeman. Don't try anything heroic yourself.'

'All right,' Harry said, and got unsteadily to his feet.

Mooney took his arm.

'I'm right with you, kid,' he said. 'Take it easy and lean on me.'

When they had gone, Parkins stared thoughtfully at Dawson.

'I think it'd pay us to keep an eye on that young fellow,' he said. 'He knows more about this than he says. Now, I wonder what made him lie like that? Put Jenkins on to him for the next few days. I think it might be interesting to find out who his friends are.'

V

Although Harry made out he wasn't badly hurt, he did feel shaky, and the shock made him restless and nervous. He was quite pleased to spend a day in bed, and when Mooney told him to take the rest of the week off, and not to come to the studio until Monday, he didn't need any persuading.

Mrs Westerham volunteered to provide him with meals, and Ron moved his typewriter to a friend's office in Fleet Street.

'You rest and sleep,' he said to Harry. 'I won't disturb you. After a couple of days you'll be as fit as a flea again.'

But Harry didn't feel like sleeping. He was worried about Clair. Was it possible, he kept asking himself, that her companion of last night had had anything to do with the tow-headed chap? Had he told the tow-headed chap to get the film from Harry? If so, why?

Harry had said nothing to Ron about Brady. He felt that until he had asked Clair for an explanation, the less he told anyone the better. It occurred to him that as Clair had cut him last night, she might not want to see him again, and that thought sent his temperature up.

Mrs Westerham was continually popping in and out. She was a tall, bony woman, as thin as a bean stick, with a mass of greying hair done up like a cottage loaf on the top of her head. Harry liked her, but he didn't feel in the mood to listen to her endless gossip, so most times when she came in he pretended to be asleep.

'What would you like for lunch, Mr Ricks?' she asked, slipping into the room without warning. 'I've a nice bit of cod or you could have an omelet; only those Polish eggs are very doubtful. There's nothing else I can offer you.'

'The cod sounds all right,' Harry said doubtfully. 'That'll do fine. I'm so sorry to be such a nuisance.'

'Don't you worry,' Mrs Westerham said. 'You rest and get well. You might 'ave been killed. That's what Mr Mooney said.'

The morning seemed endless, and when, just before noon, Harry heard the front door bell ring, he wondered hopefully, if Mooney or Doris had come to see him. He wanted company, and perhaps a little sympathy, but company before anything.

Someone was coming up the stairs. A tap sounded on the door, and he called 'Come in,' half expecting Mrs Westerham.

The door opened and Clair entered: Clair, radiant in a smartly cut coat, hatless, her hair caught back with green ribbon, looking very young and bright, and ladened with parcels.

'Hallo,' she said, and shut the door with her foot.

Harry felt himself turn red, then white, then red again; too surprised to utter a word.

'How's the head?' Clair asked. She dumped her parcels on the bamboo table, and seeing how confused he was, walked across the room to take a quick look at herself in the fly-blown mirror to give him time to recover. Then she turned and smiled at him.

'Well, say something,' she said. 'Don't gape at me as if I were a ghost. You'll make me think I shouldn't have come.'

'You startled me out of my wits,' Harry said, his pulse leaping and jumping. 'What on earth are you doing here? How did you know where to find me?'

She came over to the bed, and stood close to him, looking down at him.

'Aren't you pleased to see me?'

'Oh yes,' Harry said. 'Of course I am. Only you're the last person I expected to see – and I was thinking about you too. It is wonderful of you to have come.'

'How are you?'

'I'm all right,' Harry said, conscious that his pyjamas were old and faded, and the room looked horribly drab. 'I've a bit of a headache, of course. How did you know?'

'It's in the paper. As soon as I saw it I thought I'd come and see you. I rang up the studio, and Mr Mooney gave me your address. He asked me if I was your girl friend, and said he had heard a lot about me.'

'He's an awful liar,' Harry said hastily. 'You mustn't believe a word he says.'

'Well, I told him I was your girl. I didn't think he'd give me your address otherwise. Do you mind?'

'Mind?' Harry said. 'No, I don't mind. I don't mind a bit.'

'And I told the old lady who let me in I was your sister. I didn't think she would let me come up unless I said that,' Clair said, and giggled.

'I bet she didn't believe you,' Harry said, grinning. 'You know this is marvellous. What made you come?'

She took off her coat and dropped it on a chair.

'Oh, I hadn't anything better to do, and I thought you might like something to eat. You didn't sound as if you got much when last we met. I told the old lady I was going to give you lunch. She seemed quite relieved. I've even brought you a bottle of whisky if you feel like a drink.'

'But, look, Clair – I suppose I may call you Clair?'

She smiled.

'You may. But look – what?'

Harry struggled to sit up.

'This is crazy. Why, we only met the other night . . . '

'You mean you don't want me?' she asked, and her eyes hardened. 'Do you want me to go?'

'Of course I don't. I didn't mean to sound ungrateful. But I'm – well, I'm just bowled over. Can't you see? That a girl like you should bother to come here . . . it's fantastic.'

'Is it? Then let's not talk about it. I'm here. Stop looking like a startled ghost and tell me about your head. Does it hurt very much?'

'A bit, but it's all the better for seeing you.'

She sat on the bed and began to open her parcels.

'Who did it, Harry?'

'I don't know. I wish I did. He was after a roll of film I had taken,' and he told her about his idea of night photography, of his success and how the tow-headed man had attacked him.

'Nothing else was stolen except the film. The police think I must have taken someone's picture who didn't want it taken.'

'You – you went to the police?' Clair said, still busy with her parcels.

'They found me and took me to the station. The inspector said perhaps I had photographed someone working with this chap, and he asked me if anyone had objected to having their photo taken.' He was watching her closely now, but her expression didn't change. She seemed intent on unpacking plates and knives and forks from the picnic basket she had brought with her.

'Did anyone?' she asked casually, unwrapping slices of smoked salmon and laying them on two plates.

'I told the inspector no one had, but it wasn't true.'

'That looks tempting, doesn't it?' she said, showing him the smoked salmon, then frowned and turned to stare at him. 'What was that? What wasn't true?'

57

'That no one had objected: someone did.'

She looked searchingly at him, and then caught her breath sharply.

'Oh, Harry, what a fool I am! It was you who took my photo last night? What must you be thinking of me? I didn't recognise you. Honestly, I didn't. It was you, wasn't it?'

'Well, yes,' Harry said awkwardly.

'I'm so sorry. I – I saw some man pointing a camera at me. I didn't particularly notice him and it was dark. I didn't think you worked at night. Then the flashlight went off and blinded me. It startled me too. Oh, Harry, I am so terribly sorry.'

'It's all right,' Harry said, smiling. 'I was a bit fed up at the time, of course. I thought you had cut me.'

'I'd never do that,' Clair said, and put her hand on his. 'You must believe me, Harry.'

'Of course I do.' He hesitated, and then went on, 'Your friend didn't like what happened. In fact, he was pretty rotten about it.'

Clair laughed uneasily.

'Who – Robert? Oh, you don't have to worry about him. He's always like that. Was that why you didn't tell the police the whole story?'

'It was in a way. I thought they might start asking questions, and I didn't want to drag you into it.'

'It wouldn't have mattered,' she said, and drew the bamboo table to the bed. 'I assure you he had nothing to do with it.'

'I didn't think he had,' Harry said, not entirely convinced. 'But you know what the police are. Who is he, Clair, or shouldn't I ask?'

'Oh, he's my boss,' she said carelessly. 'Come on, let's eat.'

'Your boss?' Harry said, taking the plate of smoked salmon she handed to him.

'That's right. My agent. His name's Robert Brady.'

'Did he say anything about me?'

'Oh, no,' Clair returned. 'I had a feeling he might make a scene so I just walked on. He's always making scenes. He's even horrid to me sometimes.'

'Is he?' Harry said indignantly. 'Well, if I ever run into him again . . .'

'You mustn't. You're not to have anything to do with him. I don't want him to know anything about you. If he knew I was seeing you he'd be beastly about it. I get a lot of work through him so you won't make things difficult for me, will you?'

'Does he mean anything to you?'

'Not a thing! I think he's a fat, conceited ape. But he happens to be my boss so I have to be careful.'

'But he has no right to interfere with your private life,' Harry pointed out. 'Even if he is your boss.'

'He thinks he has. Up to now it hasn't mattered. But now you've come along – well, I'll have to be careful.'

This was so unexpected that Harry stared at her.

'Do you really mean that?'

'Mean what?'

'What you said about me coming along.'

She smiled at him.

'Well, haven't you come along?' She leaned forward and hooked her finger into his pyjama coat pocket. 'If you want to see me, then I want to see you.'

Harry pushed his plate away, and slipped his arms round her. Then he was kissing her, holding her to him, feeling her trembling, her mouth hungrily against his.

VI

For the next three mornings, Clair came to see Harry, bringing food, cigarettes, magazines and flowers. Although Harry protested that he couldn't accept her gifts, she overrode his objections. He was an invalid, she said, and it was the recognised thing for visitors to spoil invalids. If he was going to be stupid about it, she would stay away.

In the few hours they spent together during those three days, a link was forged between them that would have taken any other couple months to achieve. Once she was sure Harry reciprocated her love, she made no attempt to hide her feelings for him, and he was bewildered and dominated by her possessiveness.

By Saturday he had completely recovered, and except for a scar across his forehead, none the worse for his experience.

Before he returned to work, Clair said, he must have a day in the country, and she promised to call for him in her car on Sunday.

Ron had heard all about Clair's visits, but had not seen her.

When she called for Harry on the Sunday morning, Ron was still in bed, but as soon as Harry had left the room to go down to her, he jumped out of bed and watched Harry greet her on the doorstep. She looked particularly lovely and young in a white sweater and bottle green slacks, and Ron saw at once why Harry was so infatuated with her.

'A girl with those looks,' he thought, watching Harry get in the emerald green sports car, 'could twist any man round her finger. Anyway, they look happy enough. I hope it lasts.'

Harry had never had the opportunity to learn to drive a car, and was impressed by the speed at which Clair drove. She whisked him through Sloane Square, out to Hammersmith to Shepherd's Bush and on to Western Avenue in no time.

After forty minutes of fast driving, she pulled up in a narrow country lane, surrounded by woods and high grassy hills, as quiet and as lonely as if they were the only two people left in the world.

'Let's park here,' she said, getting out of the car. 'We can go over that stile and have lunch in the wood. Then after lunch we can walk up that hill and look at the view. From there you can see nearly all the Home Counties.'

They climbed the stile, and after walking through the quiet shady wood, they came upon a clearing surrounded by bluebells.

'How's this?' she asked, flopping down on the grass and smiling up at him. 'Let's eat. I'm starving.'

Later, when they had finished lunch, and Clair was repacking the basket, Harry said, 'You know, Clair, I can't believe it. I keep thinking there must be a catch somewhere.'

'Now, what?' she asked, glancing up and frowning.

'It beats me what you see in me,' he said. 'What have I to offer you, Clair? There must be hundreds of men you could have fallen in love with. Why did you pick on me?'

'Darling, you've said that so often,' she returned, patting his hand. 'Can't you believe I find you different from other men? Don't ever change, Harry. Always be as you are now. And let me do things for you.'

'But that's the trouble,' Harry said, worried. 'You do too much for me. I want to do things for you too. I've been thinking. I'll have to get a better job.'

'But why?' She looked sharply at him.

'Because I can't give you the things you are used to on six pounds a week. And I want to give them to you.'

'But I don't want them from you!' Clair exclaimed. 'Don't you understand that I have everything I want? Even if I hadn't I could find dozens of men who'd give me money and presents and a good time. But I don't want anything of that. I'm sick and tired of men who want to give me things!' She rested her head on his shoulder. 'Now, look, Harry, you've got to be sensible. For a start, it's no good thinking we're going to get married. I've told you how I feel about that. I must have my freedom. I know this sounds hard, but it's the only way we can really be happy together. I love you. I'm all yours. But I can't give up my present life. I can't run a home for you. If I could, I would, but I know myself too well. It'd last about a month; but it wouldn't last longer. I couldn't stand it. You don't know me as I really am. I don't want you to, and you soon would if we lived continuously together.'

'But, Clair . . . ' Harry began, sitting up.

'It's no use. You've either to accept me on my terms or we mustn't meet again.'

'But I love you! I want to marry you. Not at once, of course, but when I have a new job, and I'm earning more money. I want to provide for you and look after you. If two people love each other . . . '

'It won't work, darling,' she said, her eyes hard. 'I have my work to do, and I'm not giving that up. If you knew what a struggle I've had to be independent you wouldn't expect me to give it up. If something went wrong, I couldn't start all over again. I just couldn't. You must accept me as I am or not at all. And you must get marriage out of your mind. Let's meet wherever we can, Harry. Let's find happiness and have fun together. Don't worry about money. You won't need money with me. We can go for a ride in the car or stay at the flat. I don't want to be taken out or given things. I promise you, darling. I won't cost you a penny. All I want is you, to be around when I'm lonely, to talk to, to rely on. And, Harry, it won't be one-sided. I'm all yours to take and to have whenever you want.'

Harry looked at her in despair.

'But it's all wrong. It's not natural. If two people love each other, there can be only one way to live. This – this idea of yours is wrong. It has no foundation.'

'Nor have I,' she said with a sudden bitterness that startled him. 'It's no good, Harry. You must accept me as I am or we must forget about each other. I don't want to do that, but you

can't make me something I'm not. You never will be able to.'
She jumped to her feet. 'Come on, let's snap out of this. Let's
go to the top of the hill.'

Harry caught hold of her.

'Do you really love me, Clair?'

'You know I do. Be patient with me, Harry. Let me have my
own way in this.'

'All right,' Harry said, and kissed her. 'I suppose I'm lucky
to have this much. I'll be patient. But I want it to be permanent.
I'm scared of losing you.'

'You're far more likely to lose me if we're tied together,' she
said. 'Now, do snap out of it, Harry. It's no good going on and
on . . .'

'You're not afraid to marry me because of this agent of
yours?' Harry asked abruptly.

She looked away, but not before he saw an odd expression in
her eyes.

'I'm not afraid. That's not the word,' she said curtly. 'But it
wouldn't help. I wouldn't get any more jobs if I married you.
And I can't live on air. Robert rather looks on me as his own
property. I let him kid himself. It doesn't hurt me. Now, don't
look like that. He doesn't mean a thing to me. Honestly, Harry,
he doesn't.'

That rather spoilt the day, although Harry tried hard not to
let it. At least, he told himself as they climbed the hill, she was
honest with him. She had concealed nothing. But how he
loathed this Robert Brady. What right had he to regard Clair as
his property?

In spite of what Clair had said Harry was still determined to
marry her.

The thing to do, he told himself, was to get down to the job
of making money. It was time he pulled himself together. It
was time he stopped messing about at street corners for six
pounds a week. Perhaps, after all, it would be an idea to open a
portrait studio. Worked properly it might make money, and
then he could go to Clair and offer her what she wanted and
she'd marry him. It would take time, but in the meanwhile he
could go on seeing her, go on gradually breaking down her
objections, and do what he could to keep her away from Brady.

They had tea in a field that sloped gently away towards the
main road to London, and sat watching the cars moving towards
London as the crowds began their return home.

The cars looked like toys from where they were sitting, and they were both conscious how completely alone they were.

'Happy, Harry?' Clair asked, suddenly.

'Yes. I've had a wonderful afternoon; only it's gone too quickly. Would you like to go to the movies when we get back? We could have supper at a place I know in Soho.'

She shook her head.

'No, I don't want to go to the movies, nor do I want supper out. I have lots of food at the flat. We'll go back in a little while, and you can talk to me while I iron some dresses. That's what we'll do.'

'But are you sure you wouldn't like to go to the movies?' Harry asked, disappointed. He had the lover's urge to do something in return for the outing she had arranged.

'I hate going to the cinema on Sundays. It's so crowded, and you have to queue. No, let's go to the flat, and you can keep me company.'

'All right. We needn't go yet, need we? It's only just after five. Or would you rather go?'

'No, I want to stay; and Harry . . .'

He looked at her, and there was something he saw in her eyes that sent his heart pounding.

She pulled him down beside her, holding his face in her hands while she kissed him.

'Now, Harry! I don't want to wait. We mustn't ever wait for anything,' she said fiercely, and her hands slid under his coat and moved down the muscles of his back, and her lips parted against his.

CHAPTER THREE

I

Alf Mooney scarcely believed his ears when Harry told him he had changed his mind, and if Mooney was still willing, he would go into partnership with him.

During the few days Harry had been away from the shop, business had been so bad that Mooney was doubtful if he would have enough money to pay wages on the following Friday. He had discovered it was Harry who kept the shop going, and that the other two photographers didn't earn their keep.

And now, just when he had decided the only thing to do was to shut down the business and cut his losses, here was Harry offering new capital. Mooney very nearly threw his hat in the air.

'I've been thinking about what you said, Mr Mooney,' Harry told him, 'and I think perhaps, after all, I might make a go of it.'

Mooney struggled out of his chair and clasped Harry's hand, his eyes bright with emotion.

'Call me Alf, kid,' he said feverishly. 'Make a go of it? Of course you will! Why, damn it! If I had one I'd give you a cigar!'

If Mooney hadn't been so excited he might have noticed quite a change in Harry since he had been away. He looked a little older, more solid, less vague, and there was a determined look in his usually placid brown eyes.

'Please don't get too worked up about this,' Harry said. 'You may not agree to my terms.'

'Worked up?' Mooney said, trembling from head to foot. 'I'm not worked up.' He mopped his face with his handkerchief. 'Damn it! This is the best bit of news I've had in weeks.' Then he shot Harry a suspicious look. 'Terms? What terms?'

'I've been thinking pretty hard about what you said,' Harry returned, 'and if I'm allowed to do it my way I'll put down a hundred pounds. I'm not putting down any more.'

Mooney was so hungry for money he would have accepted half that sum, but for the sake of his reputation and from habit he began to quibble.

'A hundred pounds? But that's chicken feed, kid. If you want to go big, you've got to think big. Now, come on! Make it two-fifty, and have a splash. Damn it! The camera will cost sixty; even if we're lucky to find one.'

'The camera's not going to cost us a penny,' Harry said firmly. 'We'll use the Leica we're using now. All we want is a good enlarger for thirty pounds, and the lights won't cost us much more than twenty. We can use this office for the studio. The alterations will cost about another twenty. That'll leave us thirty pounds for art paper, frames, mounts and running expenses.'

Mooney sat down heavily. He had the look of a man who has found a snake in his bed.

'A pretty narrow margin, kid,' he said, pushing his hat to the back of his head and scratching his forehead. 'What's that about using *my* office for the studio?'

'Where else can it go?' Harry asked, sitting on the edge of the desk. He had spent a sleepless night planning the studio, and had kept Ron awake until the small hours, arguing whether or not to sink his capital in Mooney's business. Ron had been against the idea, but Harry, thinking of Clair, had finally talked him into agreeing. 'Doris wants the back room for developing and finishing. I'll have to help her and I'll need a desk in there. We want the outer office as a waiting room and to make appointments. We'll have to put up a partition to make a dress-ing room. This will have to do for the studio. It's only just right for size as it is.'

'What do I do then? Sit in the street?' Mooney asked, blankly.

'Well, I thought you'd be in the outer office, making appointments and persuading the customers to have a whole plate instead of a half plate, and getting out the accounts.'

'Why, damn it! That's Doris's job!'

'Doris is going to be busy. If she isn't, then she'll have to go. We haven't any room for seat warmers, Mr Mooney.'

'What's that?' Mooney demanded, sitting bolt upright. 'Are you calling me a seat warmer?'

Harry grinned at him.

'I'm just saying that everyone will have to pull their weight. That's all.'

'That's all, eh?' Mooney said bitterly. 'Now look here, before you start giving orders let's see the colour of your money. You're not a partner yet, you know.'

'I'm buying the equipment,' Harry said quietly. 'And I shall pay the bills for the alterations. It's not going to be a question of seeing my money, but seeing the results of my money. Of course, if you don't want to go ahead on those terms, then we won't say anything more about it. I'm still not at all convinced it will work.'

Mooney opened and shut his mouth, then pulled at his long thin nose and scratched his forehead. He realised he had caught a Tartar, and there was not much he could do about it.

'We'll have to have some working capital, Harry,' he said, keeping his voice mild with an effort. 'I haven't enough to pay the wages on Friday.'

'I'll pay them,' Harry said. 'It's agreed I take fifty per cent of the profit, and you pay me five per cent on my capital?'

This was too much for Mooney.

'Hey! Wait a minute!' he exclaimed, starting out of his chair. 'Those were my terms if you put up three hundred, but I'll be damned if you stick me like that if you're only putting up a paltry hundred!'

'It's not the case of sticking you,' Harry said. 'It's business. If two partners go into business together, both of them usually put up an equal share of capital. I could ask for seventy-five per cent of the profits as I'm putting in all the new capital.'

Mooney clutched at his hat with both hands and wrenched it off his head.

'You – you young robber!' he bawled. 'What about the goodwill and the lease? What about the blasted furniture and the cameras? They're worth hundreds!'

'Well, all right, Mr Mooney, but I thought you said just now you couldn't pay the wages?'

Mooney flung his hat on the floor and kicked it.

'It's that girl!' he cried, thumping the desk. 'She's put you up to this! I can smell it a mile off. Before you met her you were a nice, decent kid, now you're nothing but a man-eating shark!'

'She doesn't know anything about it,' Harry said, and grinned. 'The fact is I'm sick of being short of money. I want to get married.'

Mooney retrieved his hat and began to brush it sadly.

'I knew it! Getting married, eh? Well, it's your funeral. But it's a nice thing I have to be your pall-bearer. Okay, kid, the floor's all yours. I'll accept your terms and I'll get out of the office. I'm too old and worn out to fight you, Harry. I don't mind telling you I'm hurt. I never thought I'd live to see the day I'd be kicked around by you. Never. You've taken advantage of an old, broken man.'

'Even that little act won't persuade me to change my mind,' Harry said quietly. 'It's pure corn, and you know it.'

Mooney gaped at him, struggled with his feelings, and then grinned.

'Well, damn it,' he said, 'I wouldn't have believed it possible. Say, let's meet this girl of yours. If she can do this to you, maybe she can do something for me.'

'I tell you she doesn't know a thing about it,' Harry said, sliding off the desk. 'Well, if you agree, I thought we might go along to a solicitor's, and get it fixed up; then I'll get the equipment. If we work fast we might make a start in a couple of days.'

'Solicitors?' Mooney repeated, his eyes growing round. 'We don't want to waste money on solicitors' fees, kid. You and me can trust each other, can't we?'

'If we're going to do this properly, we must have it down in black and white. It's not that I don't trust you, and I hope you trust me, but I want a partnership deed, and I intend to have one.'

Mooney put on his hat and got slowly to his feet.

'I don't know what's got into you. What have you been doing over the week-end?'

'Oh, nothing special,' Harry said. 'Shall we go?'

Mooney put on his coat.

'Perhaps I'd better persuade some thug to knock me over the head,' he said gloomily. 'It might do me a bit of good.' He brightened up suddenly. 'How about lending me a quid, kid? Now we're partners we ought to help each other. I'm a little short right now.'

'I'm sorry, Mr Mooney,' Harry said, 'but I'm short too. I have a lot to do with my money.'

67

Mooney shook his fist at the ceiling.

'Women!' he exploded. 'It's always the same! When a mug gets mixed up with a woman, he's ruined, and everyone suffers. Come on then, feed me to your sharks,' and he stamped out of the office.

II

Tired but satisfied, Harry returned to Lannock Street a few minutes after seven o'clock. He was not so triumphant as he might have been as Clair had told him she was working that evening and couldn't see him. She seemed to be in a hurry to get off, and the telephone conversation which Harry had hoped would be a long one was all too short. But at least she had promised to see him the next day, and had invited him to her flat.

As he groped his way up the dark stairs and through the inevitable smell of boiling cod, he hoped Ron would be in. The new partnership called for a mild celebration.

Ron was in, but was preparing to go out. He was putting on his trench coat as Harry entered the room.

'Are you going out?' Harry asked, disappointed.

'Hallo,' Ron said, turning. 'Yes, I'm just off. How did you get on?'

'It's all fixed,' Harry said, sitting on the arm of a chair. 'Mooney and Ricks: a sign writer's putting the name on the shop front now.'

'Good show,' Ron said, smiling. 'I bet old Mooney's feeling a bit depressed. Did you make him toe the line?'

'Had my way in everything. I say, must you go out? I thought we might celebrate.'

'Celebrate with your girl friend or is she going out too?'

'She's working.'

'She keeps odd hours. I didn't think models worked as late as this. Well, I'm sorry. I'm meeting a man who I hope will give me some information. But I don't have to meet him until nine. Why not come over to the local and have supper with me?'

This suited Harry, and together they went down the stairs and into the street. As they walked to the pub at the corner, he told Ron how he had negotiated the partnership.

'I've been rushing about like a lunatic ever since. It's all going fine. I've found a grand enlarger, and I managed to pick up a small lighting unit that'll give me the results I want. Mooney and I have been fixing up the studio. Now he's recovered from the shock, he's almost as keen as I am.'

They pushed into the crowded pub and struggled towards the snack bar. There were fewer people in there, and they managed to find two stools at the far end of the counter.

'I must say this girl's made you pull up your socks,' Ron said as he sat down. 'I was getting worried about you, Harry. You seemed to be in a rut.'

'I was. You see, Ron, I hope to marry her. I just had to do something about earning more money. I can't marry her unless I can give her the things she's used to.'

'That's the wrong way to begin a marriage,' Ron said, shaking his head. 'If two people love each other – '

'Oh, I know,' Harry broke in, frowning. 'But that's not the way it's done these days.'

Ron began to argue, then changed his mind.

'Have it your own way, Harry,' he said. 'But watch out.'

He rapped on the counter to attract the barman's attention and ordered a plate of corned beef and pickles.

'What are you having?'

Harry said he would have the same, and ordered two pints of beer.

'Well, here's luck,' Ron said, when the beer arrived. 'Here's to Mooney and Ricks: may they make a fortune!'

'What are you doing tonight?' Harry asked as they began their meal. 'Did you say you were working?'

'That's right. I think I'm on to something interesting: something that'll make a good article for my series,' Ron said with his mouth full. 'I don't suppose you know, but there's a gang working the West End, picking pockets. It's been at it now for the past year, and the police haven't been able to catch any of them. Believe it or not, twenty to thirty people lose something of value every night in the West End. No one quite knows how the system works. I was talking to your pal Inspector Parkins about it, and he thinks they work in pairs. His idea is that girls are doing the actual stealing, and pass the stuff to an accomplice. Several girls have been taken to the police station and charged by men who have picked them up, but the missing articles are never found on them, and of course the charge doesn't stick.

'I've been nosing around for some time trying to get the inside dope on this gang, and I think I've found a chap who's willing to talk. I'm meeting him tonight at the Red Circle café in Athens Street.'

But Harry was too preoccupied with his partnership plans to be interested in pickpockets, and he didn't pay much attention to what Ron was saying. At the back of his mind he was wondering if he should tell Clair what he had done or whether to wait and see if the partnership proved successful or not. He decided to wait.

After they had finished their meal they parted, Ron going off to the West End, and Harry reluctantly returning to Lannock Street.

He spent an hour or so making rough sketches of the studio, plotting his lights, marking on the sketch plan where he would need new switches and plugs. He would get an electrician to tackle the job first thing in the morning. If only he could persuade some famous actress to sit for him, he thought, as he undressed; someone like Anna Neagle or Gertrude Lawrence. With a photograph like that in the window he was sure business would roll in.

As he lay in bed, racking his brains how to solve this problem, it suddenly occurred to him that a portrait of Clair might do as well. He knew just how he would light her, and could see the effect in his mind as clearly as if he had already taken the photograph. He decided he would talk to her about it the next night.

With so much on his mind he didn't get off to sleep until past midnight, and then it seemed to him he had slept only for a few minutes when he woke with a start at the sound of someone knocking at the door.

Sleepily he groped for the light switch and turned it on. He looked at his watch: it was after half past one. The double knock sounded again, and then the door opened.

Harry scrambled out of bed and grabbed up his dressing gown as Mrs Westerham, also in a dressing gown, looking very odd with two plaits hanging over her shoulders, and her eyes big and alarmed, entered the room. Behind her loomed a man in a trench coat and homburg hat.

'What's up?' Harry asked, startled, then he recognised

Inspector Parkins, and his heart gave a lurch of alarm.

'Right-ho,' Parkins said to Mrs Westerham. 'You get back to bed. Sorry to have disturbed you. And sorry to have disturbed you too, Mr Ricks.'

Harry sat on the edge of his bed, gaping at Parkins as he gently but firmly shepherded Mrs Westerham from the room.

'Well, young man,' Parkins said, coming over and standing before Harry. 'I have a bit of bad news for you. Your friend Ronald Fisher's had an accident.'

'Ron?' Harry exclaimed, starting up. 'What's happened?'

Parkins pulled up a chair and sat down, facing Harry.

'Same thing that happened to you. We picked him up in Dean Street about an hour ago. He's been bashed across the head with a bicycle chain.'

There was a long silence. Parkins sat still, watching Harry, his big, fleshy face expressionless.

'Is he badly hurt?' Harry asked at last.

' 'Fraid he is. You remember I told you one of these days this basher would hit someone with a thin skull – well, he's done it.'

Harry looked at the inspector in horror.

'He's – he's not dead, is he?'

'No, he's not dead, but he's in a very bad shape. I've just come from the hospital. He's as bad as he can be.'

'Can I see him?'

'Oh, no. I don't think anyone will be able to see him for a long time. The end of the chain caught him at the back of his neck. The damage may result in paralysis. It's too early to say yet, but if he lives it looks as if he mightn't be much use for years.'

Harry sat still. He felt sick.

'I didn't appreciate him,' he thought. 'He and I have been around together for years. We've had good times together, but we did take each other for granted. And now – well, I shall miss him. It's going to be awfully flat and dull without him. Poor devil! And it might have happened to me! That swine! To have done that to Ron. But, why? Why did he do it?'

'Has he any relations?' Parkins asked, breaking into Harry's thoughts. 'I came here because this address was in his wallet, but if he has a wife or relations I'll have to send someone to break the news.'

'He has a wife,' Harry said. 'Perhaps I'd better see her.'

'Just as you like. She'll have to be told. I'll send an officer if you'd prefer it.'

Harry shook his head.

'No, I'd better go. I expect I'll find the address somewhere amongst his papers. Then his editor will have to be told. The paper ought to do something for him.'

'Well, all right, now that's settled, let's have a little talk,' Parkins said. 'It looks as if the chap who hit you, hit your friend. Any idea why?'

'No. I was wondering myself.'

'What was Fisher doing in Soho at twelve o'clock at night?'

'I can tell you that. He was after information. He said he was meeting a man who could tell him something about this pickpocket gang.'

'That's right.' Parkins looked interested. 'I was talking to him last week about the business. He wanted to do an article about it, and came to me for information but I hadn't much to give him except the bare facts. Who was this fellow he was meeting?'

'He didn't say.'

'Well, where was he meeting him?'

'Some café in Soho. He did mention the name, but I – I can't remember it. You see, I wasn't really interested, and I didn't listen very attentively. It was a café in Athens Street I think he said.'

'You must remember,' Parkins said curtly. 'Now look here, Ricks, you haven't been too helpful about this business nor about your own accident. You haven't told me all you know. Someone did object to being photographed that night, didn't they?'

'Well, yes,' Harry said, changing colour. 'But he had nothing to do with this business.'

'How do you know?'

'I know who he is. He's an advertising man.'

'What's his name?'

'Robert Brady,' Harry said sullenly, wondering if Clair would be furious with him for giving her boss's name to the police.

'Why didn't you tell me this before?'

Harry hesitated, then said, 'Well, he was with a girl I know. I didn't want her dragged into it.'

'Who's she?'

72

'My fiancée. I'm sorry, but I'm not giving you her name. She has nothing to do with this business; nor has Brady.'

'Your fiancée, eh?' Parkins gave him a long, searching stare. 'You know Brady?'

'I don't exactly know him. He's my fiancée's agent. He doesn't like his photograph taken.'

To Harry's relief, Parkins seemed to lose interest in Brady.

'Let's get back to the café,' he said, resting his big hands on his knees. 'I want the name of it. Now come on; think.'

Harry thought, but couldn't remember what Ron had told him.

'I'm sorry, but it's no use. It's gone out of my mind.'

Parkins looked at his watch. It was ten minutes past two.

'All right. Suppose you hop into your clothes and come to Athens Street,' he said. 'We'll walk down both sides of the street and see if you spot the place. I have a car outside. We'll be there in twenty minutes.'

'What, now?'

'Yes, now,' Parkins said curtly.

'Well, all right,' Harry said, and began to dress hurriedly.

Parkins lit a cigarette and rested back in the chair.

'Fisher was a good lad. He came to me for help a number of times, and I liked him. I'm willing to bet he found out something about this gang, and they've silenced him. The Doc says he may not recover consciousness for weeks, so it's no use waiting for his statement. I'll have to move fast if I'm going to catch this chap.'

'Do you think the fella who hit me has anything to do with the gang?' Harry asked, struggling into his coat.

'I should say he's one of the ring leaders. That's why I'm anxious to find out why he stole that roll of film off you. I think it's likely you took one of the gang's photographs. Maybe they were working in the background, and you didn't see them. It was something like that. Are you ready?'

Harry said he was, and followed the inspector from the room.

Although it was after two o'clock, Mrs Westerham lurked in the front room. She popped out as soon as she heard footsteps, and turned pale when she saw Harry coming down the stairs with the inspector.

'He's not taking you away?' she gasped, clutching Harry's arm.

'It's all right,' Harry said. 'Ron's met with an accident. I'm

73

just helping the police. I'll tell you about it when I get back.'

He shook his arm free, forced a smile and hurriedly followed the inspector out of the house.

'I believe she thought you were arresting me,' he said as he climbed into the car and sat beside Parkins.

Parkins grunted, and told the uniformed driver to go to Athens Street and to be quick about it. It was surprising how quickly they got there. The roads were practically deserted, although as they rushed along Piccadilly there were still a few street prowlers to be seen, and looking out of the window, Parkins snorted at the sight of them.

'Those are the fellows who give us so much trouble,' he said. 'They hang about the West End looking for a girl, and when they find one and she picks their pockets, they come squealing to us. If they'd only keep out of the West End they wouldn't lose their money – the damned fools!'

And suddenly Harry felt a cold prickle run up his spine. He remembered Sam Wingate. He had picked up Clair and had lost his wallet! Could Clair . . . but that was impossible! His mind jumped to Brady and to the tow-headed chap. Ron had been after information about the gang, and had been silenced by the tow-headed chap. He suddenly wanted to be sick. Was Clair tied up with this gang? She had passed the wallet to him. He remembered Ron had said that was their method. He refused to believe it, pushing it out of his mind. It was a coincidence. It must be! But he would have to warn her. She must never give way to such a dangerous, stupid impulse again. She might have been hauled to Vine Street.

The car slid to a standstill in Dean Street and Parkins got out.

'We'll walk the rest of the way. It's down here. Now keep your eyes open. There are about a dozen cafés here. See if you can recognise the name.'

Athens Street was a narrow, dimly lit thoroughfare, lined on either side with shops, cafés and public houses. One or two loafers stood under the street lamps, but at the sight of Parkins's burly form they melted into the darkness.

Harry walked down the street, peering at the darkened shop facias. He noticed at the far end of the street a big American car standing outside a building. As they approached he saw a sign hanging over the door, and he caught hold of Parkins's arm,

'That's it!' he said excitedly. 'The Red Circle café. I remember now.'

'Sure?'

'Positive.'

'All right. Now you hop back to the car and wait for me. I'm going inside.'

'Can't I go with you?'

'Not with that scar you can't,' Parkins said shortly. 'You keep out of sight. That'd properly give the game away.'

Harry stood on the edge of the kerb and watched Parkins walk towards the café, wanting to follow him, but realising what Parkins had said made sense.

As the inspector drew near the café, the door suddenly opened and four girls came tumbling out. The quiet of the night was disturbed by their loud laughter and high-pitched voices.

One of them, a dark girl in a fur coat, was screaming with laughter, and staggered slightly as she moved across the pavement, hanging on to another girl's arm. The four of them behaved as if they were drunk. They went laughing and pushing each other towards the car.

A man got out of the car and opened the rear door. Harry recognised him at once – Robert Brady! Even in the dim light of the distant street lamp, Harry was sure he was Brady. The arrogant air, the tilt of the homburg hat and the big, powerful shoulders were unmistakable. With a sudden sinking heart, Harry looked again at the girl in the fur coat. It was Clair.

Brady had taken hold of Clair's arm and had given her a rough little shake. She fell against him, still laughing, while the other girls bundled into the car.

Parkins had slowed down and was watching the scene. Brady seemed aware of him. He said something to Clair, and her high-pitched laugh suddenly stopped. She looked over her shoulder at Parkins, and then hurriedly scrambled into the car.

Brady followed her, and slammed the car door. The engine roared and the car moved swiftly away.

The next morning Harry was late at the studio. He found Mooney sitting at his desk in the front room laboriously going through the accounts.

'Hey!' Mooney said, looking up. 'What's the idea? You're late. Just because you're a partner . . . ' He broke off, seeing Harry's pale, worried face. 'What's up, kid?'

'It's Ron. He had an accident last night,' and Harry told Mooney what had happened.

Mooney liked Ron who had often called in when he was in Soho for a chat, and he was shocked at the news.

'Have you had a word with the hospital?'

Harry nodded.

'I rang them on my way here. There's no news. He's still on the danger list, and they don't expect him to regain consciousness for a week or so,' he said, sitting on the edge of the desk. He fingered the scar across his forehead, frowning. 'It's an awful thing. Poor old Ron. Inspector Parkins thinks it's something to do with this pickpocket gang.'

'You keep clear of it, Harry,' Mooney said, pulling at his moustache. 'You don't want another bang on the head.'

'I must see Mrs Fisher. I'm on my way now, but thought I'd drop off and tell you the news. Look, here's the sketch plan of the studio. Would you get an electrician to put the plugs where I've marked them on the plan? The chap next door will do it. I may not be able to get back here until after lunch.'

'You're not going to neglect the business?' Mooney asked, alarmed. 'I'm relying on you, Harry. I've always been a damned Jonah, and if you're going to leave it to me – '

'I must see Ron's wife. But I'll be here after lunch. I'd better get off now.'

Mooney looked searchingly at him.

'Is there anything else on your mind, kid?'

'This is enough, isn't it?' Harry said shortly. 'You'll probably be busy this morning. Those night cards will be coming in. You'll have to explain the roll was destroyed or something. See if you can book anyone for a portrait when they do come in. The electrician should be through by tomorrow. You can make appointments for Thursday. I'll be ready then.'

Leaving Mooney to look after the studio, Harry caught a bus to Charing Cross, and took a ticket at the Underground station for Walham Green. He had found Sheila's address in a notebook of Ron's. In the notebook was a record of payments Ron had been making his wife. He had been paying her six pounds a week. Harry wondered how she would manage now this source of income had dried up. He was pretty certain that Ron hadn't saved any money.

During the journey, his mind darted from Ron to Sheila, from the studio to Clair. He was afraid to think too much about Clair. What he had seen the previous night had shocked him. What in the world had Clair been doing with those three other girls and Brady at that time of night?

Parkins had seen her, although he had said nothing to Harry about her. Parkins hadn't discovered anything at the café. The owner and the waiters declared they knew nothing about a man with tow-coloured hair, nor did they remember seeing Ron Fisher there.

Harry was still worrying about Clair when he arrived at Sheila's house in a side street near Walham Green station. It was a dark, grey stone house, with dirty, untidy lace curtains at the windows.

As Harry mounted the steps, he was aware that he was being inspected by a sharp-featured woman who was shaking a door mat from the next door porch.

'You'll have to ring 'arder than that,' she said scornfully as Harry pressed the bell. 'She don't get up 'til 'eaven knows when.'

Harry muttered his thanks, and rang again.

After nearly a five minutes' wait, and having rung two or three times, the front door suddenly jerked open, and a girl in a soiled pink dressing gown stood glaring at him.

'I'm sorry to disturb you,' Harry said, feeling hot and embarrassed. 'Are you Mrs Fisher?'

'What if I am?' the girl demanded in a shrill, hard voice. 'What a time to call! You got me out of bed!'

'I'm very sorry,' Harry said. 'I'm Harry Ricks, Ron's friend.'

'Oh!' The hard little face with its painted eyebrows and smeared lipstick broke into a smile, and when she smiled she looked much younger and prettier, and Harry could understand

77

why Ron had fallen in love with her. 'I've heard about you. You'd better come in.'

He followed her down a passage into a back room.

'It's in a mess, but I don't suppose you care,' she said, going over to an armchair and sitting down. She yawned, and ran her fingers through her ruffled, blonde hair.

The room was in a mess. There were saucers full of cigarette butts and ash dotted all over the room. Dirty glasses, a couple of empty bottles of gin and a half-empty bottle of whisky stood on the table. Silk stockings and underwear lay scattered over the floor. A dirty suspender belt was under the table. Dust lay over everything, and the empty fireplace was choked with a fall of soot. On the floor by a gramophone was a pile of records, some of them broken.

'Had a party last night,' she explained, rubbing her eyes. 'I feel like death this morning.'

Harry looked around the room for a chair to sit in, but the only other armchair was so smothered with cigarette ash he decided to stand.

'I'm afraid I have bad news for you,' he said, hoping the disgust he felt for her didn't show on his face.

'Oh?' She looked sharply at him. 'What?'

'Ron's met with an accident.'

The doll-like face hardened.

'You mean – he's dead?'

Harry was shocked to see no sign of consternation on the hard little face, only a look of inquiry and suspicion.

'No, he's not dead,' he said quietly, 'but he is very bad. It may be weeks before he even regains consciousness.'

'Oh.' She got up and poured a stiff whisky into a dirty glass. 'Have some?' she asked, glancing at him.

'No, thank you.'

'Was he run over or something?'

'No. Someone hit him over the head with a bicycle chain.'

She drank some of the whisky, gave a sudden giggle, and spluttered over her drink.

'That's rich! He was so respectable too. What did they do that for?'

'I don't know,' Harry said, suddenly furious with her. 'Does it matter to you?'

She looked at him, surprised, pouted and sat down again.

'I suppose not. What's going to happen to my money?'

78

'I don't know, and I don't care,' Harry said. 'He's in Charing Cross hospital if you want to see him, but it's no good going for several weeks yet.'

'Oh, I don't want to see him,' she said, shrugging. 'It's all very well for you to say you don't care about my money, but something's got to be done. I can't live on air. When do you think he'll start work again?'

'Not for a long time,' Harry said. 'He's very ill. I don't want to frighten you, but he may die.'

She grimaced.

'Oh, hell! That's just like Ron. You needn't look so shocked. It isn't as if we meant anything to each other. We've been separated for four years now – thank God! Only the money did come in handy.' She slipped her hand inside her dressing gown to scratch. 'Oh, well, I dare say I'll manage. If he pops off it'll let me out of a hole. I want to get married again.'

Harry stared at her, disgusted.

'I should have thought you would have had a little feeling for him. After all he is your husband.'

She gaped at him as if she couldn't believe her ears, then burst out laughing.

'That's rich! Why, he means no more to me than you do. What's he ever done for me?' Then a shrewd, calculating expression came into her eyes, and she smiled at Harry. 'I tell you what,' she said, 'I'm damned hard up at the moment. I don't suppose you could lend me a fiver?'

Harry felt the colour rush to his face.

'I'm afraid I can't,' he said. 'I'm hard up myself.'

She got out of the chair and sidled over to him.

'Well, a couple of quid then. I wouldn't mind giving you a good time. I like you. Come on, be a sport. I'm a sport too. Let's go into the other room and have fun.'

Harry backed away, feeling sick.

'I'm sorry . . .'

She stared at him.

'Don't be a fool,' she said. 'Ron won't know. Make it a quid, then.'

She was between him and the door, but pushing her roughly aside Harry crossed the room and jerked the door open.

'I'm sorry,' he repeated.

'Then tell him to hurry up and get well,' she said angrily. 'If he doesn't send me some money soon I'll take him to court.

He can't walk out and leave me without a thing. You tell him that. I'll give him a month, and if he hasn't sent me anything by then I'll give him something to think about.'

Harry was so disgusted and angry that he went out of the room without a word. As he reached the front door, she shouted after him, 'And don't give yourself airs, you little twerp. You're nobody from the look of you. Just like all his wet friends . . . '

He hastily shut the door behind him and ran down the steps into the street.

'What a ghastly woman!' he thought as he walked quickly towards the Underground station. No wonder poor Ron had been so bitter about women. He wouldn't have believed such women existed.

He paused outside a telephone box, hesitated, then entered and dialled Clair's number.

There was a long pause as the bell rang, and just when he had decided she was out, he heard a click on the line and Clair's voice.

'Hallo? Who is it?'

There was a sharp note in her voice that startled him.

'This is Harry.'

A pause, then she said, 'Oh, hallo, Harry. Darling, you woke me up.'

'Did I?' Harry looked at his wrist watch. It was nearly noon. 'Well, I'm sorry. I thought you would be up by now.'

He heard her yawn, and for a moment the vision of Sheila's crumpled, painted face came to his mind.

'I went to a party last night,' she said. 'It was hectic. I have a hangover you could lean against.'

'I'm sorry. Will it be all right if I come tonight? Will you be feeling like it?'

'Of course, darling. I'll be fine then. Come about eight.'

'Yes.' A sudden feeling of tenderness came over him. 'It seems ages since I've seen you, Clair –'

'I know. Well, come and see me at eight. I'm going back to sleep now.' She yawned again. 'I feel ghastly. Good-bye, darling,' and the line went dead.

Harry came out into the sunshine and stood thinking. He was suddenly depressed. Every time his mind dwelt on Clair he saw, instead of her, the yawning, untidy, blowsy Sheila.

He gave a grimace of disgust and went down the steps to the trains.

IV

But there was nothing about Clair to remind Harry of Sheila when she opened the front door of her flat that night. She was very spruce and wide awake, and looked attractive in a pair of black slacks and magenta coloured sweater.

'Hallo, darling,' she said, taking his arm and leading him into the big luxurious room which was as neat and clean as Sheila's room had been untidy and dirty. 'Oh, what a long time it seems since Sunday, doesn't it?' She slipped her arms round his neck and kissed him, her lips soft and yielding against his. 'Have you missed me?'

Harry held her to him.

'Yes, I missed you,' he said, thinking how beautiful she was. 'I've thought so much about you. Sunday was the most wonderful day I've ever known.'

She smiled up at him.

'Well, I don't have to go out tonight. So you can stay as long as you like. If you want to you can stay the night.'

Harry immediately forgot about Ron, Inspector Parkins and the Red Circle café, and when she pushed him into an armchair and sat on his lap, her face against his, nothing mattered except his hunger for her.

But later, when she was preparing supper, he came to the kitchen door, ready to talk to her. Before he could begin, she looked at him, smiling, and said, 'Oh, Harry, I have something for you. I clean forgot about it. It's over there in that drawer. No, not that one . . . that one.'

He opened the drawer and found a small parcel done up in tissue paper.

'Is this for me? What is it?'

'Open it and see.'

He unwrapped the paper and inside found three neckties. He had never seen such ties: ties that must have cost the earth, he thought, startled.

'Why, Clair! You can't mean these for me?'

'Of course they're for you. Like them?'

'They're marvellous. But, Clair, they must have cost an awful lot of money. I don't know if I should accept them.'

6

'Don't be silly.' She came over to him and stood by his side. 'They didn't cost me anything. I used to work for the makers, and I thought you could use a few decent ties so I wrote to them and asked them to send me some samples. They sent these. Are you sure you like them? I know how fussy men are about ties.'

'Do you mean firms give their stuff away like this?' Harry asked, bewildered.

'Well, not all of them, of course. A lot of them do, especially if the advertising manager has an eye for a pretty girl.'

'Oh, that's how it's done, is it?' Harry said. 'Anyway, I think they're marvellous, and I can't thank you enough. I'm going to put one on right away.'

They spent some minutes choosing the one he was to wear, then when he had adjusted the knot in the mirror, he turned for her approval.

'You do look smart,' she said. 'You know, Harry, you're quite good looking. I'd like to give you a suit. I think I could get you one from another firm I've worked for. Would you like me to try?'

'A suit?' Harry said blankly. 'It's nice of you, Clair, but I couldn't accept a suit from you.' He moved uneasily, shifting from one foot to the other. 'It's time I gave you something. Up to now you've done all the giving.'

'What does it matter?'

'Oh, but it does.'

'But look, darling, let's be sensible. You need a good suit. If I can get you one why not have it? It's not as if it'll cost me anything.'

'No, I'm sorry,' Harry said firmly. 'I can't accept any more presents.'

She sat on the arm of a chair and studied him thoughtfully. 'Why not?'

'Well, it's not done,' Harry said, reddening. 'Men don't accept presents from girls. You know it's not done.'

'Who says so?' Clair asked sharply. 'Don't be so conventional, Harry. Who cares what's done and what isn't done? And besides, I love you. I want to make you happy. It so happens I have more money than you. I have more useful friends than you. Why shouldn't you share with me? Why shouldn't I have some pleasure? I want to give you what you need.'

'But can't you see, Clair, it'd make me feel like a gigolo. I know these things don't cost you anything, but that's not the point. It's not as if I can give you anything in return.'

Colour swept into her face and her eyes hardened.

'What a narrow mind you have!' she said impatiently. 'All right, if that's how you feel about it, don't take anything from me. I'm not going to beg you to. And don't come here if you feel like a gigolo. You'll be saying I'm keeping you next.' She got up and went into the kitchen, her back stiff with anger.

Harry looked after her in dismay. He hadn't expected her to fly off like this, and the thought he might lose her frightened him. He followed her into the kitchen.

'Clair . . . please . . . '

She swung round and he was startled to see tears in her eyes.

'I'm sorry, Clair. Please don't be unhappy.'

He went to her, but she pushed him away and turned her back on him, and began preparing a salad, bending over the sink so her dark tresses hid her face.

'I didn't mean to hurt you,' Harry said miserably.

'It's all right,' she said in a curt, hard voice. 'Forget it. I was just being soft. Look, the tray's over there. Will you lay the table?'

He turned her.

'I love you, Clair. I didn't mean to hurt you, and I'll do anything you wish.'

'That's what you say.' She tried to pull away, but he held her, and suddenly she put her arms round his neck. 'Oh, Harry! I love you so.' The desperate urgency in her voice startled him. 'I want to do things for you. I've never been able to help anyone before. I've never wanted to.'

'And I want to do things for you too. And I will when I get some money.'

She pushed away from him so she could see him.

'I keep telling you, Harry: I don't want your money. I want you. If only you'd get that idea into your dear, silly head. I have everything I want except you. Can't you forget your pride? That's all it is. We can have a lovely time together if you'll only share things with me. What does it matter who has the money so long as one of us has it? Can't you see that? What does it matter?'

'It matters to me. I want to be the one to give you things.'

'But how can you until you earn more money?' she asked, impatience creeping into her voice again. 'When you have enough money I'll share it with you. I won't be too proud to take your presents. Harry, please let me help you for the time being, and when you begin to make more money – as I'm sure you will – then you can do all the paying.'

As Harry began to protest, she interrupted him sharply.

'If you can't do this for me, then I don't believe you love me!'

'Of course I do,' Harry said helplessly. 'Well, all right, but it won't be for long. I'm making plans to do something better. All right, I'll share things with you.' He kissed her. 'I won't make a fuss if you want me to have things, but don't overdo it, will you?'

'Do you mean that?' she asked, brightening. 'Honest?'

'Yes; honest.'

'Then I have a surprise for you.'

She ran out of the kitchen and into her bedroom.

It's quite fantastic, Harry thought. If only Ron could know about this. He always said women took and never gave. In spite of his reluctance to accept presents from Clair, he couldn't help being elated. She had taken the trouble to write for those ties, and she wanted him to share everything with her. That must mean she loved him.

She returned with another small parcel done up in tissue paper.

'I was going to give you this on your birthday, but I'm not going to wait. I want you to have it now. It used to belong to my father.'

She stripped off the tissue paper and put a gold cigarette case in his hand. He nearly dropped it with surprise. It was the most fascinating and beautiful thing he had seen.

'Open it,' she said, watching him.

He thumbed the catch and the case opened. Inside was an inscription: *For Harry: all my love: Clair.*

He looked at her, his eyes shining.

'What can I say?' He turned the case over in his hand. 'It's a beauty, and of course, something I've always wanted. But honestly, darling, if it belonged to your father, should you part with it?'

'I want you to have it. Take care of it, Harry, and think of me every time you use it.'

He caught her in his arms.

'I can't thank you enough, and I don't know what to say,' and he kissed her.

'So long as you're happy I don't care what happens,' she said.

'You will always love me, won't you, Harry? You won't get tired of me and leave me?'

He lifted her and held her, looking down at her.

'I'll love you whatever happens, and for always,' he said, and carried her across the room.

'But, Harry . . . supper's ready,' she said, as he pushed open the bedroom door and carried her in.

'Hang supper,' Harry said, and kicked the door shut behind them.

V

The grey light of dawn filtered through the half-drawn curtains, and Harry stirred and opened his eyes. He lay for some moments, looking at Clair by his side, and as if she felt him watching her, she moved closer to him and murmured sleepily, 'It's early, isn't it?'

'About five.' He slid his arm round her. 'Clair, are you too sleepy to talk? There's something I want to tell you. I should have told you last night.'

She opened her eyes and smiled up at him.

'Go ahead. I'm not sleepy. What is it?'

'You remember my friend, Ron? The chap I share my room with? He was knocked on the head the night before last.'

He felt her stiffen against him.

'Is he badly hurt?'

'Yes. It was the same chap who hit me. The police asked me a lot of questions.' He hesitated, then plunged on. 'I told them about Brady.'

She lifted her head from the pillow and looked at him. In the dim light her face was hard and set.

'You told them about Robert? But, why? What's he to do with it?'

'You remember when I was hurt? I told you they wanted to know if anyone objected to being photographed, and I said no. Inspector Parkins had an idea I wasn't telling the truth, and when Ron was hurt, he asked me again. I was rattled, and told him.'

'Did you tell him I was with Robert?'

'I wouldn't give him your name. I said you – you were my

85

fiancée, and he seemed to think that was all right,' Harry said wretchedly. He felt she had suddenly withdrawn from him, although she still lay in his arms.

'What did they say about Robert?'

'Parkins lost interest in him when I told him he was an advertising agent and your boss.'

'You talked a lot, didn't you?'

'I hope I didn't say too much. You see, Clair, there's a gang of pickpockets working the West End, and Ron was trying to get information about them for an article. He got a tip to go to the Red Circle café, in Soho. The police think that's where he was attacked.'

She sat up abruptly and pulled away from him, reaching out for a packet of cigarettes on her bedside table. She lit a cigarette and flopped back on the pillow, but she was away from him now.

'Why tell me all this? I couldn't be less interested,' she said curtly.

'Parkins and I went to Athens Street last night. He wanted me to point out the café. We arrived there about two o'clock, and you and some other girls were coming out. Brady was there too.'

In the half-light the red glowing tip of her cigarette burned brightly.

'Well, what about it?'

'That's all,' Harry said, wishing he hadn't started this. 'I thought I'd tell you.'

'Did you point me out to your policeman friend?'

'Of course not. He had left me and was going into the café. I – I don't think he even noticed you.'

'I couldn't care less if he did.'

There was a long awkward pause.

'I've been worrying about you,' Harry said. 'The police think girls are responsible for these robberies. They hang about the West End and pick up well-to-do men, then rob them and pass the stuff to an accomplice.'

She stubbed out her cigarette.

'I can't see why you should tell me all this, and why I should worry you. What exactly are you driving at?'

Harry sat up in bed and tried to take her hand, but she jerked away from him.

'Surely, Clair, you can see why. You haven't forgotten

86

Wingate, have you? Don't you see this gang works in the same way. If Wingate had given you in charge, as he might well have done, the police would have thought you belonged to the gang. You took his wallet and passed it to me. That's how they work.'

'Oh, I didn't think of that,' she said. 'You don't think I'm a thief, do you, Harry?'

'Of course not! But you must never do anything like that again. And, Clair, tell me the truth: is Brady anything to do with this chap who attacked me and Ron?'

'What on earth are you talking about?' she said. 'Why should he be?'

'Well, don't you see, Brady objected to being photographed, and five minutes after the film is stolen. It kind of hooks up.'

'Oh, rot!' she said angrily. 'Really, Harry, how can you suggest such a thing? Of course, Robert's nothing to do with it. For goodness' sake don't go telling the police that. I'll lose my job if he finds out you've been gossiping about him.'

'Of course I won't,' Harry said. 'I won't mention him again. Don't look cross, Clair.'

'It's enough to make anyone cross.' She forced a laugh. 'You had me rattled for a moment. Robert would be livid if he knew you had given his name to the police. You're sure they're not going to question him?'

'I don't think so. Why should they?'

'Are you seeing the inspector again?'

'I hope not, but I don't know.'

'Well, if you do, be careful what you tell him about me, won't you. I don't want the police to come here. Promise me you'll never give them this address?'

'Of course I promise,' Harry said, bewildered. 'I won't even give them your name. But it's all right, Clair, I'm sure they're no longer interested in either you or Brady.'

'I don't trust policemen. They're so damned suspicious. If they knew I was living alone here they might watch me. I know what they are. They pick on girls like me.'

'But, surely, Clair –'

'But they do!' she exclaimed irritably. 'I know more about this than you do. If they found out you spent the night here they'd tell my landlord and he might throw me out.'

'I don't see why.'

'You can't be too careful if you live in the West End. They'd probably try to make out that this was a brothel.'

'Well, of course I won't say a word.'

She suddenly moved into his arms again.

'Dear Harry. You're not worrying any more, are you?'

He said he wasn't, although he felt uneasy and not entirely satisfied, but thought it best to change the subject and asked her if she would sit for a portrait.

'I want to try my hand at portrait work again,' he explained, 'and if I could make a good study of you and put it in the window it might encourage trade. Would you mind, Clair?'

'No. I'd love to help you.' She seemed glad he had changed the subject. 'Do you mean you're putting money into the business after all?'

'I'm putting in a hundred pounds to equip the studio. I didn't mean to tell you. I wanted it to be a surprise. Mooney and I are partners now. It's a gamble, but I think it'll come off. If you would sit for me I know it would help.'

'When shall I come, and what would you like me to wear?'

'I won't be ready until this afternoon. I want to be sure of my lighting, and I don't want to keep you hanging about. I'll get Mooney to be your stand-in. Let's have lunch together, and then we'll go on to the studio.'

'I can't lunch. I have a business date. I can get along about five. Will that do? What would you like me to wear – a bathing dress?'

Harry laughed.

'Oh, no. I want to take the kind of picture anyone seeing it would say "That's how I want to be photographed." It has to be just theatrical enough to be glamorous, but no more than that. I'll try a head and shoulders study, I think. If you have a picture hat and a summer dress; that'd be fine.'

'I'll show you,' she said, and scrambled out of bed.

'Wouldn't I love to take a picture of you like that,' Harry said, looking at her with shining eyes. 'You'd make a perfect nude study.'

She caught up a wrap and covered her nakedness.

'Not to put in a shop window, thank you! I can see the queues now.'

And at five-thirty in the morning with all the lights in the bedroom ablaze, Harry witnessed a mannequin parade. He lay in bed while Clair brought out dress after dress and frock after frock, putting on one after the other and parading before him.

He finally chose a frock that would photograph well: a

88

flimsy, floral-patterned dress that reached to her heels, and a big straw picture hat that enhanced her beauty.

It was arranged she should come to the studio at five and change there. Harry was relieved to see she was as excited as he was, and seemed to have forgotten about Inspector Parkins and Brady.

Mooney arrived at the studio just after nine and found Harry surrounded with trailing wires and lights.

'What are you up to?' Mooney asked, standing in the doorway.

'I have a model who's going to pose for a portrait,' Harry told him. 'We'll make a big enlargement and put it in the window. I think it'll attract trade.'

'Is this *the* girl friend?'

'That's right. She's coming this afternoon about five.'

'I wish I'd known,' Mooney said gloomily. 'I would have put on a clean shirt.' He went to inspect himself in the mirror. 'I could do with a shave too.'

'You don't have to worry,' Harry said, hiding a grin. 'She doesn't care for old men. It's the young men she likes.'

Mooney jerked round, then seeing Harry's grin, grinned too.

'Don't be too cocky, my lad,' he said. 'It's the old 'uns who know all the tricks.'

'Suppose you sit on that stool for a moment? I want to arrange my lighting and I need a model.'

'What's Doris doing that she can't help you?' Mooney demanded, always reluctant to make himself useful.

'Doris is developing yesterday's films. I'm not asking you to do much. All you have to do is to sit on that stool.'

Mooney grinned slyly.

'Go ahead,' he said airily, and sat down. 'Don't say I'm not co-operative. But I object on principle. This is no job for a senior partner.'

Harry ignored this, and busied himself with his lights. He took some time getting just the effect he wanted, and Mooney began to fidget.

'If you're going to take this long over every photo,' he complained, 'we'll never get anywhere.'

'But don't you understand? This is going to be *the* portrait,' Harry said, pulling a spot light a few inches closer. 'Once I have set up the lights all I have to do is to log them and I have the lighting scheme for good and all.'

Mooney groaned.

'Well, all right, but these damned lights are blinding me.'

When at last Harry was satisfied and had plotted his lights, he still wouldn't let Mooney leave his seat.

'I've got to get the exposures right now,' he said. 'I'll run off half a dozen films and get Doris to develop them.'

'What I have to do in a good cause,' Mooney grumbled. 'I suppose you want me to look pleasant?'

'I couldn't care less how you look,' Harry said. 'All I'm interested in is getting the exposure right. You can make faces if you like.'

'In that case I'll have a look at the four-thirty runners,' Mooney said, reaching for the midday paper. 'Just buck up, that's all I ask.'

Harry fired off six films, slightly altering the exposures of each and making a note of them.

'Right-ho,' he said. 'That's all. We'll leave the lights for Clair. I'll get Doris to develop these right away.'

'Is that all the thanks I get?' Mooney asked and crawled away to his desk in the shop and sank down with a grunt of exhaustion. It had been the hardest day's work he'd done in months.

Immediately after lunch Harry went into the dark room to examine the prints Doris had made. He found her examining them as she moved them about in the hypo bath. She glanced up and smiled at him.

'You've got something here, Harry,' she said. 'This is a wonderful portrait.'

Harry came round the table and stood by her side.

'It's the exposure I'm interested in. Which do you think is the best one?'

'This.' She fished out a limp print with a wooden paddle and laid it on the drying board. 'The exposure's good, but the composition is absolutely first class.'

Harry studied the print and was startled. She was right. It was the best portrait he had ever taken. Because Mooney had been so bored, not caring whether Harry photographed him or not, he had come alive in the photograph in a most extra-ordinary way. Here was a man, disillusioned, bored, sad, fed-up, going broke, worried sick and miserable. The expression, the droop of the head, the limp, hanging tie, the battered hat, resting on the back of his head, the open waistcoat, the dead cigar built up a character that was as intriguing as it was natural. 'Why, it's terrific!' Harry exclaimed. 'It's an absolute winner! And to think I wasn't even thinking about Mooney. We can't go wrong on this.' He stood away from the print to examine it more critically. 'We must use it. Now look, this is what we'll do. We'll make a twenty-four by thirty-six enlargement on a soft Gauveluxe paper, mounted on board and I'll get a bead frame for it. We'll call it "This Year of Grace" and we'll put it in the window. Not a word to Mr Mooney. Have we any of that Gauveluxe paper or shall I have to get some?'

'We have three sheets they sent in as samples,' Doris said, who knew her stock. 'Shall I work on it right away?'

'Rather,' Harry said excitedly. 'Scrap the rest of them. When you've got it in the enlarger, call me. We must get the exposure exactly right. I don't want to waste a sheet that size.'

'I'll make a strip test,' Doris said. 'It'll be all right.'

Harry knew he could leave the enlargement safely to her, and he returned to the office where Mooney was dozing.

'All right?' Mooney asked, opening one eye.

'Yes,' Harry said with elaborate indifference. 'Doris is taking care of it.' He sat on the edge of the desk, took out his gold cigarette case and lit a cigarette.

Mooney's eyes snapped open.

'Hey!' he exclaimed, sitting up so violently he nearly upset his chair. 'That's gold! Where the heck did you get that from?'

Harry put the case back into his hip pocket.

'Oh, a present,' he said airily.

Mooney blinked at him, then relaxed back in his chair.

'Did *she* give it to you?'

'If you must know; she did.'

'And very nice too.' Mooney produced his gold watch and dangled it on its chain. 'A girl once gave this to me. Must be thirty years ago.' He examined the watch affectionately. 'Rum animals – women. Not many of them give presents, but when they do, they're usually good ones. Look after that, kid. It'll be your turn to pawn it when we run out of money. It's time my watch had a rest.'

'I'll never pawn it,' Harry declared sharply.

'Never's a long time,' Mooney returned, settling down and closing his eyes. 'I hope this portrait stunt works. Business is getting lousier every minute. Those two punks don't bring in a

91

quarter of what they should. I shouldn't be surprised if they spent most of the day in a pub.'

'Well, why don't you go out and check on them? Tom works in Oxford Street and Joe in the Strand. It wouldn't take you long.'

'What – me?' Mooney said, horrified.

VI

While Clair was changing in the partitioned off cubicle, Mooney came into the studio where Harry was making last-minute adjustments to the lights.

'Now, she's what I call a remarkable girl,' he said, propping himself up against the doorway. 'What she sees in a young hobble-de-hoy like you defeats me.' He shook his head, genuinely puzzled. 'I think I've made an impression on her,' he went on as Harry took no notice of him. 'You mightn't believe it, but when I was your age, girls flocked round me. I had a way with me. Call it technique if you like. Why, damn it, I believe I could cut you out even now if I tried.'

'Then you'd better not,' Harry said, grinning. He stood up and dusted his trouser knees. 'Still, I'm pleased you approve. I think she's coming now.'

Clair entered the studio, swinging her big picture hat and smiling.

'Will I do?' she asked, posing for the two men.

'You look lovely,' Harry said enthusiastically, while Mooney blew her a kiss. 'Will you sit here?' He looked at Mooney. 'Did you say you were going to keep an eye on the shop?'

'That's right,' Mooney said bitterly. 'Kick an old man around.' He gave Clair a sly wink. 'If you ever feel in need of a change my dear, call on me. Old wine is reputed to be better and more satisfying than young.'

Clair giggled.

'I'll remember,' she said, and when he had gone, she went on, 'He's quite a pet, isn't he? But I bet he doesn't do much work.'

'He doesn't,' Harry said, leading her to the stool under the lights. 'Now, I'll leave this to you. You've much more experience than I have. Let's try a lot of poses. I have a camera full of film, and we'll run off the lot. Now, what do you suggest?'

She sat down and folded her hands in her lap.

'Oh, I'll leave it to you,' she said, and he had a sudden idea she was nervous. 'You know what you want. I always do as I'm told.'

'I bet you don't,' Harry said, smiling. He stepped away from her and looked at her critically. It was extraordinary, but she looked both awkward and camera conscious, just like any young girl about to be photographed. 'Relax, darling,' he went on. 'You're actually looking shy.'

'Am I?' She didn't seem to like this, and her eyes shifted away from him.

'Look over my shoulder,' he said, surprised he should have to tell her what to do. The effect was strained and unnatural. A prickle of apprehension ran up his spine as he looked at her. What was the matter with her? he wondered, puzzled. 'Well, I'll try that,' he went on, hoping that when he began work she might catch his mood and relax. He released the shutter and wound on the film. 'Now let's have one with your hat on. Imagine you're coming up the road.'

'How do I do that, for goodness' sake?' she asked, putting on her hat and inspecting herself in the mirror.

'Look expectant, darling. You know the kind of thing.'

'Like this?'

'Oh, no,' Harry thought, 'not like that at all.'

'Not bad,' he said, worried now. 'But don't look quite so happy.'

'If I was expecting you I would look happy,' she returned, and her voice sounded cross.

'Yes, I suppose so. But I wanted to get the idea of uncertainty. You're hoping to see me, but you're not sure I'm coming.'

She contorted her features and peered at the opposite wall as if she was short-sighted.

'How's this?'

'Yes, that'll do,' Harry said, his heart sinking. 'I'll take that. Hold it.'

And so it went on. Harry tried every pose he could think of without success, and it gradually began to dawn on him that she had never posed before in her life. She had every amateur trick without one professional mannerism. She was camera-conscious, awkward, and her attempts to follow his instructions were embarrassing.

In the past, Harry had attended a school of photography and had photographed professional models. He knew something about the art of posing. It was obvious that Clair had no talent in this direction, and the discovery frightened him.

'I say, darling, will you be much longer?' she asked, plaintively. 'These lights are giving me a headache.'

'Let's have a rest,' Harry said, his face shiny with perspiration. He turned off the arc lights and came over to offer her a cigarette.

'But surely you have taken enough by now?' she asked, and he caught an impatient note in her voice. 'It's after six and I've a date at seven-thirty.'

'Oh. Aren't I seeing you tonight?'

She patted his hand.

'Not tonight, Harry. I promised a girl friend dinner at the flat. I'd ask you along too, only she's a frightful bore, and besides, she wants to gossip.'

'All right,' Harry said, feeling depressed and worried. 'How about tomorrow night?'

'Of course. I'll tell you what we'll do. Come round about six, and if it's fine we'll drive out to Richmond and look at the river. Would you like that?'

'Yes,' Harry said, his mind in a whirl. 'If she wasn't a model, then what was she?' he asked himself. 'How in the world did she manage to live on such a scale unless – '

A tap sounded on the door and Mooney came in. Harry was so worried he welcomed the diversion.

'That copper's outside,' Mooney said, closing the door. 'He wants a word with you. I told him you were busy, but he says he'll wait.'

'What does he want?' Harry said, frowning. 'Well, I suppose I'd better see him. Will you excuse me, Clair?'

Looking at her he was startled to see she had lost colour and had risen to her feet, her eyes alarmed.

'Don't let him know I'm here,' she said in a whisper. 'I don't want to meet him.'

She was so obviously perturbed that both Harry and Mooney stared at her in surprise.

'It's all right,' Harry said, feeling it was far from all right. 'He'll be gone by the time you've changed.' He stubbed out his

94

cigarette, forced a smile and with a growing feeling of uneasiness, went into the office. Mooney followed him.

Inspector Parkins, still wearing his baggy tweed suit, was examining the big frame of street photographs.

'Hallo, Mr Ricks,' he said, glar.cing round. 'These are interesting. It might pay me to look in from time to time and go through your pictures. I've spotted a couple of old customers just in this little lot.'

'You wanted me?' Harry said. 'I'm rather busy, Inspector. Is it important?'

Parkins lifted his busy eyebrows. There was a bland look in his eyes that Harry didn't like.

'Well, no, it's not important. I was passing so I looked in. You haven't seen our tow-headed friend again?'

'If I had I should have told you,' Harry said shortly. He was anxious to be rid of the inspector.

'Yes, I suppose you would.' Parkins seemed in no hurry to go. 'By the way, when we went along to the Red Circle café the other night, there was a fella outside with a big American car. He was joined by four drunken tarts if you remember.'

Harry went scarlet.

'They weren't tarts!' he said angrily, and then caught himself up. 'At least, they didn't look like that to me.'

Parkins eyed his angry flushed face with mild interest.

'Didn't they? Well, you surprise me.' He felt in his pockets and took out a carton of cigarettes. He opened it, found it empty and tossed it in the near-by wastepaper basket. 'I thought they were tarts. They behaved like tarts, but maybe I was mistaken. Even a police officer makes a mistake now and then,' and he laughed. 'You wouldn't have a cigarette on you, would you?'

Impatiently Harry took out his gold case, opened it and offered it. Parkins took the case out of his hand, and as he selected a cigarette with deliberate care, he said, 'Was that fella with the car Brady?'

Harry felt himself change colour.

'I don't think so. I – I really didn't notice.'

'Didn't you? That's a pity. I was under the impression he might have been Brady.' Parkins closed the case and turned it over in his hand while he examined it with a look of bland interest. 'Nice case this. New?'

'Yes,' Harry said shortly, and held out his hand for it.

'Where did you get it from?'

'That's not your business,' Harry said, angrily. 'May I have it, please?'

Parkins opened the case and read the inscription.

'What's this girl's other name?'

'Now, look here,' Harry exploded, 'this has gone far enough. Please give it to me.'

'So you think it's gone far enough?' Parkins said and smiled. 'Well, so do I. This case was stolen last week. Did you know that?'

'Stolen?' Harry said, and suddenly felt sick. 'It wasn't! You – you're making a mistake.'

'Oh, no I'm not,' Parkins said. 'We have a complete description of it, even down to the small scratch on the back. A young gentleman up from the country ran into a nice-looking girl in Piccadilly a few nights ago. He bought her some drinks, and thought he was set for a riotous evening, but she disappeared and his cigarette case went with her.' He dropped the case into his pocket. 'Unlike many young men he did the sensible thing. He came to me. I have a description of the girl, and I'm looking for her.' He suddenly pointed a finger at Harry. 'She slipped the case to you, didn't she?'

'I don't know what you mean!' Harry said, the truth dawning on him. Here then was the explanation. His first suspicions were correct. She was working with this gang! The discovery horrified him, but even now, he was determined to protect her if he could.

'Oh, yes, you do,' Parkins said, suddenly losing his bland air. 'I've been watching you ever since you lied about Brady. We're on to him, too. He's another of them. You're sleeping with this woman, aren't you? You're the fella she passes the stuff to. We know all about you, Ricks. She's keeping you, too.'

'That's a damned lie!' Clair said from the doorway. She came into the office like a furious little hurricane, pushed Harry aside and faced Parkins. 'You keep your dirty mouth shut! I took the case! I gave it to him as a present! He didn't know it was stolen! He doesn't know anything about anything! Leave him out of this! Do you hear? Leave him out of this!'

PART TWO

CHAPTER ONE

I

The clock hands on the dashboard of the car pointed to five minutes to eight. Rain ran down the windscreen, and the ancient wiper creaked to and fro, pushing the stream of water aside, keeping clear a small arch through which Harry could see the entrance to the prison.

It was a cold, bleak morning, and sodden grey clouds moved sluggishly in the chilly wind.

Harry smoked uneasily, resting his hands on the driving wheel, his eyes intent on the tall, wrought-iron gates that had separated him from Clair for the past nine months. She was due out at eight o'clock. During those long months while she had been serving her sentence, Harry had neither seen nor heard from her.

After she had been sentenced he had spoken to her for a few minutes. Parkins had beckoned to him, and had led him along a passage tiled in white, and which had reminded Harry of the entrance to a public convenience. Clair was in a cell, waiting to be taken to the prison at Aylesbury. She had been quiet and cold and as hard as granite. It had been like saying good-bye to a stranger.

'Don't ever come to see me,' she said, standing away from him and looking straight at him, 'and don't ever write. I don't want to be reminded of you. I won't see you if you come. I won't read your letters if you write.'

'All right,' Harry said, 'but I won't forget you, Clair.'

She had given a sneering little smile when he said that.

'You'll forget all right,' she had said.

Then a uniformed policewoman had come in. Clair had given Harry one long, searching look as if she wanted to impress his face on her mind, then she had gone with the policewoman, her head up and her mouth set.

He didn't write to her or visit her because he knew she had meant what she had said, but she remained as alive in his mind as she had been when he held her in his arms for the first time.

Parkins had said she had been lucky to have got off with a year. She had told them nothing about the gang, admitted she had been stealing for over a year, but refused to incriminate anyone else. She had cleared Harry of suspicion, and since she had been in prison no other cases of pickpocketing had been reported. The gang was lying low.

To Parkins's angry disappointment there was no evidence to connect Robert Brady with Clair. She admitted he was a friend of hers, but denied he was a member of the gang. Brady had slipped away like a ghost at the first sign of trouble. Parkins told Harry he had left the country and was probably in America.

'I doubt if he'll show his nose in London for some time,' Parkins had said. 'Pity; I would have liked to have hooked him.'

And the tow-headed chap also disappeared.

While Clair was waiting trial Harry had been desperately busy trying to raise money for her defence. She had told him to sell everything she possessed, but he kept some of her clothes and stored them in his room. The car was sold; so was the radiogram and the cocktail cabinet. Her jewellery had been taken by the police and returned to its various owners. There was very little left after they found her guilty: some clothes, a few books, a fountain pen and a handbag. Harry kept these things in his room.

'I'm going to make a home for her,' he told Mooney. 'I have nine months to make money in, and I'm going to make it.'

But the partnership didn't succeed. It was as Harry had suspected. The people of Soho had better things to do with their money than spend it on a photograph.

The enormous enlargement of Alf Mooney failed to attract customers.

'With that face,' Mooney said gloomily, 'you're driving custom away.'

But Harry knew it was a fine study. He knew it proclaimed him as an outstanding photographer, and he was reluctant to take it out of the window. He was back on his beat now, taking photographs in the street. Tom and Joe had gone. Doris had obstinately refused to go, accepting half-wages until they had weathered the depression. Mooney was suicidal, and kept telling Harry to give up and close the shop.

Then came the lucky break that Harry had been praying for. He happened to be in the shop with Mooney one wet afternoon, standing in the doorway, staring up at the lead-coloured skies and wondering when he would be able to get out on the job, when he noticed a well-dressed man pause to look at Mooney's portrait.

Harry regarded the man enviously. He was immaculately dressed, dark and good looking. His age might have been forty or even fifty. There was an air of confidence about him that told of success, riches and good living. He studied the photograph for some minutes, and then looking up, caught Harry's anxious eyes.

'Who did that?' he asked.

'I did,' Harry said.

'Have you any more like it?'

'I'm afraid I haven't. I've only just started that kind of work.'

'Would you care to take some portraits for me?' the man asked, and took from his wallet a card. 'You may have heard of me if you are at all interested in the theatre.'

Harry took the card. Allan Simpson! The best-known and most successful theatrical producer in London! He felt himself turn hot, then cold with excitement.

'Why, yes, Mr Simpson. Of course I would.'

'I'll tell you what we'll do,' Simpson said. 'Come up to the Regent Theatre tomorrow afternoon with your kit, and we'll try some shots. If you do as well as this we might get together. Would you care to do that?'

That was five months ago, and now Harry worked exclusively for Simpson at a salary of twenty-five pounds a week. It was unbelievable, of course. Even now, as Harry sat in the shabby little Morris he had bought second-hand, he couldn't believe his good fortune. The work wasn't arduous. He was responsible for taking all the stills to dress the outside of the theatre, and all the portraits for publicity purposes. When a new show was being produced he was kept busy, but once it was running he had more time on his hands than he cared about. Simpson had made him sign a contract to do no other work except the work Simpson wanted him to do.

Because it was due to Mooney's portrait that his luck had

changed, Harry offered Mooney the job as his assistant, and persuaded Simpson to pay Mooney five pounds a week which Harry made up to ten out of his own pocket. Mooney grudgingly accepted the offer. His job was to carry the equipment, set up the lights under Harry's directions, keep people from making a noise while Harry worked, and make himself generally useful which he seldom did. Doris processed the films, made the enlargements and mounted them. Harry paid her five pounds a week out of his own pocket. Even at that, he was now earning fifteen pounds a week which was more than double what he had ever earned.

Out of what was left to him after income tax had been deducted he managed to save a few pounds a week. He remained with Mrs Westerham, and his only extravagance was to buy the second-hand Morris from a bankrupt firm in Soho and which he got for ninety pounds, not perhaps such a bargain as it seemed for as it turned out, it was more luck than skill that kept the engine running.

However, it got Harry to the Regent Theatre when he had to work late, and somehow it had brought him all the way from Sloane Square to this country road just outside Aylesbury to bring Clair back in triumph.

She had said he would forget her, but he hadn't. His love for her had grown more solid and had taken deeper roots during her absence. He had thought about her a great deal. He had wondered about her. She had deceived him and lied to him; she was a thief. These things he forgave. She was in love with him; of that he was sure. It was because she loved him and wanted to keep him that she had lied to him. Would she still be in love with him? That worried him more than her past. Would she be glad he was here to meet her or would she be angry and ashamed?

He had talked to Mooney about meeting her. Mooney liked her. That she was a thief didn't disturb him. That she gave herself away to the police because she wanted to keep Harry out of their hands pleased him.

'A girl who can do that's all right,' he had said to Harry. 'Go and meet her. If she doesn't like it now, she'll remember it later. A girl likes attention.'

So here he was on a bleak, wet morning, sitting in the wheezy, broken-down Morris waiting for his love. The minutes dragged by. Eight o'clock came; the clock hands moved on slowly to five past. Then there was a sudden rattle of iron against iron and one of the big gates swung inwards. Clair came out into the wet, lonely road.

She came out as she had gone in, her head high, her mouth set. She was wearing the smart coat and skirt she had worn when she had come to sit for her portrait. She carried her smart little hat in her hand. A wardress appeared, said something to her and patted her arm. Clair paid no attention. She began to walk quickly towards Aylesbury and towards the waiting car.

Harry's heart was beating so rapidly that he felt suffocated. He couldn't move, but watched the trim figure coming towards him in a kind of emotional stupor, and it was only when she was within a few yards of the car that he pulled himself together, opened the door and scrambled out.

She stopped short at the sight of him, and they looked at each other.

'Hallo, Clair,' Harry said huskily. He had an absurd feeling he was going to cry.

'Hallo, Harry,' she said, her face hard and expressionless. 'What brings you here?'

He paused close to her, longing to take her in his arms while she looked past him down the long and empty road.

'Didn't you expect me, Clair? I've come to take you home.'

'I have no home,' she said in a cold, flat voice.

'Don't let's stand out in the rain; you'll get wet,' Harry said, trying hard to speak normally. 'Let's get in. I bet you could do with a cigarette.'

Although her face remained hard, he saw her lips begin to tremble, and she put her hand to her mouth.

'I don't think I'll get in. It's all right. You don't have to bother. I – I'd just as soon walk.'

He put his hand on her arm, and at his touch, her face suddenly twitched and she looked hastily away, but she allowed him to lead her to the car and help her in. He ran round to the other side, slipped under the steering wheel. 'Here, have a cigarette,' he said, dropping a packet of Players and a box of matches into her lap. 'I'll start the car. It usually takes hours.'

While he was coaxing life into the engine, he looked straight ahead, feeling her trembling against him. She ignored the carton of cigarettes that lay in her lap, and out of the corner of his eye he could see her fists clench tightly, and then suddenly she gave a harsh sob that seemed to be wrenched from her in spite of her efforts to control it.

Still not looking at her, Harry reached out and took her hand and she held on to it desperately. Then she began to cry.

'It's all right, darling,' he said, putting his arm round her shoulders and pulling her to him. 'I'm here. I love you. It's all going to be all right. Oh, Clair, my darling . . . my darling . . .'

II

As luck would have it Mrs Westerham had a vacant room opposite Harry's room, and Harry had rented it for a couple of weeks. He, Mooney and Doris had spent their spare time making it 'nice' as Doris called it. They had rearranged the furniture, put up new curtains, bought a coverlet for the divan and arranged flowers on the window-sill.

As Harry pushed open the door and led Clair into the room he thought at least it looked clean, comfortable and bright. It couldn't compare to the luxurious room in the Long Acre flat, but it did somehow look homely and inviting even though the carpet was worn and the wallpaper was past its prime.

'This is only until we get something better,' Harry said. 'The bed's comfortable, anyway. I've tried it.'

Clair scarcely looked at the room. She dropped her hat and bag listlessly on to the bed and wandered over to the window. All the way back to London, they had said little to each other. She had looked through the windscreen, her eyes hungry for the sight of people, traffic, the houses and streets from which she had been locked away for nine months.

Harry hadn't attempted to make conversation. He was content to sit at her side, to glance at her occasionally, and take her as quickly as the ancient Morris could go to Lannock Street.

'I'll leave you for a moment,' he said, watching her. 'You'll want to tidy up. When you're ready, will you come into my room? It's right opposite. I'll have some coffee ready.'

She didn't turn.

'All right,' she said.

Harry went into his room and half closed the door, took off his raincoat and hung it in the cupboard. He lit a cigarette, moved to the window and stared down into the rain-swept street. It was now half past nine, and he felt as if he had been up for hours.

Of course she was bound to feel strange, he thought. He must be patient, but if only she had come to him, let him comfort her instead of being so hard and distant.

He waited for more than half an hour, then worried, crept over to his door and listened. There was no sound from Clair's room. He crossed the passage and looked round the half-open door. She still stood by the window as he had left her, motionless, her head resting on her arm. But there was a sag to her shoulders and a weariness about the way she stood that tugged at his heart.

He went to her, turned and pulled her to him.

'Darling Clair,' he said. 'It's all right now. Come and sit down. You look so tired.' He sat in an armchair and pulled her on to his knees. She lay limply against him, her hands in her lap, her head against his shoulder. They sat like that for some time, neither of them saying anything, and as the minutes passed, he felt her relaxing against him.

'I thought you were certain to forget me,' she said suddenly. 'I couldn't believe it when I saw you get out of the car. It's the loveliest thing that's ever happened to me.'

He slid his hands over hers.

'You didn't forget me, why should I forget you?'

She lifted her shoulders.

'Who else had I to think about? And there was so much to take your attention away from me.'

'Well, I didn't forget,' Harry said happily. 'I've been counting the days. In my room there's a calendar with every day marked off since you went away.'

She pushed away from him, sat up and looked at him. Her eyes searched his face.

'Still the same old Harry. You haven't changed. You're still nice and kind and different. I worried myself sick you'd've changed, but you haven't.'

He was looking at her. Well, *she* had changed. There was a hardness in her eyes that worried him. She looked older, not quite so pretty, and there were lines each side of her mouth that gave her a cynical, bitter expression.

'Go on, say it,' she said. 'I know I've changed, but so would you if you'd been kept in a cage like an animal for nine months.'

'It'll all come right, darling,' he said, taking her face in his

103

hands. 'Only try not to be too bitter about it. I can guess what it must have been like, but it's over, and you've got to try to forget it. You will, won't you?'

She kissed him, and at the touch of her lips, he felt a wave of tenderness and desire run through him, and he caught her to him, kissing her, hoping to arouse in her the same urgent longing that gripped him. But she pushed him away, got off his lap and wandered over to the window.

'Not yet, Harry,' she said. 'Be patient with me. I feel cold and hard inside. Be patient with me.'

For a few seconds he sat trembling, disappointed, then he got to his feet.

'Sorry, Clair, of course. There's lots of time.'

She swung round on her heels to look at him.

'I don't know what I should have done without my thoughts of you,' she said. 'Later, Harry, I promise. Just give me time to get over all this.'

'Of course, Clair . . . Let me make you some coffee. Come into my room. It's bigger than this, and there's a better view. I was wondering if you would like it instead of this one. Come in and see it.'

She linked her arm through his, looked up at him and for a moment he caught a glimpse of the old Clair.

They went into his room, and while he heated coffee she wandered around looking at his things.

'Who's that?' she asked suddenly, standing before a photograph. 'He looks nice.'

'Ron – Ron Fisher,' Harry said, pouring the coffee into cups.

'Oh.' She turned away, her face hardening. After a moment's silence, she went on, 'What happened to him?'

'He's in a home in Brighton,' Harry said. 'The newspaper he worked for is looking after him.'

'A home?' She looked at Harry, then away. 'Isn't he all right now?'

'He won't ever be quite well,' Harry said quietly. 'Here, sit down and try this. You do have sugar?'

'They didn't catch the man who did it?' She took the cup of coffee and sat down. There was a cold, impersonal look on her white face.

'No.'

'I suppose you want to know if I had anything to do with him?'

'No, I don't. I don't want to know anything about the past, Clair.'

She stirred the coffee, her mouth pursed, a frown creasing her forehead.

'Tell me about yourself, Harry,' she said promptly. 'What have you been doing?'

So he told her about Alf Mooney's portrait and how Allan Simpson had seen it and had given him a contract.

'Of course it's unbelievable,' he said, smiling at her. 'I'm now earning fifteen pounds a week, and I've been saving like mad for the day when we'd meet again. Simpson is pleased with my work, and I think when my contract runs out I'll get better terms. I want to break the monopoly clause. At the moment I can't work for anyone else, nor can I do private work. If I can get him to agree to dropping that clause I should make a lot more money.'

'The wheel turns,' she said with a bitter little smile. 'You're now making more than I. It's your turn, isn't it, Harry?'

'But you mustn't mind,' Harry said, taking her hand. 'You remember you once persuaded me to share with you? You were right when you said it didn't matter who had the money so long as one of us had it. Clair, darling, ever since you've been away I have been planning to do things for you. The past doesn't matter; nothing matters except we love each other. I want you to marry me. Will you? Will you marry me and help me and share with me whatever I have?'

'I don't want to get married. I'll live with you, Harry, but not marriage.'

'But why? We're only asking for trouble if we don't marry, Clair. Why are you scared of marriage?'

'What's going to happen to me?' she asked, avoiding his question. 'There's nothing I can do. I can't run a home, and yet you ask me to marry you. I don't know enough about anything to earn a living. All I'm good at is picking pockets. Who wants a wife like that?'

'I do, Clair,' Harry said. 'We'll take a service flat somewhere and you can help me in my work. I'll teach you. Mooney's no good at lighting. You'll find it interesting. You'll meet all the stars. It'll be fun darling.'

'Fun for them to meet an old lag?' she asked, raising her eyebrows.

'You must stop being bitter, Clair. No one will know about

your past. You can trust Mooney. He's the only one who knows, and he likes you. He won't talk.'

She shifted her shoulders in a hopeless gesture.

'How can I help you?'

'After a couple of weeks you'll know all about lighting. It's simple enough and interesting too. Seriously Clair, will you marry me? It's the only answer. I won't expect you to do a thing in the flat. All I want is to have you with me for always. Say yes, darling.'

'But Harry, this is ridiculous. You don't know anything about me. How can you want to marry me?'

'I know all I want to know. We'll make a fresh start. It'll be all right. So long as you love me, nothing matters.'

'I love you enough to want to keep you happy, and marrying will only bring you unhappiness, Harry.' She got up and moved restlessly about the room. 'I'm no good. You may as well know it now because you'll find out before long for yourself. I was never any good, and I never will be any good. It's the way I'm made.'

'That's nonsense,' Harry said. 'If you know what's right and what's wrong, and obviously you do, you can get yourself straightened out.'

She shook her head.

'You're such an old-fashioned darling.' She came over and sat on the floor at his feet. 'It's not as easy as that. I don't want to get straightened out as you call it. I have a kink. Ever since I can remember I've been in trouble. You wouldn't think to look at me that my father was a labourer on the railway, would you? Well, he was. We lived in a council house. My mother wasn't quite all there. She couldn't read or write; and she scarcely ever did anything to the house. It was a pigsty of a place. I was allowed to run wild, play in the streets, do what I liked. When I was fifteen, my father got drunk one night and came to my room. My mother caught us, and there was a fight. She was thrown downstairs. She broke her back. They gave my father five years, and he got another five years for nearly killing another convict. They put me in a home, but I didn't stay long. I ran away and got a job in a laundry. That cured me of working for a living.' She reached for a cigarette, lit it and tossed the match angrily into the fireplace. 'I'm sorry to be so sordid, Harry, but you must know what you think you want to marry. I and another girl palled up. We worked the big stores, shop lifting.

It was a good racket while it lasted. She was caught and given a year. That scared me and I gave it up. Then the war came, and I made friends with an American officer. I lived with him until he went overseas. He introduced me to a pal of his, and I lived with him. If he didn't give me money – and he was mean sometimes – I stole from him. He had so much he never missed it. He was a ghastly little squirt, but I put up with him because of his money. I hoped he would take me back to America with him. I wanted to go to America. But he went without telling me, and I was left high and dry. For a week or so I had a bad time. I was broke and hadn't anywhere to live. I spent my nights in air raid shelters and walked the streets for money.' She didn't look at Harry. 'Sorry, darling, but there it is. You've got to know the truth. I ran into another man. He was a crook. He taught me to pick pockets. He had three other girls working for him. It was a marvellous racket while it lasted. I've never made so much money. Then I met you, Harry. You didn't realise it, but you saved my neck that evening. That was the first and only time I had a pang of conscience. I hated myself for making you my stooge. I still hate myself.' She stubbed out the cigarette, frowning. 'It was my luck to slip up over the cigarette case. I should have given it to Rob . . . to the man I was working for, but it was such a beauty I couldn't resist making you a present of it. It was a mad, stupid thing to have done. But then most things I do are mad and stupid.' She made an angry, impatient gesture. 'I'm not trying to excuse myself. I'm bad, and until I met you, I didn't give a damn what I was. Well, that's the story. Pretty, isn't it? And don't think I'm a poor little girl who hasn't had a chance. I've had dozens of chances. I was offered a job once in a hat shop. I could have earned four pounds a week, but picking pockets brought me in thirty to fifty pounds, and I preferred to pick pockets. It was much more exciting and much more profitable, and I was my own mistress. The court missionary wanted me to get a job in a factory. That was sweet, wasn't it? From eight to five, at five pounds a week. No, thank you! I told her to go to hell. Then some old lady took a fancy to me and wanted me to be her companion. Can you imagine me as a companion to an old lady? Oh, I've had lots of chances, but I preferred the easy way. That's the way I'm made. Well, now you know. So don't let's talk about getting married. It's hopeless.'

Harry had listened to all this in silence.

'I really don't care what you've been, Clair,' he said when she had finished. 'What I want to be sure of is you really love me. I think you do. You have said so, but I'd like you to say it once more.'

'Yes, I love you,' she said, looking up at him. 'And there are moments, Harry, when I wish I didn't. I've never loved anyone but you. Why I should have to pick on you I don't know. Why couldn't I have fallen in love with one of my own kind? Someone as worthless and as rotten as I am.'

Harry took her in his arms.

'Please, Clair, don't talk like that. If you really want to make me happy, marry me. I know you and I will make a go of it. The past doesn't matter.'

'Do you really mean you want to marry me after what I've told you?' she asked blankly. 'You can't mean it, Harry.'

'But I do. Nothing matters so long as I have you. I want you more than anything in the world.'

She studied him for a moment, then dropped her hands in her lap with a gesture of resignation.

'All right; if that's what you want. But I warn you. I'm no good and I'll never be any good.'

Harry didn't believe her.

III

The next three weeks were full of bustling activity for Harry. With Doris's aid – and she walked herself nearly to a standstill – he found a two-room service flat, well enough furnished, in a quiet Kensington street. The rent was four guineas a week – more than he wanted to pay.

'If your wife cares to look after the flat,' the agent told him, 'you can have it for three guineas. It's small and compact and wouldn't be difficult to run.'

But Harry had promised Clair she wouldn't have to do any housework. To have service for the extra guinea was worth it, he told himself, although Doris was scandalised. She admired Clair's looks and the way she dressed, but felt she should buckle down to a little housework.

'It's not as if it would kill her,' she said to Mooney.

'You leave her alone,' Mooney said. 'She's all right. There're some girls who're fitted to slave in a house. That one isn't.'

It was lucky for Harry there was little work to be done at the theatre during those three weeks, and he spent most of his time in Clair's company. She was restless and wanted to go out continuously, and they spent more money than Harry could afford. But he told himself that this was just a fling until she had got used to her freedom.

He seldom saw Allan Simpson, and took his orders from Val Lehmann, Simpson's business manager. He told Lehmann he was getting married.

'My contract comes up for renewal at the end of the month,' he said. 'I was wondering if Mr Simpson would consider cutting out the monopoly clause. I have a lot of spare time, and I'd like to be able to do some portrait work for myself.'

Lehmann, a serious-looking young man, prematurely bald, whose weak eyes hid behind the thick lenses of his spectacles, said he would have a word with Simpson.

'He doesn't like the staff doing outside work,' he said, 'but in your case he might make an exception. Suppose, instead, I try and get you a raise? What are you getting now?'

'Twenty-five, but out of that I have to pay my two assistants. I'm not clearing much more than ten by the time tax is deducted.'

'Suppose I push him up to thirty? Any good?'

Harry hesitated.

'I'd prefer to do private work, Mr Lehmann, if I can. I want every shilling I can earn.'

Lehmann smiled. He liked Harry, and thought his work was sound.

'All right. I'll speak to him. What are you marrying – an extravagant wife?'

The marriage was to take place at the Kensington Registry. Only Mooney and Doris were invited. Clair said she didn't want any fuss. Harry had been disappointed by her attitude towards the coming wedding. She behaved more like a patient facing a serious operation than a bride.

On the morning of the wedding, as he was shaving, she came into his room.

'Hey!' he said, turning to smile at her. 'This isn't allowed. The groom isn't supposed to see the bride on the wedding morn. It's bad luck or something . . . ' But he broke off, seeing how pale and worried she looked. 'What's the matter, Clair?'

She began to say something, stopped, and looked helplessly at him.

'I know,' he said, wiping off his lather. 'You've got cold feet, haven't you?' He went to her and put his arms round her. 'It's all right, Clair. Go and get dressed. We'll have a damned big drink before we go. It's going to be all right.'

'You're sure this is what you want, Harry?' she said, looking searchingly at him. 'I'll live with you without marrying you. You don't have to do this.'

'I want it,' Harry said. 'Don't fuss, darling.'

She pulled away from him and wandered over to the mirror and inspected herself.

'I don't know why I'm acting like this,' she said impatiently. 'I thought I was tough, but this worries me sick. If this is really what you want I'll go through with it, but, Harry don't have regrets after, will you?'

As he was going to her the door opened and Mooney appeared resplendent in a new hat and tie.

'What's all this?' he said, genuinely shocked. 'You go back to your room, young lady. Doris is waiting for you. Damn it! One doesn't marry every day, and one's got to observe the conventions.'

They were married at noon. The sun shone for them as they came out of the registry, arm-in-arm, both quiet, both a little fearful in their minds.

Mooney and Doris followed them down the steps. Mooney whistled Mendelssohn's Wedding March under his breath, but he too wasn't over happy.

'Like a damned funeral,' he whispered to Doris. 'We've got to get some drinks into these two or they'll burst into tears.'

They had agreed not to go away for a honeymoon, but to have lunch with Mooney and Doris at the new flat, and then Harry thought it would be nice to drive into the country for the afternoon. He felt it would be romantic to return to Wendover where they once spent such a happy Sunday. Clair rather listlessly agreed.

With Mooney in charge of the drinks, the wedding lunch turned out to be quite a success. Thanks to his overpowering cocktails, Clair came out of her moody depression and joined in Mooney's hilarity and Doris's valiant attempts to keep the conversation going. But it was a relief to Mooney and Doris when they saw them off in the Morris, they having volunteered to stay

110

behind and clear up the room and put everything in order for their return.

'Well, we've done it,' Harry said triumphantly as they drove through the traffic around Shepherd's Bush. He had got over his feeling of depression, and was now happy and possessive. 'I'm glad we did it, Clair darling. I've never been so happy in my life.'

She patted his arm affectionately, but didn't say anything. Now that she was sobering up, her fears of the future returned. She felt cold in the draughty little car and the roar of its worn-out engine gave her a headache. She wasn't looking forward to the long drive out to Wendover in this bumping, noisy rattle-trap, but Harry looked so happy she hadn't the heart to suggest they turn back.

Harry was fully occupied in coaxing the car along at a speed of twenty miles an hour and didn't notice Clair's growing irritation. He was thinking how wonderful it was that within such an amazingly short time he had acquired a wife, a car and a service flat. Just because he had taken a photograph of Mooney! It was like a fairy story, he told himself.

'Harry darling, isn't it time you got a better car?' Clair said suddenly, shattering Harry's day dream. 'This one's falling to bits.'

'Oh, it's not as bad as all that,' Harry shouted above the roar of the engine. 'Of course it's a bit noisy, but it gets me where I want to go.'

'There's a frightful draught going up my legs,' Clair complained, holding her skirts down. 'We can't keep this much longer. You are thinking about getting a new one, aren't you?'

Harry was startled. He thought they were lucky to have a car at all. The idea of buying a new one hadn't entered his head.

'Well, I don't know. I don't think we could afford one just yet. Later, of course, when I make a bit more money, we can think about it. But there're lots of things we want besides a car, darling.'

'You could get it on the never-never. Let's do it. I'd love another M.G., wouldn't you?'

'Wouldn't I!' Harry said, his face clouding. 'But we'd never run to it. I'm afraid we'll have to make do with this for a while. At least, it goes.'

He should have known better to have tempted providence with such a remark. As they went through the gates of the White

City towards Western Avenue the engine suddenly died in a flurry of rasping gasps and the car came to a standstill.

'Oh Lord!' Harry said, his heart sinking. 'I spoke too soon. Oh, damn it! She's been going so well all this week.' He got out and lifted the rusty hood.

Clair looked bleak. She was impatient of anything that caused her physical discomfort, and it was cold and draughty in the car and the spring in the seat was sticking into her. Black clouds were creeping over the horizon. She didn't think from the look of the car roof that it would be watertight.

'You better buck up,' she said, leaning out of the window. 'It's going to pour. I think we ought to turn round and go home.'

Harry, who had just burned his hand on the over-heated engine gave her a wan smile.

'We will if I can get her to go again,' he said, peering doubtfully at the engine. 'Would you mind getting out for a moment? You're sitting on the tools.'

'No wonder the seat feels like a lump of iron,' Clair said, getting out. She hunched her shoulders against the rising wind. 'It's getting cold and horrid. Please don't be long.'

Harry collected the tool kit.

'I'll do my best. I don't really know what's wrong.'

Clair got back into the car. It infuriated her to see the other cars going past. She felt sure the drivers were looking contemptuously at the ancient Morris. There was a time, she thought bitterly, when she could have out-paced any of these smug devils in her M.G., and she stamped her feet because she was angry and her feet were cold.

After some minutes, Harry came to the window.

'Blown a gasket,' he said gloomily. 'I'm afraid we're stuck, darling. I'll have to get a tow.'

'Oh, Harry!' Clair's face hardened. 'Isn't this sickening? That's what comes of putting an old crock like this on the road. And now, look, it's beginning to rain.'

'Well, you wait here,' Harry said. 'I'll find a garage. There must be one quite close. I'm awfully sorry, Clair.' He looked so woebegone that she forced a smile.

'Just one of those things, darling,' she said. 'I'll be all right. It's not your fault. Anyway, this settles it. We must get a new car.'

As Harry closed the hood and put away his tools, a big Buick slid to a standstill by them. It was a long, glittering car with white rimmed wheels, a waving wireless mast, and a battery of enormous headlamps.

The driver leaned out of the window.

'Hallo, Ricks, are you in trouble?'

Harry looked up, startled.

'Why, hallo, Mr Simpson,' he said, and walked over to the Buick. 'Yes, I'm stuck. The gasket's blown.'

'I'll give you a lift into town if you like or to a garage,' Simpson said. 'I'm on my way back.' He glanced with an amused smile at the Morris. 'About had her day, hasn't she?'

Harry grinned ruefully.

'I'm afraid she has. My – my wife's with me, Mr Simpson. We would be grateful for a lift.'

Simpson raised his eyebrows, looked again at the Morris and met Clair's steady stare of interest.

'I didn't know you were married.' He opened the car door and got out. As usual he was immaculately dressed and Harry felt a twinge of envy. If only he could afford to dress like that, he thought.

'Actually, we got married this morning. May I introduce you?'

'Congratulations.'

Harry was aware that Simpson was looking at Clair with increasing interest. He seemed oblivious to the light rain that was falling.

'Are you off on your honeymoon?' Simpson went on as he strolled over to the Morris.

Seeing him coming, Clair slid out of the Morris. Harry thought she looked suddenly brighter and more lovely.

'Clair, this is Mr Simpson,' Harry said. 'He's going to give us a lift.'

Clair gave Simpson a quick, calculating look, then smiled.

'That's very nice of you,' she said, shaking hands. 'What a lovely car!'

'It's nice, isn't it?' Simpson said. There was a puzzled look in his eyes. 'I haven't had it long. Get in before you get wet.'

He made to open the rear door, but Clair had already opened the door in front and had slid into the seat next to the driving seat.

Simpson closed the door after her.

'You've found a very pretty wife, Ricks,' he said, not bother-

8

ing to lower his voice. 'You'd better get in too. Shall we find a garage?'

Harry got in the back and Simpson went around the car and sat behind the driving wheel.

'They'll have to tow it in I'm afraid,' Harry said.

'That's damn bad luck.' Simpson turned in his seat to look at Clair. 'Were you off on a honeymoon?'

'Honeymoon? Oh no. We're not having a honeymoon,' Clair said and laughed. 'We were going into the country.'

'But surely you're going to celebrate?'

'Oh, we have. We had lunch with Mr Mooney.'

Harry listened to this unhappily. Put like that it did sound a dull way of spending a wedding day.

'Mooney?' Simpson laughed. 'He's quite a character.' He started the Buick and drove towards Shepherd's Bush. 'That was a fine portrait your husband took of him.'

'Oh, Harry's very clever,' Clair said. 'You ought to let him take a picture of you, Mr Simpson.'

Harry stiffened with horror. What was she saying? He looked quickly at Simpson to see his reaction. Simpson seemed amused.

'Why do you say that?' he asked as he steered the big car through the close-packed traffic. 'What would a picture of me be good for?'

'Well, you could give it to your wife.'

'I'm not married.'

'You could hang it in one of your theatres then,' Clair said brightly.

'What do you think, Ricks?' Simpson asked laughing. 'Do you think the Regent's lobby would be all the better for a portrait of me? I doubt it myself.'

'I – I don't know, Mr Simpson,' Harry said, embarrassed.

'Of course it would,' Clair said. 'Harry's too modest and so are you. The public would like to know what you look like.'

'Here's a garage,' Simpson said, swinging the car through the open gates. 'What'll you do? Get them to tow it in and collect it later?'

'I don't suppose they'll do that,' Harry said. 'I'll have to go back with them.'

The rain was falling steadily now, and Simpson glanced out of the window, frowning.

'Would you like me to drop your wife off at home?' he asked. 'Where do you live?'

'Oh, thank you, Mr Simpson, but we won't bother you. It'll be all – '

But Clair interrupted.

'We have a flat in Kensington. Would you really take me back? It's raining so hard, and I don't want to get wet.' She turned in her seat to look at Harry. 'I'll wait for you at the flat, darling. You shouldn't be long or do you think you will?'

Harry got out of the car.

'I'll be as quick as I can. Are you sure it's not taking you out of your way, Mr Simpson?'

Simpson smiled.

'It's all right. I'm happy to be of service.' He engaged gear and the Buick slid away.

Clair waved to Harry, and he turned to watch the big glittering car edge into the traffic. He could see Clair talking animatedly to Simpson. He stood looking after them, heedless of the rain, a sudden chill at his heart.

IV

It was after six o'clock before Harry returned to the flat. He was soaked through and angry. Three times he had rung the flat, but there had been no answer. To add to his troubles, the garage at which Simpson had left him wouldn't send out for his car, and he had to go to two more before he found someone to oblige him. When he arrived with the mechanic he found a policeman waiting for him and was told he would be summoned for obstruction. After he had given the policeman the particulars he required, the mechanic who by then had examined the car, told him it wasn't worth repairing.

'Cost you more than the car's worth,' he said. 'I'll tow it to the garage, but if you took my tip you'll sell it for scrap.'

Harry went back to the garage and had the mechanic's opinion confirmed. He accepted fifteen pounds ten for the car, and then caught a bus back to Kensington.

He mounted the stairs, feeling depressed at the loss of the car and worried that Clair hadn't returned home. He opened the front door and called, but there was no answer.

A pretty fine wedding day, he thought savagely.

Doris and Mooney hadn't cleared up quite as well as they had promised. No doubt Mooney's cocktails had had an effect on them. Most of the washing-up hadn't been done, and there was cigarette ash and traces of confetti that Mooney had insisted on showering on Harry and Clair, still on the carpet.

But where was Clair?

She had left Harry at three o'clock. The drive to the flat couldn't have taken more than a quarter of an hour. It was now six-ten. Where on earth had she got to?

Harry controlled his rising anger. It was no use going off the deep end, he told himself. After all it was his own fault: he hadn't planned her wedding day very well. He couldn't blame her if Simpson had taken her to a show. Or perhaps, he thought hopefully, she was out shopping; getting something special for supper, and would be back any moment. While waiting for her to return he decided to put the flat straight.

He went into the kitchen and finished the washing-up. By the time he had put the last plate away it was six-forty, and he was struggling with a feeling of jealousy and hurt anger. He swept up the confetti, emptied the ash trays and straightened the chair and cushions. As he was putting the dustpan and brush away he heard footsteps running down the passage. A key turned in the lock and Clair came in.

'Oh, Harry! I'm so sorry,' she said. 'I had no idea it was as late as this.' She went to him and he noticed she was a little unsteady on her feet, and when she kissed him her breath smelt strongly of whisky.

'Clair!' Harry exclaimed, sharply. 'You – you're a bit on, aren't you?'

She giggled.

'I am a bit,' she said, and flopped into an armchair. 'Give me a cigarette, darling. Phew! What an afternoon!'

Silently Harry gave her a cigarette, lit it for her and then sat opposite her.

'Sorry, Harry,' she said again. 'Swear at me if you feel like it. I know you're furious with me.'

'It's all right,' Harry said. 'I – I wondered where you were. I hope you had a good time.'

She sat up and looked straight at him.

'Don't be forgiving, Harry. That's not the way to treat me. Give me a damn good slap in the face, but don't be forgiving.'

Harry lit a cigarette with a hand that trembled.

'Rot!' he said. 'Mind you. I think you might have waited for me. But you're here now, so what does it matter? Have you had anything to eat?'

'Not yet. Don't you want to know what I've been up to?'

'Why yes, of course I do.'

'Darling, you don't think I've been up to mischief, do you? Don't be so cold and distant.' She got up and sat at his feet. 'Oh, I know I had too much to drink, but I'm all right now. He can drink, can't he?'

'You mean Simpson? I don't know. I don't know much about him,' Harry said, his face hardening. 'I'm not sure I want to know either.'

'We spent the entire time in the bar of the Regent Theatre,' Clair said. 'That chap Lehmann was there too.'

Harry looked bewildered.

'Why didn't he take you home as he said he would? Why did you go to the theatre?'

'Because I asked him for a job.'

'A job?' Harry stared at her. 'But – but you're working for me.'

'No, I'm not. I couldn't be bothered messing about with lights, Harry. And besides, I wouldn't be earning anything. I'm not going to take all your hard earned money. I'm going to earn for myself.'

'What's the job, then?'

'Well, after we left you, we got talking and he told me he's putting on a cabaret at the 22nd Club. The season opens in three weeks. I saw he liked the look of me, so I asked him if he could give me a job in the cabaret.'

Harry was dumbfounded.

'But, Clair, what will you do? I didn't know you had any stage experience.'

'I haven't. That's why he's not paying me much. But he says with my looks and talent I'll soon acquire the necessary experience. Lehmann is going to coach me.'

'Talent?' Harry repeated. 'Darling, what exactly are you going to do?'

She stubbed out her cigarette before replying, and Harry had a feeling she found it difficult to tell him.

'I'm going to do what I'm good at,' she said. 'Picking pockets.'

'But darling . . . ' Harry began, shocked.

'Why not? I told him I had practised for years, hoping to go on the stage one day. He believed it. I know he did. The joke was he didn't think I was as good as I made out. When we got to the flat, I gave him back all his property. I had taken his wallet, his wrist watch, his cuff links, his cigarette case and his keys. I wish you could have seen his face! He said would I go to the Regent Theatre right away so Lehmann could see me. Well, darling. I couldn't let him get cold, so I went with him. He told me to pick Lehmann's pockets. He introduced me to Lehmann and we started drinking, and I really went to town on Lehmann. I even got his braces. Simpson said I was sensational. He's giving me thirty pounds a week, and if I go over big, he'll double it. I start rehearsals tomorrow.'

Harry felt stunned. After all his hopes and plans, his scheming and hard work to support Clair, she had again stepped in front of him and would be very soon in the position to provide for herself and for him too if he wasn't careful. Not that he begrudged her her triumph. But when would he see her? he wondered. If he had to work all day, and she half the night, what kind of a married life would they have?

'What's worrying you, Harry?'

'Well, nothing. It's a bit of a surprise, that's all. Do you really want to do this, Clair? Wouldn't you rather work with me?'

'Now look, darling. We must have money. There're so many things we need. We can't continue to live in this hole. We must get a car. As a matter of fact, on the strength of the job, I've already had a word with a car agent I know. I rang him up in the lobby downstairs. He thinks he can get us something and he'll spread the payments. He's a good friend of mine, and he'll get us something good and quickly. Together we'll be earning fifty pounds a week. That's much more like, isn't it, darling?'

'Yes, I suppose it is,' Harry said doubtfully. 'I thought you liked this place.'

'It's all right, but it's too small. We could never have a party in here, could we?'

Harry looked round the room. No, they couldn't entertain more than two people in the small room, but did that matter?

'It worries me,' he said suddenly. 'Suppose someone finds out you've been in – in – '

'That I'm an old lag?' Clair said with a hard smile. 'I'll take a chance on it, Harry.' She jumped to her feet. 'Let's celebrate!

118

After all it is our wedding day. How much money have you got in the flat?'

Harry hesitated.

'Well, I've got about ten pounds, but it'll have to last us until next Friday.'

'Oh, bosh!' She threw her arms round him. 'Don't be such an old caution. I'll ask Lehmann to give me an advance. Go and make yourself look nice, darling. We're going out and we're going to spend every penny of that ten pounds, and then tomorrow I'll pay it all back to you. This is my treat.'

'Look, Clair,' Harry said firmly. 'We're married. It's not going to be like that. I'm doing the paying now. The money you earn you must keep for yourself. I'm not having you spending your money on me.'

She looked at him mockingly.

'What does it matter who has the money so long as we have it, remember? Come on, go and get changed.'

She left him and ran into the bedroom. Harry stood undecided, then he went over to the window, and looked into the street. He felt thoroughly dejected. And he stood there for some minutes, thinking of the future. She had said if she made a success of her act Simpson would pay her sixty pounds a week. She was sure to make a success of it. Then she would be earning four times as much as he. How could he hope to hold up his end of the marriage under such conditions? With Mooney and Doris to pay – and Mooney was already hinting he could do with more money, it wasn't fair competition. They would move to a larger flat, and Clair would pay for it. They would have a car, and Clair would pay for that. He wouldn't even be able to afford to buy her clothes now she was back to her old standard.

'Harry . . .'

He turned.

Clair stood in the bedroom doorway, looking at him. She had taken off her dress and was in a flimsy slip.

'What's the matter, Harry?'

'Nothing. I'm just coming.'

'You're sore because I'm going to earn more than you, aren't you?'

'Oh, I know it's silly,' Harry said, frowning. 'But I can't help it. I've always wanted to provide for you, to look after you and – well, it just doesn't work out that way.'

She came over to him and slipped her arms round his neck.

'Harry darling, I love you. But you are a little selfish about this, aren't you? If you had your way we would only have your money, and we'd be hard up. Don't keep me out of it. After all marriage is a partnership. Can't you look on it that way? I tell you what we'll do. We'll have a joint banking account. You'll pay in everything you earn and so will I. Then we'll both draw on it for everything we want. That's the way partners do it, isn't it?'

She was right, of course. He was being selfish, and marriage was a sort of partnership. But for all that he wished frantically that he could provide for her and give her the things she would buy with her own money.

'I'm sorry, Clair,' he said, and gave her a little hug. 'I am being selfish. All right, we'll pool our resources, and see how we get on. Now, let's get ready. Where would you like to go?'

'We're not going anywhere. I've changed my mind,' she said, her face against his. 'We'll have a picnic supper and then we'll go to bed.'

'Oh no, you wanted to go out just now. Don't let's change our plans. We ought to celebrate.'

She held him closer.

'We are going to celebrate. Oh, Harry, I know I'm no good, but I'm only thinking of you. I want everything to be right for you. You can see that, can't you?'

V

The next morning, Harry had a telephone call from Lehmann, asking him to come down to the theatre right away.

'I'll come with you,' Clair said. 'I'm one of the family now. Hurry up and shave, darling. I won't be ten minutes.'

While Harry was shaving he heard Clair on the telephone. She sounded very animated and once or twice she laughed, and he wondered a little irritably who it was she was talking to. He heard her hang up, and as he was washing the lather off his face, she came into the bathroom.

'That was Maurice,' she said. 'The chap who's getting us a car. He's got a 1948 Jaguar; it's just come in. £900, and only done six thousand miles. He says it's an absolute bargain.'

'Nine hundred pounds,' Harry said, staring at her. 'But, darling – '

'Twenty-five pounds a month,' Clair said briskly. 'I said we would look at it on our way down to the theatre. I can run to twenty-five a month . . . it's nothing.'

'But you haven't got the job yet,' Harry said. 'It might fall through.'

'Then Maurice can have the car back. It's all right. I know him.' She patted his arm and returned to the bedroom and began to dress.

Harry stood motionless for a moment, then with a helpless shrug, joined her.

The bus or the Underground were far too slow for Clair that morning. It had to be a taxi.

'We're running away with the money,' Harry muttered as he told the taxi driver to go to Portland Street. 'A bus wouldn't have been much slower.'

'But, darling, we've got the money,' Clair said gaily. 'In three weeks' time we'll be worth fifty pounds a week.'

'You forget there's income tax,' he pointed out, hating himself for harping on money like this. 'We'll be lucky to get thirty a week by the time tax has been deducted.'

Clair pulled a face.

'Well, thirty's not bad, and if I go over big, we'll have even more. Cheer up, darling. After all the taxi won't be more than a couple of shillings.'

The car salesman, Maurice, turned out to be a swarthy young man with black wavy hair, a blue chin and a hooked nose. He greeted Clair like an old friend, and glanced suspiciously at Harry as if wondering who he was and what he was doing in Clair's company, and Harry was surprised that Clair introduced him as 'This is Harry Ricks', and not her husband.

Maurice showed them the glittering showy car painted cream and red.

'Special coach work and a bang-on radio,' he said. 'We'll guarantee it. Hop in and come for a run.'

'We're going down to the Regent,' Clair said. 'I'll drive.'

Because Maurice wanted to explain the controls and gadgets, Harry had to sit in the back. He was silent and moody while Clair and Maurice chatted and laughed as she drove the car along Oxford Street.

'It's a peach, isn't it, Harry?' she called over her shoulder. 'Would you like to handle her?'

'No, thank you,' Harry said.

He had had very little experience of driving cars, and was scared of the Jaguar. It was all very well driving the old Morris that couldn't do more than thirty miles an hour, but in traffic, he felt if he even touched the accelerator of this powerful monster with his unsure foot, he would send it rushing madly into the back of a bus.

'I'll give you seven hundred for it,' Clair said suddenly.

They began to argue while Harry listened, dismayed and angry that he wasn't even being consulted.

After a strenuous struggle, Clair succeeded in closing the deal at £800.

'I'll send you a cheque, Maurice, for twenty-five,' she said as she pulled up outside the theatre. 'I haven't the spare for a deposit. Okay?'

'For you, my lovely, anything's okay,' Maurice said. 'Keep her. I'll take a taxi back. The book's in the glove compartment. Better get her registered today. She's taxed and insured to the end of the month.'

He got out, beamed through the window at Clair, and looking uncertainly at Harry said, 'Well, Clair, any time you have a moment. I'll always be glad to see your pretty face. So long for now.' He nodded to Harry and went off, waving to a distant taxi.

'How do you like it?' Clair asked, turning in her seat. Her face was radiant and her eyes bright. 'This is much more like it, isn't it, darling?'

'Yes,' Harry said, and got out of the car. 'You won't leave it here, will you?'

She gave him a quick searching look.

'You don't mind, Harry? I'm afraid I was a bit high handed, but you see, I know Maurice. If you had dealt with him we should have been here hours arguing about the price. It is what you want?'

'It's very nice,' Harry said carefully.

'I'm so glad.' Her face lost a little of its radiance. 'I'll run it round to the back.'

'All right. I'll go on in.'

He watched her drive the car away, then entered the theatre. He was shocked at Clair's irresponsibility. To have bought an

122

eight hundred pound car in less than half an hour, without a thought of future payments or of the money to be found for the tax or insurance seemed to him the height of recklessness.

'If we go on like this,' he thought as he made his way to Val Lehmann's office, 'we'll be up to our ears in debt.'

Lehmann was going through a series of sketches, spread out on the top of the grand piano that took up most of the room in his office.

'Hallo, Harry,' he said, looking up and smiling. 'We've got some work for you. Mr Simpson has decided to take *Crazy Days* off. We go into production right away. Here, have a look at these sketches. They'll give you an idea of the set-up.'

While Harry was examining the sketches, Lehmann sat at his desk, and wrote furiously in a fat notebook he always carried around with him.

'Some wife you've picked yourself, Harry,' he said suddenly. 'That's a clever act she's got. It should go over big at the 22nd. Mr Simpson's delighted with her.'

'Is he?' Harry said flatly.

'Oh, and Harry, I'm sorry, but Mr Simpson won't break the monopoly clause,' Lehmann went on. 'He says if he does it with you, he'll have to do it with others.'

Harry dropped the sketch he was looking at and turned.

'But it's important to me, Mr Lehmann. I – I want the money.'

'Who doesn't?' Lehmann said, and smiled sympathetically. 'You see, Harry, there are very few, if any, photographers on a salary as you are. If you like to work on piece work so to speak and not have a contract it'd be all right, but so long as you're a member of the staff, private work is out.'

Harry hesitated. To be without the steady twenty-five pounds a week would be too dangerous. There was Mooney and Doris to be thought of.

'Yes,' he said. 'I understand. Did – did you get me a raise?'

'Mr Simpson suggested I bring that up later. Matter of fact, Harry, business isn't so hot.'

'And yet Simpson could promise Clair sixty pounds a week if she was a success,' Harry thought bitterly.

'I see,' he said and turned back to the sketches.

Clair came in a few minutes later.

'Hallo, Val,' she said, and Harry started, surprised she was already on a Christian name basis. He had never thought of calling Lehmann by his Christian name; in fact, he knew he would have been snubbed if he had done so, and yet here was Clair, after only one meeting, calmly sitting on the edge of Lehmann's desk, helping herself to a cigarette out of his box and calling him 'Val'. And what was more surprising Lehmann seemed to like it.

'Hallo, Clair,' Lehmann returned. 'What do you want? You can't come barging in here. I'm busy.'

'Well, I like that!' Clair said smiling. 'Didn't you tell me to come down for a rehearsal this morning?'

'So I did. But we're going to put on a new show, and I'll be busy. I'll have to get Oman to coach you. He's a good chap. Look, go along to his office and tell him I sent you. Work with him this morning. I'll have a look at you this afternoon. Mr Simpson has had a word with him.'

'All right.' Clair slid off the desk.

'And work like hell, Clair. You have a lot to do in a short time.'

'Don't I know it. I'll work all right.' As she went to the door, she patted Harry's back affectionately. 'Let's have lunch together, darling.'

'Yes,' Harry said. 'I'll pick you up in Oman's office.'

'Oh Val,' Clair said, turning. 'Look out of the window.'

Lehmann pushed back his chair.

'What now?' he asked with an amiable smile.

'See what we've bought.'

He went to the window.

'My word! Is that yours?' he asked, looking down at the glittering Jaguar that was parked in the alley behind the theatre.

'Just got it. It's a beaut, isn't it?' Clair said enthusiastically. 'It'll do ninety and the radio's bang on.'

When she had gone, Lehmann glanced at Harry and raised his eyebrows.

'No wonder you want a rise,' he said. 'That must have cost you a packet.'

Harry felt himself go red.

'Well, she wanted a car,' he muttered, and was glad when the door opened at this moment and Allan Simpson came in.

'Have you shown Ricks the photo montage idea yet?' Simpson asked abruptly.

'Haven't got round to it yet, A.S.,' Lehmann said. 'He's only just come in.'

'Morning, Ricks,' Simpson said, nodding to Harry. 'How do you like your wife working for a living? She's damned clever. If ever you go broke she can always pick pockets, can't she, Val?'

The two men laughed as if Simpson had made the funniest joke in the world. Harry turned away, afraid they'd see how embarrassed he was. He pretended to examine one of the sketches.

'It was good of you to give her the chance,' he said, feeling Simpson expected him to say something.

'With her looks and talent, she might make a hit,' Simpson said, lighting a cigarette. 'Anyway, we'll try her out at the 22nd and see how she shapes. Oman working with her?' he asked Lehmann.

'She's with him now.'

'Right; well, let's get to work. We'll go over the number Ricks is to work on, and then he can get on with it.' Simpson sat at Lehmann's desk. 'We want life-size enlargements of twenty girls, Ricks. They're to be framed and used as a back-cloth. The girls will be ready to be photographed this afternoon. Val will show you how we want them to pose. You'd better get the necessary bromide paper, and whatever else you need. I suppose you can tackle a job as big as that?'

'Oh, yes,' Harry said, thinking if he wasn't on contract the job would be worth a great deal of money.

'Then we want a four times larger than life-size photograph of Jenny Rand. We'd better give that to Kodaks to do. It's too big for you to handle. Get some good portraits of her and let me see them. We'll select the one to enlarge. She'll sit for you tomorrow morning. You might have a word with Kodaks and get an estimate.' He glanced at Lehmann. 'That's all for the moment, isn't it?'

Lehmann nodded.

'All right, Ricks, you get off. Be on the stage at two o'clock this afternoon.'

Harry badly wanted to ask Simpson if he wouldn't recon-sider the monopoly clause, but his nerve failed at the last moment and he left the office.

'Just my luck!' he thought as he walked down the stairs to the theatre foyer. 'I daren't give up this steady job. I might never get another. I'll have to get rid of Mooney. That'll save me five pounds a week, and perhaps I can persuade Lehmann to pay Doris instead of leaving it to me.'

He went back stage where he found Mooney lolling in a chair talking to one of the stage hands.

'I'd like a word, Alf,' Harry said. He had been on 'Alf' terms with Mooney since they had exchanged places as employer and employee. Even now, it made Harry feel embarrassed to call Mooney by his first name.

'What's biting you, kid?' Mooney asked, chewing his dead cigar. He waved the stage hand away with a lordly hand.

Harry leaned against the wings and looked at Mooney unhappily.

'The fact is, Alf. I can't afford to pay you out of my own pocket any more, I'm sorry, but getting married makes a difference.'

Mooney's eyes hardened.

'Does it?' he asked. 'What's this about Clair getting a job and earning thirty quid a week? I should have thought it would have made it easier.'

Harry reddened.

'What Clair earns has nothing to do with it,' he said. 'I have to keep my end up, and I want every penny I earn now. I'm sorry, but you'll either have to accept the fiver Lehmann pays or look for something else. I can't afford any more to make up your money.'

'What do I do – starve?' Mooney asked politely.

'You won't starve on five pounds a week, and – and . . . ' Harry broke off uneasily.

'Does Clair know about this?'

'Leave Clair out of it! It's nothing to do with her. The fact is, Alf, you don't really pull your weight, and you know it. If I could get outside work I'd keep you on, but Simpson won't let me and won't give me a raise, so I have to cut somewhere.'

'I wonder why it is,' Mooney said gloomily, 'that as soon as there's a crisis I'm the poor bastard to suffer. Don't forget, Harry, if it wasn't for me, you wouldn't have this job. I won't believe you are so damned mean as to pass me up after all I've done for you.'

Harry floundered miserably. He hated this, and Mooney knew it. Mooney knew if he kept on long enough Harry would change his mind. He wasn't going to lose five pounds a week

126

because Harry had been fool enough to marry an expensive wife.

'It's not as if you need the money,' he went on. 'Clair'll be earning soon, and you'll have more than you know what to do with. You're not going to tell me you're going to make nearly fifty quid a week and are going to begrudge me a miserable fiver. I just don't believe it.'

Put like that it did seem petty and mean, and Harry felt ashamed of himself.

'No, you're right, Alf,' he said wearily. 'Forget it, will you? It's just I hate the thought of Clair earning more than I do. I'm sorry. I shouldn't have said it.'

Mooney relaxed back into his chair.

'That's okay, kid,' he said. 'Think nothing of it. I knew I had only to point out where you were going off the rails. And that stuff about me not pulling my weight. That isn't true, you know. I'm plugging you every minute of the day. Why only just now I was telling that punk electrician what a smart guy you are. It pays to get talked about.'

'I suppose it does,' Harry said, not caring if he were talked about or not. 'Well, forget it, Alf. Now we've got to get busy. They're putting on a new show. I wonder if you'd run down to Kodaks and get an estimate for me. Mr Simpson wants it. I'll write down the details.'

'What – me?' Mooney said, horrified.

CHAPTER TWO

I

As Harry had foreseen, Clair made an immediate hit at the 22nd Club. She had insisted on doing her act in a mask and had been billed as The Masked Pickpocket. Only Harry knew why anonymity was necessary. She was taking no risk of being recognised by any of the men she had stolen from in the past who might happen to visit the night club.

The mask added to her success. She became a subject for discussion and speculation, and the members of the club continually worried the *maître d'hôtel* to find out if she was as beautiful as her figure suggested she might be.

Harry was astonished how at home she was on the stage. Her act wasn't an easy one. She had to move about the restaurant, pausing at tables, talking to the guests and picking their pockets. Then she would return the articles she had taken to the amusement of the onlookers. But the club members soon caught on to what she was up to, and were on their guard. In spite of that she invariably managed to take something belonging to them, and the act developed into a battle of wits which was another reason for its success.

A month after her opening night, Clair returned to the flat at her usual time: a few minutes after one o'clock in the morning, and instead of undressing in the bathroom and creeping into bed as she usually did, she came bursting into the bedroom and woke Harry up.

'Wake up, darling!' she exclaimed, sitting on the bed and turning on the bedside lamp. 'I've wonderful news!'

Harry grunted, blinked and sat up.

'You have – what?' he asked sleepily.

'You'll never guess. I'm going into the new revue at the Regent!'

128

'The Regent!' Harry exclaimed, now wide awake. 'But Clair, do you want it? As well as the night club?'

'Of course as well as the night club,' she said, kissing him. 'I shall be on at eight-thirty at the Regent, and I don't have to be at the 22nd until eleven o'clock. I can easily do it.'

'I suppose you can,' Harry said, and dropped back on his pillow. 'Well, darling, if it's what you want then I'm very glad for you.'

'It's what I want for both of us. We're really going places now, Harry! I've signed a contract. A hundred and fifty a week for the two jobs! Think of it! And Val says I can claim at least thirty a week expenses, and that'll be tax free of course. Isn't it marvellous?'

Well, of course it was marvellous, but Harry felt stunned and dismayed, although he made an effort to appear enthusiastic as he watched her undress and listened to her plans.

She danced around the room, shedding her clothes, looking radiant and happy: happier than he had ever seen her, and it grieved him that it was through her own efforts and not his that this had happened.

'We'll see about another flat right away,' she said as she slipped into her nightdress. 'We're not going to live in this pokey hole another week. Allan says there's a flat in Park Lane that might suit us. They only want fifteen pounds a week for it, and it's furnished.'

Allan? So she was now on Christian name terms with Simpson. A girl could get on so much faster than a man if she played her cards properly, Harry thought dejectedly. He had worked for Simpson for nearly a year and was still just an employee.

'And we're going to get rid of the Jaguar,' Clair went on as she put cold cream on her face. 'Maurice told me this afternoon he has a 1950 Cadillac just come in. He wants fifteen hundred for it, but I know I can beat him down. Think, Harry, a Cad! Won't it make Allan sit up? I just can't wait to get it,' and she came running across the room to jump into bed and hug him.

By now Harry was in despair. The gap between their incomes was a yawning chasm. It was hopeless to think of catching her up. A hundred and fifty against fifteen!

'We must be sensible about this, Harry,' she said, her head on his shoulder. 'I know how you feel about it. I know you hate me making money. You've never used a penny of mine, and you've just got to change your ideas. You've got to make up your mind to use it until you get on your feet. I've been talking to Val about you. He thinks you would do better if you worked on your own. And that's what I want you to do. Don't renew your contract. Val says they'll give you the same amount of work anyway, and they'll have to pay you more. You'll be able to do other work too. What do you think, darling? Don't you think it would be sensible not to renew?'

'But I mightn't make a go of it,' Harry said, doubtfully. 'Simpson might get someone else on contract. It's cheaper that way. After all, if I renewed I'd be sure of fifteen pounds a week.'

'But what's fifteen pounds?' Clair asked impatiently. 'On your own you might make hundreds.'

'But I might not. One of us has to be a bit cautious.'

'Oh, but you're too cautious. For a whole year we can be independent on my money. It's your chance to experiment. Can't you see that? I want you to set up a studio in the West End. I'll finance you, Harry. Then by the time my act's stale, you'll be in a position to take over. Isn't that the sensible thing to do?'

Well, put like that, it was, of course, but Harry was reluctant to take the risk, and still more reluctant to accept Clair's money.

'I have to think of Mooney,' he said, groping for an excuse to refuse her help without hurting her. 'If I give up my contract he won't be paid by the theatre, and I couldn't afford to pay him ten pounds a week out of my own money.'

'Mooney?' Clair was scornful. 'He's absolutely useless. It's about time you got rid of him. I've been watching him. He doesn't do a thing to help you. He just lolls around and pinches the chorus's bottoms. You've put up with him long enough, Harry. It's time he went.'

'But I can't do that,' Harry said, shocked. He visualised Mooney's hurt expression and the endless arguments. 'After all, it was through him –'

'Oh, bosh! He didn't even know you were taking his photograph. He has no claim on you whatsoever. You leave him to me. I know how to handle him. And Harry, will you look for a likely studio? I'll help you, of course. I'm sure Jenny Rand will recommend you if you ask her. And Val will too. I'm sure you'll make a go of it.'

'I don't think I had better,' Harry said, torn between the

desire to set up on his own and the safety of another year's contract. 'Something might happen. You might get ill or something, and then we'd be thankful to have a steady income.'

'Oh, Harry, you're impossible! But I do love you so,' Clair said. 'I do want things to go right for you. Please don't be so cautious. We'll never get anywhere at this rate. We haven't much time. We'll be old before we know where we are. If we don't do something now, it'll be too late. I may not want to go on with my act for years and years, and think how wonderful it would be if you were established in business, and we had nothing to worry about. *Now* is the time. We can afford to take risks. I have a year's contract. In that time you can get thoroughly established. It's the only thing to do. You've got to do it.'

'Well, all right,' Harry said, still doubtful. 'Anyway, I'll think about it.'

But while he was thinking about it Clair acted. A few days later she told him she had found a studio in Grafton Street, and they were going to look at it right away. She had also seen and approved of the flat in Park Lane. In spite of the high rents of both places, she bullied and bustled Harry into signing the agreements.

The studio was just his idea of what a studio should be, but the rent appalled him.

'What does it matter!' Clair said. 'It's worth it. What's seventeen pounds a week when you have an address like this? We can afford it, and before long you'll be making ten times that amount.'

'But there's the flat as well,' Harry said, distracted. 'Do you realise we'll be paying out over thirty pounds a week on rents alone? We'll have to earn more than sixty a week to pay it with income tax as it is. We shouldn't take the flat, Clair. We should stay in Kensington.'

'Oh, nonsense. It's going to be all right. Faint heart, Harry, darling. It's a short life, and it's going to be a merry one. Do stop worrying.'

But it was enough to make anyone worry, Harry thought, to see the way Clair threw her money about. She bought the Cadillac, and was paying two hundred a month for it. She spent pounds on clothes. She had something like a hundred and twenty pounds a month to find for rents as well as living expenses.

131

Now they had the luxury flat in Park Lane she was continually giving parties, and the drink bill was enormous.

The studio haunted Harry. Thanks to Clair's determined efforts and to Jenny Rand's recommendations he did have a fair amount of work to do, but after Doris's salary and the rent had been paid there was very little left for him. In fact he was several pounds worse off than when he was with Simpson.

Mooney had gone into the dry cleaning business. After Clair had talked to him he mournfully took leave of Harry. Harry hadn't been there when Clair told Mooney he must go, and Mooney was so quiet and dismal when he said good-bye, Harry guessed Clair hadn't minced her words.

'You're making a big mistake, kid,' Mooney said. 'To give up a safe job with Simpson for the risky business of working on your own is just foolishness. Well, I don't suppose you'll want to listen to an old man. No one ever does. But don't forget, if you ever get into a mess, come and see me. If there's one thing I'm good at, it's getting out of a mess. If ever you want a job, let me know. I might be able to fix you up in this dry cleaning racket. The guy I'm working for has a good business, but he's mean with his money.' Mooney sighed. 'I wonder why I'm always running into mean people? He's giving me six quid a week, and for that I have to manage a shop and three girls.' He grimaced. 'And they're as ugly as sin too. Well, so long, kid. No hard feelings. I know it's not your fault. That girl of yours is as hard as stone, but she's going to get places. When you don't care who you trample on, you usually land up at the top. But watch her; she loves you now; make sure she keeps on loving you.'

When Simpson's revue opened at the Regent, Clair made a hit. She had already made a name for herself at the 22nd, and the newspapers were kind to her, but the credit for her success was due to her own hard work and talent.

Harry saw very little of her. He went to the studio just after nine o'clock when she was still sleeping. They had supper together when he returned home. But immediately after the meal she had to get ready for the theatre, and when she returned from the night club he was asleep. The only day they had together was Sunday, and then usually Clair entertained in the evening. She often bemoaned the fact that they saw each so seldom.

'Perhaps it won't be for long,' she said one evening as she

dressed for the theatre. 'Perhaps the studio will make a fortune and I can chuck the stage. I wouldn't mind not having anything to do for a change. This routine of going every night to the Regent and then on to the 22nd is beginning to bore me. After all, it'd be fun to have an evening off sometimes. How are things going, Harry?'

Things weren't going too well.

'Mind you, it takes time,' Harry said defensively. 'But the overheads are killing. And then I have terrific competition. Look at the number of photographers there are around me, and they're established. Simpson is giving me less and less work to do. Of course I know the show is running now, but when I was under contract with him he was always finding me jobs. Now I only get an occasional portrait. I'm sure he didn't like me turning down that contract. If it wasn't for you I don't believe I'd get anything from him.'

Clair's face hardened.

'Why didn't you tell me before? I'll talk to him. Val promised it wouldn't make any difference.'

'Better not. You don't want to get into his bad books. He's a funny customer.'

'So am I,' Clair said. 'He's not going to get away with it.'

'Don't you think we should ease off spending for a bit?' Harry said abruptly. 'I've been looking at the bank statement. We've only fifty pounds in the account. Did you know?'

'There's another hundred and fifty coming in on Friday,' Clair said indifferently. 'Why worry?'

'But, darling, we haven't put anything aside yet for income tax, and there's the instalment to meet on the car. The tax will be horrific. We must start saving for that.'

'Let them whistle for it,' Clair said, and laughed. 'You worry too much. I must run, Harry. What are you doing tonight?'

'Oh, I'll read,' Harry said, shrugging. 'There's not much else to do.'

'I tell you what,' Clair said. 'We'll buy a television set. We ought to have one, and that'll help pass the time for you. I'll see about it tomorrow.'

'You'll do nothing of the kind!' Harry said, jumping to his feet. 'This reckless spending has got to stop, Clair! We can't go on and on having everything we want like this. I don't want a television, and if you got one I wouldn't look at it!'

She stared at him in surprise.

'All right, darling, don't get heated about it,' she said, and threw her arms round his neck. 'I only thought you might like it.'

'I don't want it,' Harry said, curtly. 'It's worrying me stiff we'll get into debt as it is.'

'Oh, Harry, darling, what a fuss-pot you are. What's it matter if we do get into debt? Everyone does, so what?'

'Well, I'm not going to,' Harry said. 'Now you'd better run along or you'll be late.'

She kissed him, pressing her face against his.

'You're not unhappy, are you?' she asked anxiously.

He forced a smile.

'No, only –'

'You don't regret marrying me?'

'Why Clair . . . '

'Perhaps you do?'

'No, I don't, but I sometimes wonder if you have regrets,' he said frowning. 'I'm such a damned dud beside you.'

'You're not!' Clair kissed him again. 'You're having a bad time now, but it'll come all right. You see, your luck will change. Cheer up, Harry. I love you lots. Say you're happy.'

'Yes, I'm happy.'

He watched her from the window as she entered the huge, glittering car, and then when she had driven away, he turned and sat down and looked bleakly before him. He wasn't happy. He hated this kind of life. Their standard of living, the reckless way she spent her money and the approaching income tax demand preyed on his mind.

He thought of Ron Fisher, and remembered what he had said the night he had told him about his first meeting with Clair.

He could hear Ron's quiet voice as if he were in the room: 'I don't want you to get mixed up with a glamour girl: they always spell trouble sooner or later. I know. I thought I was being smart when I married Sheila.'

If only he could talk his worries over with Ron now! He saw Ron regularly once a month, but it was like seeing a stranger. Ron was so quiet, just sitting in his wheeled chair, scarcely saying a word, brooding all the time, a fixed stare in his eyes.

Sheila was getting a divorce. Ron didn't seem to grasp that. He didn't seem to grasp anything. The only time a flicker of interest had shown on his face was when Clair went with Harry to see him. She had only been once.

'It's too damned depressing ever to go again,' she said afterwards.

Ron had looked at her intently for some moments, and then said unexpectedly, 'You're just what I imagined you'd be. Look after him, won't you? He's not much good at looking after himself,' and then he seemed to lose interest again, and the rest of the time they spent with him was just like any of the other visits Harry made.

Harry lit a cigarette and reached for his book. He had a couple of hours yet before he went to bed. It was lonely in this big luxurious flat. It was all right when Clair was here, but when she had gone, the place seemed too big. It seemed unfriendly too, almost as if it resented Harry.

He would read until eight-thirty. Then he would listen to Twenty Questions on the wireless. Clair would be in the middle of her act by now. Lehmann had said he thought the show would run another year. What would happen then? In that time the studio should be established. But would it? He tried to get his mind off his worries, but the book didn't hold him and impatiently he put it down. As he reached for another cigarette the front door bell rang, making him start. For a moment or so he sat still, wondering who it could be. No one ever called when Clair was at the theatre. He got up and went into the hall as the bell rang again.

He opened the front door.

For a moment he didn't recognise the tall fat man who stood in the passage, his navy blue homburg hat tilted rakishly over one eye; then he felt a prickle run up his spine. It was Robert Brady.

II

Faintly, from down the passage, Harry could hear Kenneth Horne introducing the Twenty Questions' team. He wanted to shut the door and turn on his own wireless: to shut out this apparition from the past and pretend he wasn't there.

In a voice he didn't recognise as his own, he said, 'What do you want?'

'It's time we had a little talk,' Brady said, and smiled, showing his gold-capped teeth. He reminded Harry of a well-groomed pig with his pink and white flesh, his small bright eyes and his heavy whistling breathing.

'What about?' Harry said, standing squarely in the doorway. 'I've nothing to say to you, and I don't want to listen to you.'

Brady waved his cigar airily.

'There are lots of things we don't want to do,' he said, lifting his massive shoulders, 'but we have to put up with them. If you think for a moment it may occur to you that I could make a lot of trouble for you. Hadn't you better hear what I have to say?'

'Yes, he could make trouble,' Harry thought, his heart sinking.

'Well, come in,' he said curtly and stood aside.

Brady entered the hall and walked into the sitting-room. He stood looking round, his eyebrows raised, his lips pursed.

'Well, well,' he said. 'You've come up in the world, haven't you, my friend? Very different from peddling pictures in the street.'

'Say what you have to say and get out,' Harry said, blood rising in his face.

Brady took off his hat and dropped it on to the table. He walked over to the fireplace and took up a position on the rug before the fire.

'Damned clever girl, isn't she?' he said. 'But clever as she is I never thought she'd do as well as this. Park Lane! My stars! When I first met her she was walking the streets.'

Harry took a sudden step forward. He had a furious urge to smash his fist into the fat pig-like face.

'Be careful, my friend,' Brady cautioned, moving out of Harry's reach. 'You can't afford to be dramatic. This is not going to be a brawl, you know. You'll have to be subtle and use whatever brains you have if you're going to crawl out of this mess. And I don't think you'll succeed however much you wriggle.'

Harry restrained himself. Better hear what he had to say. There would be time enough to hit him when he had finished.

'That's better,' Brady went on, watching him. 'Forget the violence. If you attempt to hit me it'll only make it worse for Clair. Sit down.' He sat down himself in the most comfortable chair in the room and stretched out his massive legs. 'I think

136

I'll have a whisky. You have whisky, of course? She always knows where to get everything that's in short supply.'

Harry didn't move.

'Say what you have to say and get out!'

'You know, this attitude of yours won't do at all,' Brady said, knocking cigar ash on to the carpet. 'You'll have to be brought to heel. Don't you realise that a word from me would get Clair tossed out of the theatre? Then you wouldn't be living quite so well, would you?'

'A word about what?' Harry demanded.

'Well, after all she has been in prison. The newspapers would be interested. A jailbird isn't a great attraction on the stage. I don't think Simpson could afford to make an exhibition of her.'

After a moment's hesitation Harry went to the cellaret and took out a bottle of whisky, a glass and a soda siphon and set them on the table beside Brady.

'That's much better,' Brady said and poured himself a stiff drink. 'That's much more like it.'

Harry sat down. He was calmer now. The thing to do, he told himself, was to hear what Brady had to say. If it was blackmail he would go at once to Inspector Parkins. He would know how to deal with him.

'This is really astonishing,' Brady went on, after he had tasted the whisky. 'She knows how to live, doesn't she? Just as if she were born to it, instead of spending most of her life in a slum. Of course she has me to thank for it, but I will say she was an apt pupil. When I first met her she had a squalid little room in Shepherd Market. Any Tom, Dick or Harry could have had her for a pound. I dressed her and taught her the tricks. I got her a flat off Long Acre. I taught her how to pick pockets. She learned quickly.' He gave a thin smile. 'She turned out to be my best girl. She made me and herself quite a slice of money.' He looked at Harry and frowned. 'I wonder what she sees in you.' He paused to hold the glass of whisky under his nose, sniffing at it with a look of pleasure on his face. 'She was always an impulsive creature. It's an odd thing how these tarts fall for some down-at-the-heel rat. I've seen it happen dozens of times. I suppose it's a kind of frustrated mother instinct. But most of them do it. Most of them have some worthless little horror feeding on them, taking their

137

money, whining for clothes like the parasites they are. Still, I can't understand why she's fallen for you. Usually she goes for the boys with money.'

Harry said nothing. He stared at Brady, his face white and set.

'Yes,' Brady said. 'Boys with the money. Boys like Allan Simpson.' He smiled, his small eyes on Harry's face. 'But perhaps you don't know about Simpson? I've been watching her. As a matter of fact I've been following her around for the past week or so. She goes once or twice a week to Simpson's flat. Perhaps you've never wondered what she did with herself after her act at the Regent finished and before her act at the 22nd began? Two hours to get into mischief. Two hours to spend with Simpson. Up to her old tricks, of course. She has a knack of getting things out of men. Once a tart, always a tart: the temptation is too strong for them. It's too easy.' He glanced round the room again. 'Looks as if she's come off best. But perhaps you didn't know?'

'Is that all you have to say?' Harry said, controlling his voice with an effort.

'Why, no, certainly not. I haven't started yet. I just thought you'd be interested to know how she got the job at the night club. She rolls in the hay with Lehmann too. Not that I blame her. Once you've done that sort of thing for a living you don't look on it as anything out of the way.'

'I'm not going to listen to any more of this,' Harry said, getting to his feet. 'If you don't get out, I'll throw you out!'

Brady laughed.

'Don't be absurd. Why shouldn't I tell you this? Don't you want to know? Of course you do. A man likes to know how his girl provides for him. There's a name for a man like you. It's not a pretty one, and it carries a six-months' sentence.'

'Get out!' Harry said, angrily. 'I won't tell you again! Get out!'

'But I have every right to tell you,' Brady said calmly. 'I'm her husband, too.'

Harry felt as if he had received a blow in the face. He took a step back, tried to say something, but the words wouldn't come.

'So she didn't tell you? Well, well, how odd of her,' Brady said, smiling. 'Odd too she should have married you. I imagined you wouldn't have objected to living on her without marriage.'

'Did you say you were her husband?' Harry managed to get out.

'Certainly. I've been her husband for more than five years.'

'You're lying!'

'Do you think so? A pity. Of course we didn't live together after the first year. I have no idea why we did marry. We must have been drunk at the time. It was during the blitz, and while the bombs fell she was seldom sober; nor was I for that matter. It wasn't much fun for her to walk the streets with bombs and shrapnel coming down. The only thing that kept her going was booze.' His fat finger tapped more ash on to the carpet. 'If you don't believe me, you can always go to Somerset House and check the records. She called herself Clair Selwyn then. Her mother's name, I believe.'

'I don't believe a word of it!' Harry burst out. 'She'd never marry a swine like you. Get out! If you come here again I'll tell the police!'

'My poor fellow,' Brady said, smiling. 'If I remember rightly the sentence for bigamy is about two years. Imagine how she'd hate that after all this luxury. I think we'd better leave the police out of this, don't you?'

Harry went to the door and threw it open.

'Get out!'

Brady finished his drink and stood up. He was completely unruffled.

'There's no point in staying any longer,' he said and picked up his hat. 'But I'll be back tomorrow afternoon. Tell her to expect me. I want money, of course. So long as she pays I'll keep quiet. That car of hers is fascinating, isn't it?' He looked round the door admiringly. 'Yes, she's done remarkably well. I should be able to shake her down for quite a bit.' He moved to the door. 'Bad luck for you, my friend. By the time I've finished with her there won't be a lot left for you.'

He walked through the doorway, opened the front door, glanced over his shoulder to nod to Harry, then went away, whistling softly under his breath.

Clair came into the room, bringing with her a breath of cold air, and her fur coat sparkled with rain.

'Why, Harry! You still up? Why aren't you in bed?' She paused, sniffed, looked quickly at him. 'Have you been smoking a cigar?'

Harry was sitting before the fire. Innumerable cigarette butts lay in the hearth. A cigarette burned between his nicotine-stained fingers.

'Brady's been here,' he said, not looking at her.

She was moving to the fire, stripping off her gloves as he spoke, and his words brought her to an abrupt standstill.

'Here?' she said, and her face stiffened into an expressionless mask.

He faced her and the sight of the hard, stony face, the bleak set of the painted mouth, the still, glittering eyes shocked him. He had told her a long time ago that he knew a tart when he saw one. He had said she wasn't like one in any way, but she was now. There was no mistaking the look he had seen so often on the faces of the women of the West End: that strange blend of wooden hardness and callousness that make them look sub-human.

'Yes,' he said, and looked away.

Slowly, as if she wasn't aware what she was doing, she put her hat, gloves and handbag on the table. Then she opened the cedar-wood box, took out a cigarette and lit it.

'What did he want?' she asked. Even her voice sounded wooden and harsh.

'Can't you guess? Come and sit down. He's going to make trouble.'

Instead of sitting down, she went to the cellaret, brought a glass and poured herself a drink from the bottle of whisky that still stood on the table. Although he wasn't looking at her he could tell how unsteady her hand was by the rattle of the bottle neck against the glass.

'He said you married him about five years ago,' Harry went on. 'Is it true?'

She came slowly to the fire and sat in the easy chair opposite Harry's.

'Is it true?' he repeated after a long silence.

'Yes, it's true,' she said. 'I heard he had gone to America. I thought I'd never see him again.' She drank some of the whisky and put the glass on the hearth kerb. 'I'm sorry, Harry. You wanted it so badly. I didn't want to disappoint you.'

'I see,' Harry said, and stared in the fire for a long moment. 'Oh, well, it's too late to be sorry about it. I understand, of course. It was my fault for pressing you. I wish you had told me, Clair. Couldn't you have trusted me?'

'I didn't want to lose you,' she said sullenly.

'He wants money. He's coming to see you tomorrow afternoon.'

She didn't say anything and he glanced at her. She was staring into the fire. She looked old and worn, somehow shopsoiled, as if her bright, glittering veneer had been stripped away to show what was really underneath.

As she remained silent, he said, 'It's blackmail, of course. We could go to the police.'

'Let me think a moment,' she said sharply.

They remained silent for what seemed to Harry to be a long time. She sat rigid, her cigarette in her lips, the smoke curling in a steady spiral to the ceiling. Only her eyes moved; they shifted continuously, like those of an animal in a trap.

'I want to know exactly what happened,' she said suddenly. 'Tell me everything. I'm sure he said a lot of filthy things about me, but I want to know everything.'

In a cold, flat voice, Harry told her.

'He's been watching you,' he concluded. 'He says you go quite often to Simpson's flat.'

She half-started out of her chair.

'That's a lie, Harry! You don't believe it, do you?'

He looked straight at her, and her eyes shifted.

'I don't want to believe it,' he said. 'He also said you and Lehmann . . . ' He broke off, seeing the trapped expression on her face. 'Is it true?'

'I warned you, didn't I?' she said harshly. 'I told you I was rotten. Well, I am. I don't make any bones about it. They mean nothing to me. Nothing! All right, I won't lie to you, Harry. I do go to their flats.' She reached for another cigarette.

'How could you, Clair?' He got to his feet and began to

walk aimlessly about the room. 'Haven't you any thought for me? I have to mix with them. Why did you do it?'

'How else do you think I got the Regent job? But don't you see, Harry, they can't mean anything to me! You are the only man in my life. Ever since I met you I've wanted to do things for you, but I've only succeeded in making you unhappy. I couldn't help it. It was so easy. I knew if I went with them I could handle them.'

'You put money before everything,' Harry said. 'That's where you go wrong. Oh, Clair, why did you do it? We could have been happy if you had left the money side to me. We wouldn't have had a great deal, but we wouldn't have been in this mess.'

'I suppose you hate me now,' she said in a hard, flat voice. 'Well, I don't blame you. What are you going to do? Are you going to walk out on me?'

He went to the window, pushed the curtain aside and stared down into the rain-swept street.

'Harry!' She got up and went to him, putting her hand on his arm. 'What are you going to do? Are you going to leave me?'

He shook his head.

'It's all right,' he said, not turning. 'We'll forget about everything for now except Brady. When we've dealt with him we can tackle our own problem, but not before.'

'Does that mean you're going to leave me – in a little while? I must know, Harry. I can't stand the uncertainty. Can't you see a man like Simpson couldn't mean anything to me except what I could get out of him? It's you I love. My whole life's centred around you. All I've done – this place, the car, the money I've made is for you if only you'd accept them. If you're going to leave me, tell me now.'

Harry turned and looked helplessly at her.

'How I wish you hadn't done any of this. It's all right, Clair. I'm not going to leave you. I'd be lying if I said it won't make a difference; it will, but I still love you, and if you'll try to change – give up this horrible thirst for money, we'd be so much happier. Can't you see that? Give up the stage, Clair. Let's make a fresh start. What does it matter if we're hard up? Isn't it better to be hard up than in a mess like this?'

'Do you think Brady will let me give this up now?' she asked. 'He'll want money, and I'll have to earn it. He's like a leech. He'll cling on and suck me dry.'

'We'll go to the police. It's the only way to deal with a rat like him.'

'The police? I've committed bigamy,' Clair said, her voice rising. 'How can we go to the police? Do you think I want to go to prison again?'

'But you're not going to give him money, are you?' Harry said, anxiously. 'He'll never leave you alone once he knows he can get it out of you. They never do.'

'I know I'm not going to prison. I'd kill myself first.'

'Clair ... please –'

'I would! I'd kill myself. I'd rather die than spend a week in prison. You don't know what it's like. It was awful. Worse than I ever imagined. Hellish! Shut away from everything. Made to do beastly chores. Nagged and bullied. Shut up behind bars like an animal. No, that'll never happen to me again. I'm ready this time. I'll kill myself!'

'You mustn't talk like that, Clair,' Harry said, shocked. 'We haven't the right to end our own lives.'

She gave a hard, sneering little smile.

'It's my own life to do what I want with. I know I'll never go to prison again.' She turned away. 'Come on, Harry, let's go to bed. It's late and I'm tired.' She picked up her hat and gloves and walked into the bedroom. Her shoulders drooped and she walked listlessly. Watching her, Harry felt a pang of pity for her. It was all partly his fault, he thought, following her into the bedroom. He had been weak. It was too late for regrets. Brady now controlled the situation. Unless they could think of some way out, she would either have to go to prison or pay.

'Do you want to sleep with me?' Clair said abruptly. 'I'll understand if you don't.'

He knew it was no time to pity himself or to be outraged. She had done what she had done as much for him as for herself. He knew that. He was quite sure in his mind that neither Simpson nor Lehmann meant anything to her. It was horrible that she could have behaved like that, but her background and upbringing set her aside from other women. She was in trouble. This was the time to be generous. He went to her and took her in his arms.

'It's all right, darling. Let's forget about it. We'll see this thing through together. I don't know how it will end, but whatever happens I'll be with you.'

143

The following afternoon, punctually at three 'oclock, the front door bell rang.

Clair started at the sound, scattering cigarette ash over her skirt. As she made to get up, Harry stopped her.

'I'll go. Don't let him rattle you,' he said.

She had wanted to see Brady alone, but Harry wouldn't hear of it.

'He may as well know I'm in this with you,' he had said. 'I'm not leaving you. I said we'd see this through together and we're going to.'

They had been sitting on the settee, waiting, since lunch, both smoking, both nervy, and it was a relief to Harry when the bell rang. He crossed the room to the front door.

Brady stood in the passage, expansive, smiling, immaculate and pig-like. Behind him was another man: short, square-shouldered with a mop of tow-coloured hair, a square chin, cold, steady grey eyes and a mouth which was fixed in a perpetual and humourless grin.

Harry recognised the hair at once. This was the man who had hit him with the bicycle chain and who had maimed Ron.

'Ah! So you're here too?' Brady said, showing his gold-capped teeth in an expansive smile. 'Excellent! I wanted a word with you. And Clair? She's here? A party, eh? Splendid! This is Ben Whelan. You've met him before, I believe?'

Whelan looked at Harry and his grin widened. He had small even teeth: very white and strong looking, the teeth of a professional boxer.

'Hallo, chummy,' he said.

Harry stood aside; his mouth dry and his heart hammering.

Brady walked past him into the sitting-room.

Whelan motioned Harry to follow.

'Go ahead, chummy,' he said. 'I'm keeping an eye on you.'

As Harry entered the sitting-room, Brady was saying, 'How are you, Clair? You look a little peeked, but I expect that's the excitement of seeing me again. Here's Ben. He's been looking forward to this. You were always his favourite brunette.'

'Hallo, baby,' Ben said, sauntering in behind Harry. 'How did you get on in quod?'

Clair was standing with her back to the mantelpiece. She was pale and her face was set, but she seemed to have lost her nervousness. There was a wary hardness about her now that surprised Harry.

'It wasn't a holiday,' she said shrugging. 'But then it didn't cost me anything.'

Brady laughed.

'You always did look on the bright side of things,' he said, dropping his hat on the table. 'What do you think of the lay-out, Ben? Have a look round. She won't mind.'

'The police aren't here, if that's what you're scared of,' Clair said with a sneer.

'Look all the same,' Brady said to Whelan.

Whelan wandered into the bedroom.

'Let's have a drink, Clair,' Brady said sitting down. 'We may as well be sociable. I've seen your act at the Regent. It's absolutely first rate. The idea of the mask is sheer genius. It must have made you feel very safe.'

'It did,' Clair said coolly. She looked at Harry. 'Would you get the drinks, please? Ben drinks gin.'

With hands that were far from steady Harry brought out the gin and whisky and glasses.

'And this young fellow has a business in Grafton Street,' Brady said, looking at Harry with a benign smile. 'It's astonishing how well you both have got on. To think the last time I saw you you were both working on the streets. A real success story. Just a spot more,' he went on as Harry poured the whisky into a glass. 'That's about it.' He reached for the glass. 'What do you think of it?' he asked Whelan as he came into the room. 'Pretty lush, eh?'

'Wouldn't mind it myself,' Whelan said, and sat down. He shook his head at Brady's inquiring look. 'No one hiding under the bed.' He took the glass of gin from Harry and winked at him. 'Landed yourself in a soft spot, haven't you, chummy?'

Clair went over to the table and poured herself a whisky. She gave Harry a tight little smile.

'What are you earning now, Clair?' Brady asked, stretching out his massive legs.

'A hundred less tax,' she returned promptly.

'Under paid.' Brady shook his head. 'Since this little meeting hinges on money I think it would be a good idea to have a look at your passbook.' He held out his hand. 'Let me see it.'

'It's at the bank.'

'You don't want me to make my own estimate, do you?' Brady said, continuing to smile. 'You see, Clair, the way I've worked this out is this way. I taught you the tricks of the trade. Therefore I'm entitled to a commission. If it hadn't been for my experience and skill you wouldn't be on the stage. I don't want to be unfair to you, but I'm afraid I can't trust you about your earnings. You'd better produce either your passbook or some proof of what you earn, otherwise I'll take a chance on a couple of hundred a week and let it go at that.'

Clair remained still for a long moment, then she shrugged, went to the desk, opened it, took out a buff-coloured envelope and handed it to him.

'Thank you.' He seemed a little surprised as if he hadn't expected her to give in so tamely. He looked at the passbook and raised his eyebrows. 'A hundred and fifty a week,' he said to Whelan. 'Very nice. My goodness! You've got on, haven't you? Well, then, let's come to terms.' He finished his whisky and held the empty glass out to Harry. 'Could I trouble you? I think so much better on whisky.'

While Harry poured another drink, Brady did a calculation on the back of the envelope. He whistled softly under his breath. Clair had gone back to the hearth, and was standing with her hands behind her, her face expressionless. Whelan lolled in an armchair, his eyes on Harry.

'Well now,' Brady said, taking the glass from Harry. 'Thank you so much. Well, now, let's get down to business. The position is you have committed bigamy. Being an old lag they'll probably deal severely with you. At best, you couldn't hope to get off under eighteen months. It boils down to this, are you prepared to pay for your freedom? Roughly you have about seventy pounds a week, tax free, plus say twenty-five for expenses. Let's call it a hundred. I don't want to cripple you so I suggest fifty per cent. Ben will call on you every Saturday morning, and you'll pay him fifty pounds. So long as you keep up the payments I'll keep quiet. That's my proposition.'

Clair studied him. There was a dangerous glitter in her eyes, but her face was expressionless.

'You'll be sorry, Robert,' she said. 'I played fair with you. I could have given you away. A word from me and you'd still

146

get a five-year sentence. You realise that, don't you?'

Brady chuckled.

'Don't bluff, precious. You know what happens to a squealer. Ben would take care of you if you did that. You knew he would take care of you if you had talked when you made a fool of yourself over that cigarette case.' He looked over at Harry. 'You may not be familiar with underworld methods,' he said genially. 'Perhaps you have heard of girls being disfigured by acid. It's the usual punishment for talking too much.' He turned back to Clair. 'It won't wash, I'm afraid. Even if you did squeak, I'd still get you for bigamy, and when you came out after your stretch Ben would be waiting for you. You'll have to do better than that.' He finished his whisky, glanced at his watch. 'I don't want to hurry you, but I have another appointment very soon. What do you say – fifty a week or an eighteen months' stretch?'

'I'll pay,' Clair said in a cold, flat voice.

'Splendid!' Brady said, and clapped his hands. 'Magnificent! What do you think of that, Ben? No hesitation. "I'll pay," just like that.'

Whelan grinned.

'Not much else she could do.'

'All right,' Brady said. 'Next Saturday Ben'll be along about eleven o'clock. We'll take cash. No cheques, and in pound notes. One more little thing. You've been working now for about eight weeks. It's only fair I should be paid for those eight weeks as well. Eight times fifty is four hundred. That's right, isn't it?'

Clair didn't say anything. A tightness came into her face and her eyes hardened.

'Well, then, let's start with a down payment. I don't suppose you have four hundred – or have you?'

'No,' Clair said. 'I haven't even a hundred.'

'Always extravagant.' He smiled at Harry. 'I never could persuade her to save. Well, we won't expect miracles then. Let's say two hundred on Saturday as well as the fifty. And another two hundred in a month's time. That's fair, isn't it?'

'I haven't two hundred,' Clair said.

'That's a pity. Well, you'll have to find it. There's the car. You can sell that. I don't think you really want a showy job like that. It's only ostentatious. You'll manage to rake it up if you sell the car. Anyway, it's up to you. Two hundred and fifty pounds or else, by next Saturday. Do you understand?'

147

Clair didn't say anything.

'Don't be sullen,' Brady said gently. 'It won't get you anywhere. Do you understand or don't you?'

She gave an indifferent shrug.

'Yes, I understand,' she said.

'And I would advise you not to try any tricks,' Brady said, looking sharply at her. 'Don't think you'll wriggle out of this, because you won't. You should know me well enough by now.'

She smiled.

'Bravo!' Brady exclaimed. 'So you can still smile? Well, that's fine. Now, let's see if you can keep it up.' He looked at Harry. 'Now you: oh, yes, don't think I've forgotten you. I have a little job for you. You're going to pull your weight as well. If you don't, Clair will suffer. I mean that. Do you understand?'

'You leave him out of this!' Clair snapped.

'Ah! No smile now.' Brady shook his finger at her. 'You have a soft spot for him still, have you? But he's in this and he must pull his weight. Your studio is going to be very useful and profitable to me,' he went on to Harry. 'I have some negatives I want printed. Ben will give them to you. It will be quite a big order. Five thousand of each. They're not quite the kind of pictures you've been used to handling, but they sell very well at five shillings each. You won't get paid for the work, but you'll have the satisfaction of knowing you are keeping Clair out of jail. The police aren't likely to suspect such a respectable studio as yours. It's easy enough to get the negatives, but damned difficult to produce a quantity of prints. So you're going to be busy for the next month or so. If they sell well – and I think they will – we'll have a lot more for you to do.'

'Oh, no!' Clair cried. 'He's not going to do it! That settles it! You're not going to get anything now! I'll go to prison! And I'll send you there too!'

Brady got slowly to his feet.

'He doesn't say anything, does he?' He looked at Harry. 'Don't be too hasty. I'll let you talk it over tomorrow with the negatives. You can tell him what you intend to do. I would advise you to do it if you want to keep her out of jail. It's all or nothing with me.'

'He's not going to do it!' Clair said. 'You've overplayed your hand. I'll go to the police today!'

'Come along, Ben,' Brady said. 'We have other things to do than listen to dramatics.'

Whelan got to his feet.

'Tomorrow,' Brady said, glancing at Harry. 'If she squeaks to the police Ben will take care of her. Acid makes a mess of a girl's face. It would make you sick to have to go to bed with her. You two have to make up your minds. I know what I would do.'

Clair went up to him, her face was white and her eyes vicious.

'And I know what I'm going to do! You're not getting away with this! Don't you think you are!' And she began to curse him in a high-pitched, harsh voice that shocked Harry.

'Clair! Stop it!' he shouted, went to her and pulled her round to face him. 'Stop it!'

She put her hand to her mouth, jerked away from him.

'Get out!' Harry said to Brady.

'Charming little soul, isn't she? They're all the same,' Brady said. 'Well, Whelan will call on you tomorrow. Don't forget. About eleven o'clock at your studio. So long for now,' and he sauntered out of the flat with Whelan at his heels.

'Sorry,' Clair said turning. 'I couldn't help myself.' She poured out two inches of whisky and gulped it down. 'Well, that's that. Now we know.'

'Now look, Clair . . . ' Harry began, but she raised her hand, stopping him.

'There's only one way out of this mess, Harry, and I'm going to take it. I've been thinking and thinking all this morning what I should do. I know him. I knew what was coming. Oh, I didn't know he was going to drag you into it, but I knew he'd strip me. He's ruthless. You don't know what a swine he is. Dragging you into it is the last straw. Well, this is where we part, darling. It's the only way. I've made you unhappy, but I'm damned if I'm going to make you one of his sort. No, please,' she went on as Harry began to speak, 'it's the only way. I'm dropping out of sight, and I'll take care they never find me.'

'We go together,' Harry said firmly. 'We're not parting, Clair. We can pack and get out within an hour. Let's do it. Somehow, together, we'll make a go of it.'

She shook her head.

'No, Harry, it's no good. You'll never get anywhere with me. I'm rotten, and anything I touch goes rotten. Besides, you'll have to stay and give evidence against Whelan. At least, we can put him away. Do you think Ron would recognise him?'

'Never mind about Whelan,' Harry said, sitting down and pulling her down beside him. 'You've got to listen to me. Ever

149

since we met you have held the reins, and I've done what you said. Well, it's going to change now. I'm taking over. It's time I did. If I hadn't been so weak this wouldn't have happened. We're married, and we're sticking together. We're packing and getting out, and we're going together. We'll leave everything. We'll take our clothes, and nothing more. Never mind about Whelan. Let the police pick him up if they can. Brady won't guess we'd leave everything and bolt, not if we go right away. We'll just disappear, and nobody's ever going to find us.'

Clair stared at him.

'Do you really mean that, Harry?'

'I mean it,' he said, getting to his feet. 'Come on, we're not going to waste a minute. Go and pack.'

'But wait, Harry, let's make up our minds what we're going to do,' she said, and slid her arms around his neck and hugged him. 'Oh, Harry, do you think we'll get away with it? I don't care what happens so long as we're together.'

'We must get away with it,' he said, holding her to him. 'Now go and pack. I want to go to the bank and I want a word with Mooney. He told me if I was in a mess he'd lend me a hand, and I think he will. We'll need new identity cards and ration books. It's possible he may know where I can get them.'

Clair looked different now. Her old brightness had come back and her eyes sparkled with excitement.

'This is going to be exciting! To drop out of sight and start again as someone else! I'll go blonde! You'll like me blonde, won't you, darling?'

He caught hold of her and shook her.

'Clair! This isn't going to be a picnic. We'll be short of money. We'll probably have to live in one room. We'll have to watch our step all the time. I don't think exciting is quite the word.'

She patted his face and laughed.

'I'm going to love it. Just you and I, Harry! Of course it's going to be exciting! Look, with the car we could take all we want; our clothes, the wireless and we have a case of scotch. Oh, yes, Harry, let's take the car!'

He stared at her.

'What are you thinking of? The car isn't paid for. How can you think like that? Besides, it could be easily traced. Of course we can't take it. While I'm out, write to that chap Maurice and tell him to collect it. Say you're going away suddenly and don't want it any more.'

Her face fell.

'Oh. I hadn't thought of that. Well, all right. I must say it would have been marvellous to have had it with us. But I suppose you're right. I'll fix it with Maurice.'

'I'll get off and see Mooney. Oh, damn, the bank will be closed by now. We have to have money, Clair.'

She went quickly into her bedroom and came out again in a moment, her hands full of rings and jewellery.

'Go and pop these. They're not much, but you should get sixty or seventy pounds for them.'

He took the jewellery and dropped it into his pocket.

'We'll have to say good-bye to that fifty in the bank,' he said regretfully. 'Once we leave this flat we leave it as two completely different people. There's no turning back.'

'How about Simpson?'

'Phone Lehmann and tell him you're going away. Say you're going abroad or something; only don't let on what's happened.'

She nodded.

'All right, Harry, I'll do it. Try not to be too long, will you?'

'I'll be as quick as I can. You'll be here when I come back?'

'Of course.'

'Word of honour?'

She kissed him.

'If you still want me – word of honour.'

He left her getting out suitcases and tossing clothes on to the bed. On the way downstairs he wondered a little fearfully what was going to happen to them. She didn't seem to realise what was in store for them. To start all over again would be much harder for her than for him. Already she was thinking in terms of a car. One thing was certain, he would keep a tight hold on her. She was not going to get them into another mess like this!

He passed swiftly through the reception hall, his brow creased in a worried frown. He didn't see Ben Whelan sitting in a deep lounging chair just behind a pillar, but Whelan saw him and grinned.

The dry cleaning shop Mooney managed was off Fulham Palace Road: a small, pokey little place with a steam press in the window, three girls who couldn't have been much more than sixteen, and a back office where Mooney hid himself and chewed at his dead cigar.

The three girls looked up as Harry pushed open the shop door. Mooney had said they were as ugly as sin: an exaggeration, but they weren't attractive. The three of them were pasty-faced and grimy, but there was nothing about them that soap and water and a course of vitamins couldn't put right.

'Is Mr Mooney in?' Harry asked.

The youngest of the three girls jerked her thumb at the office door. She managed to convey by that gesture that if Harry found Mooney in there with his throat cut she wouldn't grieve.

Harry knocked on the door, turned the handle and entered a dark little room furnished with a desk, a chair, and a steel filing cabinet.

Mooney lolled in the chair with his feet on the desk. It was some weeks since Harry had seen him, and he noticed a change in him. He looked older, a little more seedy and a little more hopeless. There were holes in the soles of his shoes, and his faded tie had grease spots on it. His hat, still resting on the back of his head, was a little more shapeless; his shirt cuffs were frayed and dirty. He stared at Harry, lifted his feet tenderly off the desk and leaned forward, thrusting out his hand.

'Hallo, kid,' he said, his face lighting up. 'This is a surprise. Funny thing, I was thinking about you.'

Harry shook hands.

'Nice to see you again,' he said awkwardly. 'How goes it? You're looking fine.'

'Am I?' Mooney grimaced. 'I feel awful. Here, sit on the desk. Old Gimpy doesn't run to two chairs. He doesn't like me to have visitors. I haven't a cigar for you, kid. Things are a bit tight at the moment.'

Harry sat on the edge of the desk and lit a cigarette.

'I'm sorry.'

'Yeah.' Mooney sighed and massaged his forehead with

152

fingers that were not over clean. 'Well, it's something I expected. I never get a break for long. Did you see those girls? How would you like to be shut up with that bunch all day? I miss those dolls in the chorus. The thing I hate most is the smell of an unwashed woman.'

'Yes,' Harry said absently. He wasn't paying much attention to what Mooney was saying. His mind was too preoccupied with his own worries.

Mooney eyed him thoughtfully.

'What's up, kid? Something biting you? Got it written all over your face. Anything I can do?'

'Well, yes,' Harry said, lowering his voice. 'Can we talk here?'

Mooney nodded.

'They're too dumb even to listen at a keyhole,' he said. 'What's up?'

'We're in a mess, Alf. I can't go into details. You wouldn't want to hear them anyway. It's so bad we're going to do a flit: as bad as that.'

Mooney whistled. A flit was something he had never done, although he had a feeling it wouldn't be long before he had to do it.

'Bills, eh?' he said gloomily. 'I always thought she'd run up bills. Where do I come in?'

'We're dropping out of sight, and we intend to stay out of sight. It's got to be done properly. We'll need new identity cards and ration books. Do you know where I can get them?'

'Well . . . ' Mooney paused, got up and went to the door. He opened it a crack and peered into the shop. Satisfied the three girls were busy gossiping together, he shut the door and sat down again. 'It can be done,' he went on in a whisper, 'but it costs dough. Do you want me to handle it?'

'Can you?'

Mooney nodded.

'I wish you would then. I want them quickly. A matter of hours.'

'It'll cost about thirty quid. And that's cheap. The chap who dishes them out is a pal of mine. If you went to him yourself it'd cost you fifty.'

Harry took out his wallet and counted out thirty-five pounds on the desk.

'And a fiver for yourself, Alf.'

Mooney hesitated, then shook his head.

'No, kid, if you're in that kind of trouble you'll need all your dough. I've had enough out of you in the past. That's all right. I'm glad to do it.' He pushed five of the pound notes back.

'Thanks, Alf,' Harry said gratefully. 'I do want every penny I can lay hands on. But look, here's a cheque for fifty pounds. It's all I have in the bank. I can't get it myself this afternoon so I shall have to leave it. Go to the bank tomorrow and draw it all out. Give twenty-five to Doris and keep the rest for yourself. Will you do that?'

Again Mooney hesitated. The temptation to accept the money made him perspire.

'No again, Harry,' he said, breathing heavily. 'I can get this cashed right away. There's a bloke next door who'll do it. You'll be able to use fifty quid better than Doris and me.'

'I'm not leaving Doris high and dry,' Harry said firmly. 'Please do what I ask. We can manage with what we've got. Keep it, Alf. It's all right.'

Mooney shrugged. He folded the cheque and tucked it away in his waistcoat pocket.

'Well, okay,' he said, 'and thanks. If you know how I could use twenty-five! If you're sure it's all right, it'll save my life.'

'It's all right. Now, will you get after those identity cards? I'll call back. When do you think you can get them?'

'By six,' Mooney said, consulting his watch. 'Not before.'

Harry stood up.

'All right, I'll be back. Have them made out in the names of Douglas and Helen Kent. Husband and wife. Last address 23 Sinclair Road, West Ham. All right?'

'My word! You're coming on,' Mooney said, staring at him. 'You've got it all planned out, haven't you?'

Harry nodded.

'Yes,' he said, 'and Alf, whatever happens, whatever you hear, not a word. The police may make inquiries. I don't say they will, but they may. It's as bad as that. You won't give us away, will you?'

'You don't have to ask that, kid,' Mooney said. 'It's Clair, isn't it? Not you?'

'Yes, but we're sticking together, Alf.'

Mooney scratched the side of his jaw.

'Yeah, you stick to her. She's all right. I like her. A bit wild,

154

of course. Perhaps a bit too wild, but there's nothing she wouldn't do for you.'

'I know,' Harry said. 'Well, so long, Alf, I'll be back at six.'

'Where are you going now?'

'To Grafton Street. There are one or two things I want to pick up, and I want to say good-bye to Doris.'

'To save you coming back here, I'll meet you at the Duke of Wellington at six. I have to go to Soho, anyway.'

'That's fine, and thanks, Alf.'

'That's what I'm here for, kid.' He got up and put on his coat. 'We can ride down together as far as Piccadilly. You taking a cab?'

'Yes. Will it be all right for you to leave?'

'It'll have to be,' Mooney said. He knotted his tie, straightened his hat and put the dead cigar carefully in a drawer of the desk. 'I've had that damned thing three weeks. Can't afford cigars at the price they're asking now.'

He went into the shop.

'Girls, I have to go out. One of you stick around until I get back. I shouldn't be later than half past six. If Mr Gimpy phones tell him I had to go to the dentist.'

Three blank pasty faces turned in his direction. Three pairs of dull, indifferent eyes looked from him to Harry.

'Yes, Mr Mooney.'

Out in the street, Mooney said, 'That's all they ever say, "Yes, Mr Mooney." At least those chorus girls said "no", sometimes.'

Harry waved to a taxi.

As they rattled along Hammersmith Road, Mooney said, 'How about Ron, Harry? If you're going to drop out of sight . . . '

'I'm no use to Ron,' Harry returned. 'If you ever have a moment I'd be glad if you'd see him. Tell him how it is.' He frowned, thinking of Ron, helpless in his chair. 'Tell him I'll write when I settle down.'

'I'll find time.' Mooney glowered out of the window. 'The trouble is to find anything to do with the time I have. Watch your step, Harry. For the love of Mike don't finish up the way I have. It's easy to do too. If you're not settled in a job by the time you're forty, it's curtains. Watch that. You've got to be fixed up by forty, kid. Don't forget. It's important. No one wants a man when he's over forty these days.'

Harry left the cab at the bottom of Bond Street, and walked quickly to Grafton Street. He found Doris busy on an enlargement.

'I thought you weren't coming in today, Harry,' she said, surprised. 'There've been a couple of appointments for tomorrow, and Mrs Grierson has ordered two dozen half plates of the proof we sent her.'

'Dorrie, there's been a spot of trouble . . .'

At the tone of his voice she looked up sharply, her plump, good-natured face alarmed.

'I'm getting out,' he went on with a rush. 'Don't ask me anything, Dorrie. It's just one of those things. I'm disappearing.'

'Is – is Clair going with you?'

He nodded.

'You mean – she's in trouble?'

'Never mind who's in trouble,' he said curtly. 'I've got to get out. Will you cancel all appointments, Dorrie? Will you close the place up? I shan't be coming back.'

'But you can't do that,' Doris said, going to him. 'Harry, this is daft. You're just beginning to make a go of it. Besides, there's the lease. You can't just walk out.'

'I'm walking out,' he said tersely. 'Be a good girl, and don't make things difficult for me. I've seen Mooney. He'll have twenty-five pounds for you. It's all I can afford. I hope it carries you on for a bit. I'm sorry, Dorrie. Don't look like that, please. I'm terribly sorry, but I can't help it.'

'You shouldn't have married her, Harry. All along I've been expecting trouble, and now – this. She's no good. I don't care if I do make you angry. I've got to tell you. She's no good, and she never will be any good. Leave her. Forget her. Let her go her own way and you go yours.'

'I love her, Dorrie. I know she isn't any good. She knows it too, but that doesn't make any difference. When you love someone as I love her you're caught. There's nothing I can do about it. We're seeing this thing through together.'

'But what about the equipment?' Doris wailed. 'And the goodwill? You just can't walk out . . .'

'Do what you like with it, Dorrie. If you can make a bit on it, go ahead.' He went to a cupboard, took out his Leica and a handful of films. 'That's all I'm taking. Now I'm going, Dorrie. You won't see me again. I can't say how sorry I am, and I'll miss you. But I won't forget you, Dorrie. No, don't cry. It's just one of those things.' He put his arm round her and gave her a hug, then made quickly for the door. 'So long, Dorrie. Alf will be seeing you.' He opened the door, looked back and saw she was struggling with her tears, felt a lump rise in his throat and ran quickly down the passage, down the stairs to the street.

It was only five o'clock. He had an hour to kill, and he walked briskly along Piccadilly, entered a phone booth near Simpson's and called the Park Lane flat.

Clair came on the line.

'It's all right,' he said. 'He's getting everything for us. All right your end?'

'Fine and dandy.' She sounded astonishingly cheerful. 'I've packed, and now I'm going to bleach my hair . . . '

'Not on the phone, darling,' he said sharply. 'I'll be back not later than seven. Have you written to Maurice?'

'Yes, and I've had a word with Val. He's furious. He said they'd sue me for breach of contract. I told him to go ahead and sue. Was that all right?'

'It'll have to be,' Harry said, a tight feeling round his chest. 'Well, I'll get along. See you at seven.'

After wandering the back streets of Piccadilly for what seemed to him to be hours, he eventually made his way to the Duke of Wellington.

The manager was in the bar, and glanced at Harry, frowned in a puzzled way, then came over.

'Good evening,' he said smiling. 'I haven't seen you for a long time – not since that little unpleasantness last – when was it? Last July, wasn't it?'

'October,' Harry said, pleased to be recognised. 'Time flies, doesn't it? No, I haven't been in. I've been out of town as a matter of fact.'

'Well, have one on the house,' the manager said. 'What'll it be?'

It couldn't be anything else but beer in the Duke of Wellington, Harry decided. Habit died too hard for that.

'What happened to that girl you were with?' the manager asked as he served Harry with a pint of bitter. 'What a beauty! Was she a friend of yours?'

'No,' he said shortly. 'I haven't seen her since.'

'Pity,' the manager said. 'Mind you, I don't suppose she was all she should be, but my goodness! How bedworthy she was!'

Harry grunted, took out a crumpled copy of the *Evening*

Standard, and pointedly began to glance at the headlines.

The manager took the hint, and after saying he hoped to see Harry again he went off to his office.

Already the bar was filling up, and putting down the paper, Harry looked round. The same old faces met his gaze. There were the three men in black homburg hats drinking whiskies and whispering together. There was a grey-faced man and his perky, shabby wife, sitting at a table close by, still drinking port, and looking a little more shabby. There was no sign of the girl with the flat chest who used to hold her companion's hand so possessively. No man would stand a woman who was so possessive for long, Harry thought. His eyes strayed to the table where he had seen Clair for the first time, and his heart contracted. So much had happened since then. It was quite unbelievable. And now this: dropping out of sight, changing his name, starting again.

He sat for a long time thinking about the past, and the future. The hands of the clock crawled on, reached six, crawled on again. At six-fifteen, the swing doors pushed open and Mooney came in.

'All right?' Harry asked in a low voice as Mooney joined him.

'Yes, it's all right. Had a little trouble about the price, but I beat him down. Here, stick this in your pocket. It's all in order. Don't look at it now.'

Harry put the thick envelope in his pocket.

'I can't thank you enough, Alf.'

'Forget it, kid,' Mooney said. 'You better get off. I know you want to get back to her. Well, kid, I don't suppose we'll see each other again, but here's luck. And tell her luck from me too. Take care of yourself. If ever you want me in a hurry, you can always get me by ringing this number.' He gave Harry a card. 'That's a guy who looks after my post and takes messages for me. Don't trust him with anything hot. Just say you want to get into touch with me. He'll give you my address in case I've moved. All right?'

Harry took his hand and squeezed it.

'Thanks, Alf. We may meet again. I hope so.'

'So long,' Mooney said. 'Keep your pecker up. I've been through tough times, but there're plenty of good ones too. Don't forget that.'

Harry slapped him on the shoulder and then walked quickly across the bar and into the street. He felt strangely moved at parting with Mooney. Mooney was an odd stick, but whatever else he was he was loyal.

Harry waved to a taxi and gave the Park Lane address. As soon as the cab was moving he took out the envelope, ripped it open and examined the ration books and identity cards. They were in order, and the names of Douglas and Helen Kent looked strange to him. There was also another envelope with a scrawl of writing on it. Frowning, Harry read the message:

'*I have Doris's twenty-five, and I'll see she has it. You better keep this little lot. I couldn't rest happy if I kept it and thought you were hard up. What a damned silly old sucker I'm developing into, aren't I? God bless. – Alf.*'

Inside the envelope were twenty-five one pound notes.

VI

Four suitcases and a hatbox stood in the hall. Across the hatbox lay Clair's mink coat.

Harry closed the front door. All that luggage would want a bit of handling, he thought, pausing to try one of the suitcases. It was heavy. Well, it couldn't be helped. They would be stupid not to take as many of their clothes as they could. He had no idea how long it would be before they could buy new ones.

'Clair,' he called. 'Are you ready?'

He turned the handle of the sitting-room door and entered.

'Everything's fixed, darling. Mooney's been . . . ' He broke off, staring.

Clair sat in a huddled heap in one of the armchairs. She was drunk. She looked up at Harry, her face empty, her eyes screwed up the way a short-sighted woman too vain to wear glasses screws up her eyes when she is trying to see something. Her hair was in disorder. The wine-coloured silk blouse she was wearing had a rip in one of the sleeves. One of her stockings had escaped from her suspender clips and had slipped down to her ankle.

It seemed to Harry as he stood before her that he was looking at a stranger. Into his mind, made vacant by shock, came a picture of the past. The memory of something that had happened to him built itself up in his mind the way a picture forms on a television screen. He saw the dark doorway and the old woman wrapped in newspapers sitting there, an empty bottle of gin clutched in a filthy hand, a ghastly smile of invitation on her drink-sodden face as she looked up at him. He heard again the croaking voice and her horrible suggestion. He could smell the drink and the dirt again. And he flinched now as he did then when he remembered the disgusting thing she had done.

'What's happened, Clair?' he asked.

Her face twitched; the muscles under her white, blotched skin moved the way water moves in the wind.

'I burned my hand,' she said.

He looked at her hands. The fingers of her right hand were blistered and stained a deep yellow. He saw the cigarette between her fingers, glowing red against her flesh and burning another blister, and he was horrified to see she didn't notice nor appear to feel the burning ember.

'Drop it!' he said sharply, leaning forward and slapped at her hand, knocking the cigarette butt on to the floor. As he placed his foot on it he saw holes in the carpet, burned by cigarette ends where she had dropped them.

'What have you been doing? Oh, Clair, pull yourself together. We've got to go. Why have you been drinking like this? What's the matter?'

'I want you to give me a baby,' she said, looking up at him, her face full of drunken cunning. 'I've thought it all out. They won't touch me if you give me a baby.'

'What are you talking about? Clair! Get hold of yourself! We've got to go. Don't you understand?'

'That's right, isn't it?' she said, leaning forward to peer at him. Her spirit ladened breath fanned his cheek. 'It's got to be all right! I read somewhere they don't touch you if you're in the family way. You've got to do it, Harry. If you won't, I'll get someone who will.'

He caught hold of her shoulders, dragged her to her feet and shook her.

'Stop talking nonsense!' he said angrily. 'You don't know what you're saying.'

She pushed him away with surprising strength.

'Oh yes, I do,' she said, swaying unsteadily. 'It's you who don't know what you're talking about. We're going to have a baby. At once! It's the only way out.' Suddenly she began to cry and stumbled against him, clinging to him. 'I'm so frightened,' she moaned. 'I don't know what I'm going to do.

You must give me a baby, Harry. They don't hang a woman who's carrying a child.'

Harry felt a cold prickle run up his spine. Had she gone mad? He caught hold of her arms, pushed her away and stared at her. The cold, bleak terror in her eyes turned him sick.

'What have you done?'

'He's in there. I – I don't know what made me do it. He caught me packing. He said we'd never get away. I went into the kitchen and he followed me, sneering at me. There was a knife on the table. I caught hold of it . . . ' She broke off, shuddering.

'What are you saying?' Harry said, his heart hammering against his side. 'You're drunk. You're lying! . . . '

'You've got to give me a baby,' she moaned, wringing her hands. 'I don't want to die! Oh, Harry . . . Harry . . . what are we going to do?'

He went quickly into the kitchen, paused in the doorway and then took a slow step back.

Ben Whelan lay on the floor, his knees drawn up and his hands clenched. His dead empty eyes seemed to be watching a big bluebottle that walked stiff-legged across the ceiling.

CHAPTER THREE

I

Mr and Mrs Douglas Kent lived at 43 Fairfield Road in two rooms on the top floor of a shabby boarding house in the poorer district of Hastings.

Fairfield Road lay at the back of the Old Town, a narrow, twisting hill of a road of cobblestones and small, dirty grey houses. No. 43 was owned by Mrs Jennifer Bates who had let lodgings for twenty years and prided herself there were no tricks of the trade she didn't know. Before he was knocked down and killed by one of the new Corporation trolley cars, her husband had made a fair living from a Punch and Judy show. He had been a jolly, red-faced man who had irritated his wife beyond endurance by refusing to quarrel with her. In spite of her continual bickering he left her five hundred pounds with which she bought 43 Fairfield Road.

To look at, Mrs Bates was not very prepossessing. She was short and fat and bulged in unexpected places. Her face reminded you of a stale crumpet, for it was round and dough-like, and pitted with small-pox scars. She had small inquisitive eyes, and a tight thin mouth. Her hair appeared to be about to come down, but somehow managed to stay up, although there were times when long, grey strands did escape and bob up and down behind her as she walked. She had five lodgers. The Kents and three thin-faced, elderly men, who worked on the railway. These three had been friends for a long time. Any day of the week you could see them from the London trains as they repaired the track or leaned on their shovels to talk to each other in slow, heavy voices. They rose at five o'clock and went to bed at nine. Mrs Bates seldom saw or heard them for they were gentle, kindly men who believed in making as little noise about the house as possible.

They had been lodging with Mrs Bates for over ten years, and she had at last come to the conclusion that they were to be trusted as far as anyone could be trusted, and were just the kind of lodgers any landlady would be glad to have.

But she wasn't anything like so satisfied with the Kents. It was the girl who worried her. The young chap seemed harmless enough, but the girl was another kettle of fish. She was a hard piece if ever there was one! Harder even than Mrs Bates, who prided herself on her hardness. Anyway, this girl always got the better of Mrs Bates in any verbal exchange, and there had been quite a few.

Young Kent, usually pale and worried looking, was quick to pour oil on troubled waters. He seemed afraid of offending Mrs Bates, and his fear did much to mollify her for she liked people to be afraid of her.

The trouble began when she discovered the girl was going to have a baby.

'Not in my house!' she said, pointing an accusing finger at the girl's thickening waist. 'No children! Never 'ad any, and I ain't starting now. You'll 'ave to 'op it when it comes, so make up your mind to it.'

The girl had given a sneering little laugh.

'Yap about the chicken when it's hatched,' she said, and slammed the door in Mrs Bates's outraged face.

Well, that was a nice way to talk!

And then one day when the Kents were out, Mrs Bates had gone into their rooms to satisfy herself they were keeping them clean, and had found three empty gin bottles under the sofa.

That started more trouble.

'No drinking in my house!' she stormed, shaking one of the empty bottles in their faces on their return. 'Any more of this, and you'll 'ave to go!'

'And what else don't you like? What else can't we do in this lousy hole?' the girl demanded, her face like granite. 'Go and drown yourself, you fat old bitch!'

And that had taken all Kent's tact to smooth over, but he had done it, explaining in his quiet, anxious voice that his wife wasn't well and the coming baby worried her, and if Mrs Bates would overlook the incident he would see it didn't happen again.

If it wasn't that he paid regularly and the lack of petrol was ruining the tripper trade, Mrs Bates wouldn't have had them in her house after such language, but she didn't want to lose the forty-five shillings they paid for the rooms, so she allowed herself to be mollified.

Kent had a job at Mason's, the photographic equipment shop on the seafront. He did the developing and printing, spending hours in the dark room, coming home about seven, looking white and tired. Mrs Bates had no idea how much he earned, but it couldn't have been much for he was very shabby and his shoes needed repairing and he looked half starved. The girl was better dressed. In fact, when she first came to No. 43 she had a fur coat that looked like mink. But that disappeared after a while, and Mrs Bates suspected it had been pawned. But now the girl's figure was thickening she had to have a couple of new dresses, and they looked cheap enough, Mrs Bates thought with a contemptuous sniff.

They were an odd couple. Neither of them had any friends. Although they had been in Hastings for over six months they always kept to themselves. No one ever called on them, and when they went out together they invariably went up the hill to the castle and never down to the town.

Kent had told Mrs Bates they used to live in West Ham, London. He always wanted to live by the sea, he said, and when he saw Mason's advertisement he had jumped at the chance of working in Hastings. One of these days, he told her, they hoped to have a home of their own, and when he said that there came into his eyes such a look of wistful longing that Mrs Bates was almost sorry for him.

If it hadn't been for the girl, Mrs Bates would have been pleased to have had Kent stay with her. He was no trouble, but the girl was a slut: that was the only word for her. Sometimes Mrs Bates would hear her slanging Kent, but as soon as she started raising her voice, he somehow persuaded her to quieten down, so, although Mrs Bates hurried to the foot of the stairs to listen, she never heard what the quarrel was about.

They would have to go before the baby was born. Mrs Bates told Kent he had better keep his eyes open for a place where squawling brats were tolerated. It'd be a job, she said, with relish. So he had better look sharp or they'd be homeless.

Kent said there was still three months before the baby was born, but he would begin looking immediately.

'Three months?' Mrs Bates said and laughed. 'Don't you believe it. I can tell by the look of her. It's coming before then. You mark my words. Them that drinks gin always 'as 'em quick. I know. Inside eight weeks: That's my guess and I 'aven't been wrong yet.'

Mrs Bates always remembered the afternoon the Kents arrived. She had been taking a bit of a rest in the kitchen with a cup of tea and the newspaper. She had been reading about the Park Lane murder: a real sensation if ever there was one.

A man wanted by the police had been found stabbed to death in the kitchen of a Park Lane luxury flat, belonging to a couple named Ricks. The woman, Clair Ricks, had been on the stage doing a pickpocket act and making as much as a hundred and fifty a week. The man, Harry Ricks, had a portrait studio in Grafton Street. Both of them had disappeared, and the police were anxious to find them, believing they could give them information that would lead to an arrest.

So far no trace of them had been found. Detective-Inspector Claud Parkins was in charge of the case. He said the murdered man, Ben Whelan, was believed to have been connected with a gang of pickpockets working in the West End, and he thought the motive of the murder had been blackmail.

Mrs Bates was speculating about the murder when the front door bell rang, making her start, and when she climbed the steep stairs from the basement and opened the front door she found this couple standing on the step.

With her mind still full of the murder, she showed them the two rooms. The moment she set eyes on the girl she knew she was a bad lot. A blonde, hard-faced bit, she thought, no better than she should be. Wearing a fur coat and coming to a working-class district! And the way she had looked at the two rooms as if they weren't good enough for her. But the young fellow took her fancy. He was quiet and polite, and was willing to pay two weeks' rent in advance, and she let them have the rooms.

It was a funny thing, but the girl didn't move out of the house for four or five weeks. Kent explained she wasn't well, but to be cooped up in two rooms for five weeks seemed to Mrs Bates to be going beyond a joke. However, it was her business. If she liked to hide herself away as if she was scared of showing her face in the street, that was her look-out. Mrs Bates didn't care so long as she got her money. The young fellow went out every day to business, but once he returned, he stayed indoors even though the summer was hot and fine.

After four or five weeks, and about the time when the newspapers had lost interest in the Park Lane murder, the girl began to go out.

The missing couple hadn't been found. Another murder had been committed, and Mrs Bates forgot all about the Park Lane murder and gave her attention to this new one: a girl had been found hacked to pieces in a West End hotel. That was far more intriguing than a stabbing in a kitchen, and the police knew who had done it too, and were after him, so there was a chase to add to the excitement.

Alone in their rooms, the Kents read of the new murder and exchanged glances. It meant the searchlight of publicity would shift away from Clair and Harry Ricks, and that seemed to give them comfort.

II

Even after six months, Harry didn't feel entirely safe. He had got over the sickening clutch of fear every time he saw a policeman. He had ceased to stiffen every time he heard a footfall on the stairs. But the hunted feeling persisted. He couldn't open a newspaper without a feeling of dread. It was still a nightmare to walk down Robertson Street, the main shopping thoroughfare, and if anyone came up to him suddenly his heart contracted and he had to control an impulse to run.

It was amazing how they had escaped detection for so long. Probably it was because everything had been prepared for flight, and they were able to disappear and assume new identities before Whelan's body had been found. He had not been discovered for eight days after they had left the flat.

Clair had been panic stricken. If she had been left alone she would have given herself away. There were times when Harry despaired of her ever getting back to normal. She was ready to run at the slightest thing: a step on the landing, a shout in the street, a sudden braking of a car. But now she was getting back her nerve, and realising that perhaps, after all, she need not have insisted on having a child. Her reaction to the inevitable inconvenience of pregnancy was of trapped fury. At times she would turn on Harry, blaming him for everything, venting her misery and anger on him, cursing the day she ever met him.

Harry was patient with her. His love for her had wilted, but

166

his loyalty was as strong as ever. He couldn't forget, in spite of her mistakes, what she had done had been more for his sake than hers. He remembered how she had given herself up to the police when Parkins had accused him of stealing the cigarette case. He remembered her past generosity. It was his turn now to provide for her, and how badly he was doing it! Under the circumstances he was lucky to have a job at all. At least it provided him for the first month with an adequate hiding place. The only danger had been the journey to and from the shop. Once he was there he remained in the dark room where no one saw him. But the money wasn't much. He earned six pounds a week. Forty-five shillings of that went on rent. There was food to buy. In their panic to escape from the Park Lane flat they had only taken a suitcase of clothes apiece, fearing to call a taxi to remove the heavier cases, and they were now running short of clothes.

They had thirty pounds left still from the sale of Clair's jewellery, but that was slowly dwindling as Clair insisted on having a bottle of gin a week, and Harry suspected that she was going to the pub at the corner of the road when he was at work. He had warned her that once their capital had gone, they would not be able to afford gin, and she turned on him fiercely.

'I've got to have something. Do you think I can stay in this blasted room day after day without something to take my mind off it? Oh, don't look so shocked. As long as the money lasts I'll drink as much as I like!'

And besides gin she smoked incessantly, whereas Harry had given up cigarettes.

At first he had been pathetically tender and even enthusiastic about the coming child, but Clair soon disillusioned him.

'Look at me!' she raved. 'Do you think I want it? If I had thought we'd have got away with it, I wouldn't have been such a mad fool to have had it. Look what the little beast is doing to my figure! Oh, shut up gaping at me! If it hadn't been for you this would never have happened!'

And yet, sometimes, she was different, and held him in her arms, crying, her face against his, assuring him she loved him, that she would do anything for him.

'Don't pay any attention to me, darling,' she said. 'I'm so miserable and frightened. Oh, Harry, what is going to become of us? Suppose the child is born, and then they find us? It won't stop them hanging me then! In a way I wish they'd find us now, then they couldn't kill me. Don't you see, the longer they take to find us the worse it is for me.' She pulled away from him and ran distracted fingers through her hair. 'I shall go mad! I'm so frightened of having the child. I hate pain! I'm such a stinking coward. Sometimes I think I'll kill myself. It would be the way out.'

She was continually talking of suicide now, and it worried Harry half out of his mind. She was so reckless, and at times, demented, that he feared she might try to kill herself. He did his best to comfort her, but after these bouts of tenderness and self-pity she would become once more hard and cynical, grumbling about the lack of money, complaining about the two rooms and the food, and smoking incessantly.

It was a nightmare time for Harry. He felt sure that if Clair didn't have to pass so much of her time alone, she wouldn't be in this frame of mind. She wasn't used to being on her own, and became morbidly depressed by sitting in the shabby little room with its view of the roofs of the Old Town, having nothing to do but to think of the past and the fun she had had and to brood over the coming birth.

He encouraged her to go out. At first, fearful of being recognised, she refused, but as the weeks went by and the newspapers ceased to feature the murder she finally screwed up her courage to make infrequent trips to the shops, but they never went about the town together.

'It wouldn't be safe,' Harry argued. 'They're still looking for us, and some bright policeman might spot us if we were together.'

So when they did go out in the evening they went up to the Castle where there were no policemen and sat on the hill and looked down at the ruins of the harbour and the sea front, stretching to St Leonards, and at the crowds moving along the promenade.

Then one day Harry mislaid his fountain pen, and in the search for it, he absent-mindedly opened one of Clair's drawers. What he saw there turned him cold.

He went into the sitting-room where Clair was manicuring her finger nails.

'Where did you get this?' he demanded, and held up a leather handbag. 'I found it in your drawer. It's new. How did you get it?'

Clair flushed and jumped to her feet.

'How dare you go to my drawer!'

He looked at her. She tried to meet his horrified eyes, then turned away and went over to the window.

'Did you steal it?' he said, his voice husky.

'What if I did? I've got to have some decent things. If you can't get them for me . . .'

He jerked her round roughly.

'You stupid fool!' his voice was shaking. 'Can't you see that's what they're waiting for? They know your tricks. It's just the thing that'd give them a clue. They're clever. If the shop you stole it from reports this to the police they'll wonder if it is you. Don't you see that?'

'Am I going to live like this all my life?' she cried, her face white with fear. 'My other bag's worn out. Do you think they'll guess it was me?'

'But, Clair, what is the matter with you?' Harry said hopelessly. 'Have you no sense of right and wrong? What if your bag is worn out? You can't just go out and steal another. Apart from the danger of being caught, can't you see what a rotten thing it is to do?'

'But I am rotten,' she said defiantly. 'I don't make any bones about that. Am I never to have any fun again or any nice things?'

'Give me time,' he said, desperately. 'Let's get your confinement over first. I'm watching out for something better. I'll get something, Clair. I'll get something that'll make more money. But you've got to promise never to steal again.'

She promised sullenly, but insisted on keeping the bag.

'It's not as if I can take it back,' she said. 'I don't see why I shouldn't use it now I have it.'

Harry's immediate task now was to find lodgings for the coming baby. Evening after evening he tramped the back streets, calling on every house which displayed a 'Board Residence' sign without success. No one wanted a squawling baby. Some of the landladies he saw were sympathetic. They said they would like to help him, but it wasn't practicable.

'Visitors don't like the noise of babies,' they explained as if he didn't know.

'Why must you go out and leave me?' Clair asked irritably when he returned, hot and tired from one of these fruitless searches. 'It's bad enough to be on my own all day, but then for you to go out . . .'

Patiently he explained what he had been doing.

'Why bother?' she said angrily. 'You don't think I'm going to keep the brat, do you? I'm not as crazy as that. As soon as I come out of hospital I'm going to dump it on a doorstep.'

Harry was horrified.

'You can't do a thing like that! It's our child, Clair. You couldn't do it! I won't let you!'

'Oh, don't give me that mother-love tripe,' she said. 'Do you think I'm going to feed it? I hate babies! I won't touch it! I'll throw it into the sea!'

Harry had read somewhere that women went a little queer when they were pregnant, and although Clair's attitude hurt him, he didn't take it seriously. But he did feel the responsibility for the baby's comfort and welfare would largely fall on him, and he redoubled his efforts to find a home for it.

There was a chap at the shop he was friendly with. His name was Leonard Wilkins; one of those simple, not very brainy fellows, with a moon-round face, sandy hair and a ready smile. He wore a Christian Crusader badge in his coat lapel, and was always trying to persuade Harry to become a Crusader himself.

'You don't have to go to church or anything like that,' he explained to Harry one afternoon when he came into the dark room with the morning's collection of films to be developed. 'It's a club really. We try to help each other. It's a bit like being a Mason, only it doesn't cost anything. We're having a meeting tonight if you'd care to come.'

Harry thanked him.

'I'm afraid I haven't the time,' he said, as he stripped the red wrapping from the films. 'I'm trying to find accommodation. You see, my wife is having a baby, and it isn't easy to find a place that takes babies. I suppose you don't know of anything?'

Wilkins reacted to this the way a ferret reacts to the sight of a rabbit.

'I'll ask the Crusaders,' he said. 'That's just the kind of thing we do. We'd be awfully glad if you and your wife would come along.' His face lit up as he added, 'They give you tea and cakes.'

But Harry couldn't imagine Clair at a Christian Crusader's meeting, and he tactfully made excuses.

'She's not very well. I don't like leaving her. If you can do anything for us I'd be grateful. We want two rooms, and I don't want to pay more than forty-five shillings. If you hear of anything . . .'

'We'll find you something,' Wilkins said confidently, and to Harry's surprise they did. A couple of days later, Wilkins gave him three addresses. 'Mrs Hamilton's the best. I'd go along and see her. She has four children of her own. You know where Castle Street is, don't you?'

The previous day had been wet and cold, and no films had been brought in to be developed, so Harry asked the manager if he could have the afternoon off.

'I'm trying to find rooms,' he explained. 'I've heard of something and don't want to miss it.'

'That's all right. You get off,' the manager said. He liked Harry. He liked the way Harry always finished his work before going home. He liked his willingness and his efficiency.

Mrs Hamilton's house in Castle Street conformed to the general pattern of back street seaside houses, but it looked clean and neat from the outside. Mrs Hamilton answered Harry's knock on the door. She was accompanied by four small children, who stared up at Harry with intent, curious eyes, and wrestled and punched each other as soon as their curiosity was satisfied. Mrs Hamilton was a tall, bony woman with lank hair, a distracted expression and large tired eyes. As soon as you saw her you felt she would put up with anything, and when Harry told her he was looking for rooms and his wife was about to have a baby she just nodded dumbly and asked him in.

As soon as the front door had closed behind him, the four children started into a bedlam of sound, and this continued all the time Harry was in the house. They seemed to be endowed with an inspired talent for making a sustained and continuous uproar. One of them hammered a tin tray. Another ran up and down the stairs rattling the banister with a stick. The remaining two punched each other and screamed. It was only by raising his voice to a shout that Harry could make himself heard.

Yes, Mrs Hamilton had two rooms. No, she didn't mind babies. She waved a vague hand at the quartet of sound. She had babies of her own. She thought two pounds a week would be fair. She would give them fish suppers for that, but she couldn't undertake a midday meal.

With the four children following them, they went up the

171

stairs to the top floor. The rooms were small but clean. One of the windows overlooked the sea front. At least the view was better than the one at No. 43 Fairfield Road, but Harry's heart sank at the noise of the children. He couldn't imagine Clair standing it for long.

He said he had two more places to see and would let Mrs Hamilton know one way or the other that evening. He was glad to get into the sunshine again.

But the other two places had been let so it was Mrs Hamilton's or nothing. The decision was too difficult to make without consulting Clair, so Harry caught a bus to Fairfield Road, arriving there just after four o'clock, three hours before his usual time.

To his disappointment Clair was out. The two rooms hadn't been swept or dusted and the bed was still unmade. While waiting for her he straightened the rooms, cleaned them and made the bed. As he put Clair's nightdress in the wardrobe he caught sight of something tucked away behind one of her dresses. He pulled it out and examined the feather-weight mackintosh with a sinking heart. It was new and expensive looking, and he was sure Clair hadn't bought it. So she was still at it! With a cold set face he searched through her drawers and the cupboard. The loot he discovered turned him sick. From the amount of articles he found he guessed she must have been systematically pilfering for a long time. Several empty and worn looking wallets he discovered hidden under the mattress told him she had also been picking pockets.

He was standing motionless by the bed on which he had thrown the various articles he had found when Clair came into the room. She moved slowly and heavily, and her face looked white and puffy. She was big with the child now, and she looked tired and depressed. Looking at her he suddenly realised that she wasn't pretty any more. In some extraordinary way her features had coarsened, and she looked what she was: a drab without a background.

She started violently when she saw him, looked at the bed, then back to him.

They stared at each other for a long moment of time.

'Spying again?' she said, through clenched teeth. 'What a dirty little Gestapo you are!'

Harry didn't say anything. He turned away and went over to the window, leaning his forehead against the dusty pane.

172

He heard the bed creak as she sat down.

'I shouldn't have said that,' she said. 'I'm sorry.'

'It's all right,' Harry said flatly. 'I was just going out. I'll be back about seven.'

'Don't go,' she said quickly. 'I – I can explain all this. It happened before you found the handbag. I haven't done it since. I swear it!'

Of course she was lying. Harry could tell that by her over-emphatic tone.

'It's all right,' he said wearily, and went past her into the other room.

She came to the bedroom door.

'You believe me, don't you?' she said.

'No, I don't believe you,' he returned, without looking at her. 'But it's all right. There's nothing either of us can do about it now,' and still not looking at her he opened the door and went down the stairs to the street below.

It was just after seven when he returned. She was sitting by the window; her face flushed and her eyes bright. He knew that look by now, and what it meant. The bottle of gin, thrust half out of sight under her chair was getting a familiar sight.

Neither of them spoke, and he began to prepare supper, while she remained at the window, smoking.

He was conscious of the danger: in spite of his warnings he was now certain that when she needed anything she would steal it. Something was lacking in her make-up. The only solution was for him either to make enough money to give her what she wanted or to leave her. He knew he could never earn enough to satisfy her demands nor could he leave her in her present condition. He felt trapped. It was like trying to save someone bent on suicide.

III

The reconciliation late that night revealed to him that the link that held him to her was weakening. He could see that her love for him was gradually being pushed into the background by her preoccupation with herself, her discomfort and the bleak outlook of her future. His love for her was being smothered by the

173

sick fear that through her own wanton stupidity she would attract the attention of the police to them.

The following morning, on the way to work, he looked at the newspaper with a feeling of dread. It was difficult to read the paper in the crowded bus, impossible to open it, and he had to wait until he got out at Whiterock before he could turn to the centre page, and then he nearly missed it so insignificant was the paragraph. It was headed:

PARK LANE MURDER

Inspector Claud Parkins of C Division, Scotland Yard said today that a new clue had come into the hands of the police which he thought might lead to an early arrest.

Clair and Harry Ricks, wanted for questioning, have not so far been traced, and it is thought the new clue may lead to their whereabouts.

Harry stood by the bus stop for some minutes. Was this a trick to start them on the run again or had Parkins learned where they were? That was the thing to decide. Should they make a bolt for it or should they stick it out in the hope that it was a false report? His legs felt weak, and his heart hammered against his side, giving him a feeling of breathlessness. He didn't know whether to catch a bus home or go on to work. Suppose they were already at Fairfield Road?

A man standing nearby looked sharply at him.

'Are you all right, mate?' he asked, and there was a kindly expression of concern on his face. 'Feeling a bit faint or something?'

Harry shook his head.

'It's all right,' he managed to say. 'Touch of the sun I expect. I'm all right, thank you.'

Somehow he forced himself to cross the road and walk the few yards to Mason's shop. Wilkins and the manager had just arrived.

'Did you get the rooms, Kent?' the manager asked as he wrestled with the padlock.

'Yes, thank you,' Harry said.

'You don't look well,' Wilkins said, staring at him. 'I say, Mr Bertram, doesn't he look white?'

'Got a bit of a headache,' Harry said, and pushed into the

174

shop. 'It's nothing,' and he went up the stairs to the darkroom.

He'd have to pull himself together, he thought as he entered the stuffy, badly ventilated little room. Should he say he wasn't well and ask to go home? He couldn't leave Clair on her own in danger like this. But fear of unemployment was even stronger than the fear of the police. He had already had an afternoon off. If he asked to go home now perhaps the manager might think he was slacking and get rid of him. To lose his job and be without money were to him things as terrifying as death.

Before he could reach a decision, Mr Bertram came into the darkroom and put a bundle of films on the table.

'Get cracking on those, Kent,' he said. 'We had a rush of business when you were away yesterday. They'll be in for them tonight.'

Harry waited until he had gone, turned off the light and turned on the red safety lamp. He began stripping off the film wrapping. Perhaps he could slip up to Clair in his lunch hour. But supposing, while he wasted time here in the dark room, the police went to Fairfield Road? He forced himself to begin to develop the films. If it were a false alarm, and through panic he lost his job, they would be in an awful mess, he thought. He had been unable to save a penny. He had nothing except the money he would receive tomorrow night when Mr Bertram paid the wages. He would have to wait. They couldn't bolt without money.

The morning passed in a nightmare of sick apprehension. More films kept arriving, and Harry, distracted, worked furiously.

A few minutes to half past twelve when he was ready to go to lunch Mr Bertram popped his head round the door.

'I'll get you to cut your lunch hour,' he said. 'You won't mind, will you? There's a mass of stuff coming in. I'll send Wilkins up to give you a hand.'

Harry began to protest that he had something very important to do in his lunch hour, but there was a testy, irritable note in Mr Bertram's voice and he was afraid to refuse his request.

Wilkins came up after an hour or so and worked on the printing machine.

'Just our luck,' he said with his bright smile that showed he was only grumbling for the sake of grumbling and didn't really mean it. 'The sun's shining, and everyone seems to be using their cameras. Mr B. only let me have half an hour for lunch.'

Harry grunted. He would much sooner have been alone.

Wilkins chattered away about the Crusaders, and again tried to persuade Harry to join. Then as he slid a batch of prints into the developing tank he said, 'I say, I forgot to tell you. An odd thing happened to me last night. A detective stopped and questioned me.'

Harry stiffened and nearly dropped the bottle of developer he was holding.

'A big chap,' Wilkins continued, obviously pleased with the experience. 'He asked to see my identity card. Then he wanted to know where I worked and what my job was. It's a funny thing, but he seemed to prick up his ears when I said I was in the photographic trade. He wanted to know who else worked in the shop.'

'Did you tell him?' Harry asked, fear clutching at his heart. He was thankful they were working in the light of the ruby lamp otherwise he was sure Wilkins would have seen the fear on his face.

'Certainly not,' Wilkins returned. 'I didn't think it was my business to do that. I told him if he wanted to know about the shop he would have to see the manager.'

'I see,' Harry said, restraining an impulse to rush out of the darkroom and get on a bus to Fairfield Road.

'I suppose they're looking for someone,' Wilkins said smugly. 'I once read a book about the methods of Scotland Yard. It's marvellous how they work. I wouldn't rest a minute if they were after me.'

The afternoon seemed interminable to Harry. His one thought was to get home before anything happened. He scarcely listened to Wilkins's quiet chatter.

It was towards closing time he heard what he had been waiting to hear.

'That's Mr Bertram calling you, isn't it?' Wilkins asked.

'Yes.'

Harry wiped his hands slowly on a towel, aware that his mouth had gone dry. Should he make a bolt for it? But there was no way out except through the shop.

'Kent! I want you a moment,' Mr Bertram was calling from the bottom of the stairs.

'Coming, sir,' Harry said.

With hands that trembled he reached for his coat and put it on. If it was the police, and they arrested him, what was going to happen to Clair? If only he could reach her by telephone and warn her. But it would be hopeless. Once the police had a description of her from Mrs Bates, she couldn't hope to escape.

'Mind how you go out,' Wilkins said. 'I have prints in the tank.'

Harry edged out of the room and moved on to the landing, overlooking the shop. His heart gave a lurch when he saw the big man with Mr Bertram. He had policeman written all over him.

'Hurry up, Kent,' Mr Bertram said sharply. He was obviously flustered.

'Yes, sir,' Harry said, and came down the stairs. There was still a chance, he told himself, if he kept his head. One false move now and Clair would be the one to suffer. For her sake he had to keep hold on himself.

The detective's vast bulk blocked the doorway. No chance of making a bolt for it.

'This is a police officer,' Mr Bertram said with a wan smile. 'He's making a check. Will you show him your identity card?'

Harry felt the quiet, shrewd eyes of the detective examining his face. He took out his wallet and handed his identity card to him.

'Thanks, Mr Kent,' the detective said. 'Sorry to trouble you.' Seconds ticked by while he looked at the card. Harry wondered if he could hear the thudding of his heart. 'This your address?' the detective asked.

'Yes.'

'Been in Hastings long?'

'About six months.'

'And you lived at 23 Sinclair Road, West Ham, before that?' the detective went on, looking at the card.

Harry turned cold. It would be only a matter of hours now. The time it would take for the detective to check the address in West Ham.

'That's right,' he said steadily.

'Where did you work there?'

'Jacksons, the chemist in the High Street,' Harry said, surprised the way the words came without effort or thought.

'Are you married, Mr Kent?'

'Yes.'

'Kent is expecting a baby,' Mr Bertram said, smiling. He was a family man himself.

A look of surprise came into the detective's eyes; just a momentary flicker, but Harry saw it.

'Your wife here too?'

'Of course,' Harry said. 'If you don't mind, what's all this in aid of?'

The detective's face relaxed into a smile.

'Looking for a chap,' he said, and handed Harry his identity card. 'That's all right. Sorry to have bothered you. This fellow's a photographer. We've been asked to check all photographic equipment shops.'

'Have you tried Westways?' Mr Bertram asked, always eager to be helpful. 'They're in Robertson Street.'

'Not yet.' The shrewd grey eyes dwelt thoughtfully on Harry. 'Going there now. Well, thank you; sorry to have taken up your time.' He began a slow move to the door. 'When's the baby due, Mr Kent?'

'Why ask that?' Harry thought.

'About a month. I'm not absolutely sure.'

'Worrying time,' the detective said. 'Looks worried, doesn't he?' he went on to Mr Bertram.

'I expect I looked like that when my wife was having her first,' Mr Bertram said smugly. 'It *is* a worrying time. But I've got six now. One gets used to the worry after the third, but one doesn't get used to the disturbed nights.'

'I wouldn't know,' the detective said, grinning. 'I'm a bachelor myself.' All the time he had been talking his eyes dwelt on Harry. 'Been married long, Mr Kent?'

'He is suspicious,' Harry thought. 'They must have my description.'

'Five years,' he said, his voice unsteady.

'Good for you. Well, I must get off. Can't stand around gossiping, and I expect you will want to get home.'

'We close at six,' Mr Bertram said. 'Half an hour yet. Sure that's all we can do for you?'

The detective again looked at Harry.

'That's all – anyway for the present.' He nodded and walked

178

out of the shop, mingling with the crowd that moved slowly along the pavement.

'Extraordinary,' Mr Bertram said. 'I wonder who he's looking for?'

IV

'They'll be watching the house,' Harry thought as he walked up Fairfield Road. How was he to get Clair out of the house without being seen? And where were they to go? If only he had some money! He had only three shillings on him and nothing in the house.

Suddenly he caught sight of Clair walking slowly ahead of him. Only a hundred yards or so separated her from the house. He lengthened his stride and caught up with her.

'Why, hallo, Harry . . . ' she said, turning.

'Keep walking,' he said in an undertone. His eyes searched the street for anyone looking like a policeman. 'Go past the house.'

Fear came into her face and her step faltered, but he took her arm and kept her walking.

'What's wrong?' she asked, and he could feel her trembling.

'They're after us. A detective came to the shop. He wanted to see my identity card. I'm pretty sure he suspects who I am, and he has only to check the address in West Ham to know it's false. They may be watching the house now.'

'Where are we going?'

'I don't know. I haven't thought. Have you any money?'

'Not much. About ten shillings.'

'Don't look at the house. Keep moving. They may be in there waiting for us.'

'We can't leave our clothes.'

'We'll have to.'

They went past the house.

'Oh, Harry!' she said. 'This finishes it. We can't go on. I feel awful. It's no use. I can't walk far.'

'We'll go somewhere where we can talk,' Harry said, tightening his grip on her arm. 'We'll go up to the Castle.'

'Look, Harry, leave me. You'll manage on your own. It's the only way. I'm sick of this. I'll kill myself. I'll walk into the sea.'

'Don't talk rot!' Harry said fiercely. 'We'll get out of this somehow. Just keep walking.'

'But can't you see this is the end? It's no good, Harry. We have nowhere to go, no money, no food, no clothes. Suppose the baby comes? Can't you see it's hopeless?'

'We've got to think,' Harry said. 'We're not going to give up until we've had time to make a plan. Mooney might help us. Let's get up on the cliff where we can sit down and rest. We've got to think of a plan.'

She shrugged helplessly, but continued to walk at his side. It was uphill all the way, and although he helped her along he could tell she was growing tired.

A car came grinding up the hill and he looked back, his heart racing. But the driver was a woman, and acting on the spur of the moment, he signalled to her.

The car stopped by them and the woman looked out of the window, smiling at them. She was fat and jolly-looking.

'I'm going to the golf club,' she said. 'That any use to you?'

'Thank you very much,' Harry said, and opened the rear door. 'We're going past there. It's very kind of you to stop.'

The woman gave Clair a quick look of sympathy.

'You shouldn't be walking up hills you know,' she said as Clair got into the car. 'Is this your first?'

'Yes,' Clair said.

The woman engaged gear and the car continued its slow grind up the hill.

'We're down on holiday,' Harry said. 'We only came yester-day.'

'I'm on holiday too,' the woman told him. 'I promised to meet my husband. He's been playing golf all the afternoon. Do you think you should go so far out of town? The buses don't run very frequently.'

'It's all right,' Harry said. 'We're spending the evening with friends. They'll bring us back. It was a bit of luck you stopping. We just missed the bus.'

'That's all right then,' the woman returned. 'I know what I was like when I had my first.'

They drove on for some time in silence, then the woman said suddenly, 'If you like I'll take you to your friends. I don't suppose my husband will be finished yet. It's only half past seven.'

180

'We won't trouble you,' Harry said, trying to speak calmly. 'We feel like a bit of a stroll.'

'Well, at least it's flat when you get up there. Going to look at Lover's Seat?'

'We might,' Harry said, wishing she would stop talking.

Clair dug her fingers into his arm as they overtook and passed a policeman who was walking up the hill, pushing a bicycle.

'There seem to be a lot of policemen about,' the woman said. 'That's the sixth policeman I've seen. Do you think they're looking for someone?'

'I don't know,' Harry said. 'I shouldn't think so. Isn't this the time the patrols go out?'

'Is it? There was a police car in Castle Square, and another on the sea front. You may be right. I thought they might be looking for someone. It's funny how criminals come to the sea, isn't it? There was that trunk murderer, and that man Heath. I was in Brighton last year . . .'

Harry ceased to listen. He and Clair exchanged glances. Would this woman remember them? Would there be anything about them in the evening paper to give her a clue?

'Well, we're just here,' the woman said, slowing down. 'You're sure you don't want me to take you on? I don't mind a bit.'

'No, thank you very much,' Harry said. 'We'll get along fine now.'

The car stopped outside the golf club entrance, and Harry and Clair got out. They both looked quickly down the steep hill, but the policeman wasn't in sight.

'Well, come in and have a drink.'

'We won't if you don't mind. My wife hasn't had any fresh air today. A little walk will do her good.'

'Well, then, good-bye. I hope you both get what you want.'

Harry took Clair's arm and they began to walk along the narrow lane.

'That policeman will be along in a moment,' Harry said. 'We'll have to get off the road.' He glanced back. The woman was manoeuvring her car through the club entrance. 'Come on. Through this hedge.'

They scrambled up the bank and squeezed through a gap in the hedge and into a field.

'Let him go past,' Harry said, pulling Clair down beside him on the grass. Then he caught sight of something in her hand. It was a small, navy-blue handbag. 'What's that?' he asked sharply. 'Where did that come from?'

Clair looked woodenly at him.

'It was in the car,' she said, and opened the bag to look inside.

'You mean – you took it?' Harry said, horrified.

'Well, we want money, don't we? You don't think I'd be such a fool to miss such an opportunity, do you?'

Harry caught hold of her arm.

'You stole it from that woman?' he said, his voice rising. 'Are you mad? She'll report it! She'll give a description of us. She might even tell the policeman who's coming now.'

'We had to have money, didn't we?' Clair said sullenly. 'Let me see what's she's got in it,' and she tipped the contents of the purse on to the grass. 'Hell!' she said angrily. 'Five shillings! I thought it was going to be pounds! Five shillings, not a damned thing else!'

Harry picked up the money and put it in the bag.

'Wait here,' he said curtly. 'I'm going back. I'll drop it outside the club entrance. She might think, in getting out of the car, we knocked it into the road.'

Clair didn't say anything, and watched him run back, under cover of the hedge.

He peered through the hedge when he reached the golf club entrance. The policeman still wasn't in sight, nor had the woman driver appeared. He tossed the bag over the hedge and watched it drop in the middle of the road. The policeman would see it, he thought, and would take it into the club. He turned and ran back to where Clair was waiting.

'Don't ever do that again!' he said, taking her arm and helping her to her feet. 'He's bound to see the purse, and it'll delay him. Come on, the cliffs aren't far away. We might find a cave to spend the night in.'

'What's the good?' Clair asked wearily. 'We might as well give up. What's going to happen tomorrow? What are we going to do for food?'

'Now look here,' Harry said sharply. 'You must pull yourself together. We would have been all right if only you hadn't started stealing. That brought them here. I'm sure of it. We're going back to London. Mooney will get us new identity cards, and we'll start again, only this time you're not going to do anything silly.'

She looked at him and suddenly smiled.

'Silly? You're a darling, Harry. All right, we'll go to London and start all over again. Do you know how we're going to get there?'

'We'll get there somehow. When it's dark I'll phone Mooney. With luck I'll find him in. I'll ask him to come down with some money. He'll do it. I'm sure he will.'

'Do you think he'll have any money?'

'He's bound to have some,' Harry said, knowing it was likely that Mooney wouldn't have any. 'Now, come on. We're wasting time.'

Clair shook her head.

'It would be much more sensible if you left me. I don't think we're going to get away with it this time. I have a feeling about it. I think you could, without me. Will you please leave me and go?'

'Don't be ridiculous. I'm not leaving you. Now, come on.'

'I want you to leave me,' she said. 'They haven't anything on you. It's been my fault all along. Leave me. I want to face this alone. Don't you understand, Harry? There's no way out of this mess. Why should they catch you? Look at me! How can I escape them looking like this? I can scarcely get along. If you love me, Harry, go!'

'Let's find a cave,' Harry said, taking her arm. 'I'm not going to leave you, so get that idea out of your head!'

She pulled away from him.

'Can't you see I don't want you?' she cried, her face hard. 'Get away from me! If you're with me they're certain to catch me. Alone, I can do what I like with myself.'

His love for her came surging back at the sight of her white, desperate, frightened face.

'I don't care what happens as long as we're together. I know it's hopeless, but let's see it through together. Let's have just a little longer together. Don't send me away. Our time together may be short: we're wasting it.'

'Please go, Harry,' she said. 'I love you so much. I've done you so much harm. Please go now so at least I'll know I didn't get you into trouble with the police. I can manage. I'm not afraid. I know what I'm going to do.'

He put his arms round her shapeless body.

'Let's find a cave,' he said gently. 'We have a lot to talk about before they find us.'

V

The sea came surging towards the foot of the cliff, its rollers bursting against the side of the cliff and throwing up foam and spray which came into the cave.

The back of the cave was dry and sheltered. Harry sat on the sandy floor watching the high watery walls come surging forward with a boom and a roar.

Clair lay on her side, her head resting against his knee.

'I'm glad we came,' she said. 'I feel safe here. It's exciting, isn't it?'

Harry looked at the dark, scurrying clouds, outlined against the moonlit sky. It was exciting, but he would rather have been in his bed at Fairfield Road. This was all right for one night, but what would happen the next day? He was hungry, and although they were sheltered from the wind it was cold, and the spray made a damp atmosphere in the cave.

'It'll do for tonight,' he said. 'In a little while I'm going to phone Mooney.' He peered at his wrist watch. 'It's just after nine. In another half-hour I'll try to find a phone box.'

She slipped her hand into his.

'Don't go, Harry. It's no use. Mooney won't be able to help us. I'd rather you stay here. In the morning I'll leave you.'

'We're not going over that again,' Harry said firmly. 'You're not going to do anything reckless. Let them find us if they can. I'm hoping Mooney will be able to help us. It's a long chance, but it's worth trying.'

'You're good to me, Harry. I'm sorry I've been such a slut. I wanted to do so much for you, and I've done so badly.'

'Don't talk about it. Let's try and make something of the future. Are you feeling cold?'

'A little. I wish I'd brought a coat. It seemed so hot . . .'

'And I wish I'd brought some food. If Mooney can get down here early tomorrow –'

'Don't go, Harry. It's wet and dangerous out there. You might slip.'

'I'll watch out. I've been wondering about the tides. Do you think we're high enough up?'

'Oh yes. The sea doesn't reach as far as this. The sand here is dry.'

Harry eased her head off his knee and stood up.

'Have my coat for a pillow. I don't feel cold. You should try and get some sleep.'

'It's all right.' She lay back, resting her head on her arm. 'I'm quite comfortable. You're not going now?'

'In a little while.' He went to the mouth of the cave and peered down at the swirling water. A wave came rushing up at him, he dodged back, just missing the spray. She was right. It wouldn't be easy to leave the cave now, but he had to do it. It was their only chance.

'Be careful, Harry. Don't you see? You can't go until this dies down, and I don't think it will.'

He came back to her and sat down again.

'I'll wait. There's plenty of time. Try and sleep, Clair. We may have a long day ahead of us tomorrow.'

'If it wasn't so cold.'

He took off his coat and put it over her.

'I'm fine,' he said. 'I don't feel it. Now, try and sleep.'

He sat beside her, listening to the roar of the sea, holding her hand. After a while he felt her grip slacken and he bent over her. She was sleeping, and looking at her the full hopelessness of their position struck him. How could they hope to escape? Anyone seeing her would recognise her. Mrs Bates would give the police a description of them. Together they would be hopelessly conspicuous.

He got quietly to his feet. Mooney was his only hope. He decided to go now. With any luck he might get back before she woke. He felt stiff and cold with the long hours of sitting still, and he rubbed his arms briskly, trying to restore his circulation.

A narrow path led from the cave to the cliff head. When they had come down it, it had been a fairly easy climb as there had been no wind, but now as he went to the mouth of the cave, the wind made him stagger, and sudden rising spray spattered him with sea-water.

Bending his head against the wind, he moved out on to the path. As soon as he was away from the shelter of the cave the wind pounced on him and threatened to blow him off the path into the raging sea below. He clung on to a scrubby bush growing by the path and waited, crouched down, while the wind buffeted him and spray from the heaving waves soaked him.

A few yards ahead of him was another bush, and he made a dash for it, throwing himself flat, gripping at its roots, as the wind once again threatened to have him over. He worked his way to the top of the cliff in this way. Twice he thought he was going to be blown over. Once his foot slipped, and if he hadn't been holding on he would have fallen to the sea-covered rocks below. He was trembling and breathless by the time he reached the head of the cliffs and lay flat, struggling to recover his breath, dismayed at the thought that it would be impossible to return the same way until the wind had died down.

After a while he got to his feet and moved across the scrub and grass land to the road. Once on the road he was sheltered from the wind, and he broke into a run.

It was moonlight, and the road showed up like a white ribbon. He walked on the grass verge so as to deaden his footfalls and kept his ears pricked for any alarming sound. He remembered seeing an A.A. box as they had come up the road to the cliff. There would be a telephone inside if he could break in.

After what seemed to him to be an endless distance, but which was only a mile or so, he caught sight of the A.A. box. It was locked, and he looked around for something with which he could smash in the door. A big flint stone in the ditch caught his eye and he picked it up, balancing it in his hand.

'I shouldn't do that, Ricks,' a voice said out of the shadows, and a big, familiar figure stepped from behind the A.A. box.

With a startled gasp Harry dropped the stone and turned to run, but facing him were two policemen, and one of them caught hold of his arm.

'All right,' Detective-Inspector Parkins said. 'He's not going to make trouble, are you, Ricks?'

'No,' Harry said.

'That's fine. Where is she? Where have you left her?'

'We've parted,' Harry said, trying to keep his voice under control. He spoke in a husky whisper. 'I don't know where she is now.'

One of the policemen flashed an electric torch into the darkness, and almost immediately the headlights of a hidden car were turned on, flood-lighting the road.

'Spread out and keep your eyes open,' Parkins called into the darkness. 'She may be right near you.'

There was a movement and swishing of grass as a number of men hidden by the high hedge moved about in the field. The car came up slowly and stopped by Harry.

'In you get,' Parkins said. 'Don't let's have any nonsense.'

'It's all right,' Harry said, in a low voice. He was thinking of Clair, alone in the cave. Would it be better to tell them? She couldn't get out without help. He had had to support her on the way down. The way up was much more difficult. He couldn't leave her there to starve. Suppose she had her baby?

He allowed himself to be pushed into the car and Parkins sat beside him.

'Have a cigarette?' Parkins said amiably.

'No, thank you.'

'Well, you've had a run for your money, haven't you?' A match flared up as Parkins lit his cigarette. He tossed the match out of the car window. It made a tiny spark as it twisted through the air and fell into the grass. The flame flared up and went out.

Harry thought of Clair. He couldn't let her die alone. She had said she would kill herself if she was cornered. It would be better for them to go together.

'Have you been in Hastings all the time?' Parkins asked.

'Yes.'

'You might have got away with it if she hadn't started her old tricks. I thought she might. Every police station in the country has been waiting for her to start. Where is she, Ricks? Come on, she's not in a fit condition to be left on her own. She's having a baby soon, isn't she?'

'Yes.'

'You don't want to leave her to look after herself, do you? Where is she?'

'What will happen to her?' Harry asked anxiously.

'How should I know? She'll stand her trial. She killed him, didn't she?'

'I don't know.'

'Yes, you do. You needn't worry, Ricks. We know you hadn't anything to do with it. I'm not saying you won't be charged with being an accessory; you probably will. But you're clear of the murder. Funny thing: Brady cleared you.'

'Brady?'

'Yes. We arrested him a couple of nights ago. We caught one of his girls and she squeaked. He'll get about five years with any luck. He seemed anxious to clear you and involve Clair. He said he had been following you as he was expecting you to skip. He said you and Mooney met at a pub about the time Whelan died. I've seen Mooney and he supports this. When you got back to the flat I suppose you found she had killed him?'

Harry didn't say anything.

'Where is she?' Parkins went on. 'Don't make things difficult for us.'

'I tell you I don't know. We parted . . .'

'We thought you might be in one of those caves up there. The local chap tells me the sea comes up at high tide. Is that where she is?'

'No,' Harry said.

'High tide's in about half an hour. If she's there, you'd better say so.'

Harry didn't believe him, but what was the use of lying? She couldn't be left alone. He suddenly felt very tired. She said there was no way out of this mess. There wasn't. He couldn't leave her in the cave.

'She's there,' he said in a flat voice. 'I'll take you to her.'

'Now you're being sensible,' Parkins said. He leaned out of the car and shouted into the darkness. 'Bring your men, Jackson. We're going up to the caves. She's up there.'

The car began to move slowly up the road. After a while, Harry said: 'It's near here I think.'

The car stopped.

With two policemen each side of him, Harry walked across the grass to the cliff head.

'Down there,' Harry said, pointing into the darkness. 'I don't know if you can get down.'

One of the policemen leaned forward and sent the beam of his flashlight along the wet, slippery path leading to the cave.

'We'll need a rope, sir,' he said, looking over his shoulder. 'That chalk won't give us a foothold. You couldn't get down there without a rope.'

Parkins swore softly. The wind buffeted him and he felt cold. 'Where can you get one?'

'There's a coastguard station not far from here,' the policeman said.

188

'Well, take the car and get it, and look sharp about it,' Parkins snapped.

Two policemen ran off into the darkness.

Parkins went to the cliff head and flashed his torch along the path. Peering forward at his side, Harry caught sight of Clair standing in the mouth of the cave, looking up at them.

'All right,' Parkins shouted. 'We're getting a rope. We'll get you out of that in a moment.'

'Is Harry there?' Clair asked, her voice thin and faint against the roar of the sea.

'I'm here,' Harry cried. 'It's no good, Clair. Just wait until they bring a rope. Are you all right?'

He could see how white and tense her face was in the brilliant beam of the torch.

'I'm going to jump, Harry,' she screamed. 'Oh, darling, I'm so sorry. It's been all my fault.'

'Don't be a fool!' Parkins bawled. 'Stay where you are!'

'Clair!' Harry cried, then darted forward and was on the path before Parkins could grab him. 'I'm coming, Clair. Wait for me! We'll go together!'

'Come back!' Parkins raved. 'Here, give him a light,' he thrust the torch into a police officer's hand.

Harry went sliding down the path, clutching at the wet bushes to check his progress.

'Go back!' Clair screamed at him. 'You'll fall!'

Harry had anchored himself to the roots of a small tree, growing out of the cliff face. The path began to crumble under his weight.

'Help him!' Clair cried, leaning forward to peer up at the light shining down on her. 'He'll fall!'

'Don't move,' Parkins shouted to Harry. 'Hang on until we get the rope.'

A shower of stones and chalk came down on Clair as Harry's feet suddenly slipped from under him. He swung out slowly away from the cliff face, his legs hanging in space, his hands supporting his weight, gripping the shrub, which began to bend.

Clair left the cave and began to climb towards him.

'I'll hang on for you, Clair,' he shouted. 'Come on, darling, we'll go together.'

'I'm coming,' she said, then stopped with a scream as the wind nearly sent her over. She looked down at the raging sea

189

below and fell on her knees, her hands digging into the thick tufts of grass.

'Clair!' Harry shouted. 'I can't hang on much longer.'

But she didn't look up or answer him.

Harry felt the shrub coming away from the cliff face. He tried to swing his legs back on to the crumbling path, but the extra strain was too much for the tree roots. He had a brief glimpse of Clair crouching on the path with the sea spray lashing her. He wondered about his unborn child. A second before the roots came away he prayed she would jump.

But she didn't. She didn't even see his fall. Blind with terror she was still crouching on the path when the rope arrived and Parkins went down to her.

THE END

BELIEVE THIS . . . YOU'LL BELIEVE ANYTHING
by JAMES HADLEY CHASE

Clay Burden had married his sluttish young wife, Rhoda, because he was tired of being on his own. Val had walked out on him – and if he couldn't have Val, maybe marriage would make him forget her.

Six years later, working in Paradise City, Clay met Val again. Married to the powerful and sinister Henry Vidal, she had changed . . . still beautiful and passionate, still compelling . . . but tense and nervous, driven by odd fears and anxieties . . .

When Clay left his job and joined the Vidal empire, what had begun as a sneaking feeling of unease hardened into stone-cold certainty. Val must be released from the hypnotic influence exerted over her by her husband – even if Clay had to murder to set her free . . .

0 552 10275 X – 60p

SHOCK TREATMENT by JAMES HADLEY CHASE

Terry Regan, who'd dropped into the Delaney's cabin up at Blue Jay lake to sell them a TV set, took in the situation at a glance. Jack Delaney was a vicious, hard-drinking cripple imprisoned in a wheelchair . . . and his wife Gilda was a lovely, sexy dish.

Things would have stayed that way . . . if Gilda hadn't indicated her availability – and her unhappiness. She needed Delaney out of the way – permanently. There'd be plenty of money coming to her at his death – enough for her and Terry to start a new life together. Once Terry had made up his mind to kill Delaney the rest was easy. Gilda's husband would be murdered by the controls on his own TV set . . .

0 552 10226 I – 50p

A SELECTED LIST OF CRIME STORIES
FOR YOUR READING PLEASURE

☐ 00000 0 **A LOTUS FOR MISS QUON** *James Hadley Chase* 40p
☐ 10275 X **BELIEVE THIS, YOU'LL BELIEVE ANYTHING**
James Hadley Chase 60p
☐ 10226 1 **SHOCK TREATMENT** *James Hadley Chase* 50p
☐ 09934 1 **THE THINGS MEN DO** *James Hadley Chase* 45p
☐ 09819 1 **SAFER DEAD** *James Hadley Chase* 40p
☐ 09675 X **NO NEED TO DIE** *John Creasey* 40p
☐ 09676 8 **A LIFE FOR A DEATH** *John Creasey* 40p
☐ 10103 6 **A HERALD OF DOOM** *John Creasey* 50p
☐ 09921 X **THE TOFF ON ICE** *John Creasey* 45p
☐ 10059 5 **THE OLD MASTERS** *William Haggard* 45p
☐ 09623 7 **THE EXECUTIONER: SAN DIEGO SIEGE**
Don Pendleton 40p
☐ 09205 3 **THE EXECUTIONER: ASSAULT ON SOHO**
Don Pendleton 40p
☐ 09204 5 **THE EXECUTIONER: MIAMI MASSACRE**
Don Pendleton 40p
☐ 09728 4 **THE DESTROYER: SUMMIT CHASE**
Richard Sapir & Warren Murphy 40p
☐ 09801 9 **THE DESTROYER: MURDER'S SHIELD**
Richard Sapir & Warren Murphy 40p
☐ 69595 8 **THE DESTROYER: DEATH THERAPY**
Richard Sapir & Warren Murphy 40p
☐ 10156 7 **THE DESTROYER: JUDGEMENT DAY**
Richard Sapir & Warren Murphy 60p
☐ 09072 7 **SHAFT'S BIG SCORE** *Ernest Tidyman* 30p
☐ 09056 5 **SHAFT** *Ernest Tidyman* 30p
☐ 09710 1 **ME HOOD?** *Mickey Spillane* 35p
☐ 09709 8 **KISS ME DEADLY** *Mickey Spillane* 40p
☐ 09707 1 **MY GUN IS QUICK** *Mickey Spillane* 40p
☐ 09272 X **THE FLIER** *Mickey Spillane* 40p
☐ 09111 1 **THE ERECTION SET** *Mickey Spillane* 50p

All these books are available at your bookshop or newsagent, or can be ordered direct from the publisher. Just tick the titles you want and fill in the form below.

CORGI BOOKS, Cash Sales Department, P.O. Box 11, Falmouth, Cornwall.

Please send cheque or postal order, no currency.

U.K. send 19p for first book plus 9p per copy for each additional book ordered to a maximum charge of 73p to cover the cost of postage and packing.

B.F.P.O. and Eire allow 19p for first book plus 9p per copy for the next 6 books, thereafter 3p per book.

Overseas Customers. Please allow 20p for the first book and 10p per copy for each additional book.

NAME (block letters) ....

ADDRESS ....

(JUNE 77) ....

While every effort is made to keep prices low, it is sometimes necessary to increase prices at short notice. Corgi Books reserve the right to show new retail prices on covers which may differ from those previously advertised in the text or elsewhere.